The Soviet Network

Amerigo Merenda

The Soviet Network

© 2016 Amerigo Merenda

ISBN: 978-1-5457-6038-3

Cover design by Phil Rose

Printed in the United States of America by
Mira Digital Publishing
Chesterfield, Missouri 63005

Dedication

Living in a police state is an experience we Americans may find difficult to comprehend.

Our forefathers created a government founded on democratic principles and a written constitution that protects us from tyranny and injustice. Our democracy is based on citizenship participation, compromise, tolerance and equal justice under the law. An interesting perspective of democracy introduced by Winston Churchill claimed that democracy is the worst form of government there is, except for all the rest. It is a profound assertion that we Americans and all democracies should remember when our system fails us. Regretful outcomes can ultimately be traced to vagaries within our political cultures.

Unfortunately our world is filled with millions of citizens who continue to live under fear of persecution, torture, imprisonment and murder whenever they attempt to speak out in defense of their human rights. They would prefer to take their chances with democracy with all its imperfections. For these reasons, I dedicate my novel, THE SOVIET NETWORK, to all citizens around the world who are suffering for their quest of liberty, especially our brothers and sisters who live in "independent" republics of the former Soviet Union. This story is especially written for you.

Amerigo Merenda

Preface

For Commander Rypchensky, living in a police state for over half his life had reached its limits. Privileges afforded him by his rank as supreme leader of the soviet army, as well as his status in the Communist Party were no longer acceptable excuses for his compliance with ideologies he could no longer accept. With a PH.D in physics, this highly educated and cultured Ukrainian made a decision that would change his life and the lives of millions in the Soviet Union.

He preferred a career in science, but chose a military path, believing his chances for transforming an incompetent communist government filled with corrupt bureaucrats would be enhanced. Deliverance from totalitarianism was his noble goal. Using the art of persuasion was his preferred strategy. However Russian political models did not embrace democracy. Therefore any transformation of power would have to include military force to root out an entrenched oligarchy.

Forty years of professional service to his country introduced him to thousands of power brokers, whose authority expanded throughout fifteen republics. He also befriended hundreds of commoners along the way, men and women who admired and respected his charismatic leadership. From this vast array of citizens, the underground movement known as The Soviet Network was born.

Beliefs shared among like minds cultivated strong bonds over time. The commander's core belief in liberty was not concealed, nor was it publicized. He shared his democratic beliefs with individuals, both powerful and common from which lists of patriots were organized for specific purposes. Many were also members of the communist party who rejected hardline ideology. Membership provided them with cover from intense scrutiny. In fact, most network members, some with positions of power, were members of the communist party who secretly planned with underground leaders. Dissident communist members were branded as moderates or even liberals. As totalitarian policies instigated more public resentment, network operatives grew more determined. Gradually as glasnost opened political dialogue, liberal factions assumed power in both legislative bodies.

Personal lives and relationships became trapped by imminent revolutionary events. Men and women in loving relationships struggled to find ways to escape their web of secrecy. Reading THE SOVIET NETWORK, a historical novel, will reveal failures of totalitarian culture interspersed with personal romantic tragedies that propel readers to the very end.

Amerigo Merenda

Chapter 1

Captain Rypchensky was evolving into a dissident who harbored contempt for the Communist Party. In 1963, he began to formulate a strategy for altering the status quo within the Soviet Union. The best pathway for incapacitating a corrupt and incompetent system was from within. His thoughts persisted, even as he read the story of David and Goliath to his son, Kristoff. The youngster loved the story as much as his father enjoyed embellishing his version of the tale. Stories about giants could be indelible moments experienced by a four year old boy. He wondered whether his son would someday recognize the meaning of "giant killers" in another context. He also wondered whether, by expanding this story, he was displacing his resentment toward a detested political system. Kristoff was always overwhelmed by the power of Goliath and how David managed to overcome his disadvantage in size. The captain showed his son a picture that portrayed Goliath after being struck a mortal blow. Kristoff responded.

"How can this happen, father? The giant is so big and strong." The captain, a rising military officer, realized the formative years of his son's education would be in part determined by his example. He was conflicted about placing too much drama into his son's frame of reference at this age, but also knew that his moral compass was being framed by his words and example.

He squeezed his son gently and quietly explained.

"Sometimes even giants can be weak. We must be strong, not weak." Then looking at his son's curious stare he said: "If you ever have to choose between being afraid of giants and being afraid of weakness, be afraid of weakness." His wife Monique was listening in and was not amused with the direction of his embellishment. But his son's interest continued to pique.

Kristoff was amazed at his father's response, as young boys would imagine the enormity of Goliath. "Why, father?" Like many young children, Kristoff asked why many times.

His father was pleased with his curiosity. "Well, sometimes you have to fight people who are bigger and stronger."

Without hesitation, Kristoff responded, "How can you win? The big person is too strong."

The captain smiled. "It depends. David defeated Goliath because David was smart and brave."

Captain Rypchensky's wife Monique waited for the right moment to lead her four year old son off to bed.

"Are you smart, Father?" Kristoff asked.

For a fleeting moment, the captain had a pang of fear he did not understand. "Smarter than whom?"

Kristoff looked at his father. "Smarter than Goliath."

Monique must have sensed the story had reached a point where she should intercede when her husband responded, "Only if I have to be".

His story telling approached a point where he could place his family under surveillance if he allowed political views to expand his son's thinking. Four year olds have no filters and could reveal parental sentiments outside the home. Living in a police state had to include this possibility. As much as the captain wanted to satisfy his son's curious mind, he realized he was treading in dangerous currents. Then his son asked another question.

"Are there any giants like Goliath today?"

Once again, he wondered, how far should he allow his son's imagination to probe. "Well, not exactly. As you get older, you will learn about giants."

However, this was not enough to satisfy young Kristoff.

"Why can't I learn now?"

His mother's instincts took over, motivated by her personal experiences of life in a police state. She reached down and lifted her son with her answer.

"Because it is time to go to bed; give your father a kiss goodnight."

Kristoff resisted. "Why can't I learn now?"

Monique embraced her son before she repeated with more authority, "Because it is time to go to bed. Now give your father a kiss good-night."

The youngster persisted.

"Father, please tell me more about giants." The captain embraced his wife and son with his massive arms.

"Maybe another night. Goodnight, my son."

Childhood memories often surfaced for Kristoff, revealing a segment of his father's psychological profile, portrayed through childhood stories. It was during moments of solitude when Kristoff vividly remembered episodes where his father would portend ominous thoughts within a story. As a child, he didn't realize his father was speaking to him subconsciously, almost as a way of planting a reality that would reveal itself in his adult years. Now as an adult journalist for Pravda, Kristoff explored his father's hidden messages. He also discovered his father purposely isolated him from political drama to protect him. Kremlin walls shielded dangerous and hidden messages. Kristoff understood there were few if any adults living in the Soviet Union who could share personal thoughts, political or otherwise, with their children. Totalitarian fear bred secrecy and anxiety.

As he matured, Kristoff began to realize how much of his adult life was spent thinking about his father, now with the rank of commander, one of the most powerful men in the Soviet army. Their relationship changed after his father's promotion. Intrigue that surrounded Commander Rypchensky was too dangerous for his son to explore. Kristoff had a problem with that because now, at age twenty-seven, his career in journalism, at his father's insistence, required avoidance of domestic politics. His frustration was building, but he understood his father's wisdom and would never endanger their careers and relationship, with political jargon that could be easily misinterpreted. Journalism in the Soviet Union was without question an arm of the state, with little demand for a journalist's true literary skills, except for the purpose of propaganda. Religion and politics were toxic subjects, topics wisely avoided in public circles. However, Kristoff sensed his frustration was also discretely shared by his parents. There were signs of dissonance within Kremlin political families. Frustration was steadily building.

Monique, Kristoff's mother, was born in Russia. Her French mother was married to a Russian artist, who developed a style of avant-garde painting that became very popular in Western Europe. Mysteriously, he disappeared during one of several purges during the Stalin era. Monique had repressed memories of her father that were very painful for her as a child. Now, as an adult, she, like thousands of other citizens, suffered in silence. She desperately wanted to share her discontent with others but feared dire ramifications. Her father's mysterious disappearance still haunted her. Repression was a very common defense mechanism in Russia. It was necessary for survival. Kristoff sensed this when he continued to probe his grandfather's life. His mother would cut him off or change the subject. Once he saw tears in his mother's eyes when his questions were persistent. At that moment, he realized her painful psychological threshold had reached its limit; he learned never to question her again.

Kristoff's family name was Rypchensky. His father's traditions were culturally Ukrainian although his father's mother was Russian. As a child, Kristoff didn't know why cultural attachments mattered until later in life when he became aware of tension between the two republics. Stalin's policy of forced migration of Russian populations into other republics, some thousands of miles away, was enforced to maintain cultural superiority. A priority was forcing Russian language on inhabitants. Ukrainians maintained their dialect. They also preferred Western European cultural habits. Their associations with cultural hubs in Warsaw, Berlin, Paris, and Rome, exposed Ukrainians to material amenities. Kristoff's father made sure his son was informed of Ukraine's unique traditions. His father's ethnicity was reinforced by Russian arrogance directed toward other social traditions. Cultural distinctions became more apparent as he matured into adulthood.

The Soviet Union's vast land mass has eleven time zones, containing fifteen republics, with over forty languages. Eastern republics have large Muslim populations that can present major obstacles to Russian hegemony. The Russian war in Afghanistan was instigated by religious zealot's plans to create a theocracy. If religious and cultural divisions continued to clash with Communist autocrats, Russia's eastern empire was threatened. Religious-cultural wars breed contempt and longevity. Avoiding this possibility is a primary objective of communist leaders who had little choice but to allow for cultural-religious traditions. However when communist authorities realized the rebirth of jihadism spreading from Afghanistan to Soviet republics containing large numbers of Muslims, they invaded Afghanistan. Their efforts failed in part because mujahideen fighters were determined enemies. Rugged geography was another factor.

Alexander the Great and the British experienced similar results. What may have been the most critical factor in Russia's defeat was the introduction of stinger missiles provided by the United States. Without air power, Russia could not control territory.

Controlling eastern republics with large Muslim populations required mixing Russian settlements with native populations. This policy began with czars and continued with twentieth century dictators. The success or failure of these policies will eventually be determined. The communist goal is to encourage a moderate political ideology that maintains cultural equilibrium. Assimilation of cultures has introduced a different demographic. However, on occasion, military force has been used when native populations protest against violations of their political and cultural traditions. Basically, Russian domination has been maintained with force. One important factor insisted upon by Russia is linguistic uniformity. A Russian common language taught in schools, creates common bonds that can transcend culture. Ethical and moral justification of policies used for Russification will weave their way into lives of Soviet citizens with mixed results. The Soviet Union's western republics had different concerns, Ukraine in particular.

The Rypchensky's status elevated their privileges. Because of her husband's rank, and the large communist Party in France, Monique was allowed to attend school at the Sorbonne where she was professionally trained in impressionism. Her intellectual capacity was wasted in Moscow. She always looked forward to touring Western Europe with her husband where art dealers from all over the world would convene. Her mother's family resided in Paris, allowing opportunities for French cultural attachments. Paris was the antithesis of Moscow. She could sense contrasts while browsing shops, often stopping to peruse or make purchases in charming boutiques, followed by dining in French cafes. Paris was liberating. On occasion, Kristoff would accompany his mother. He became fluent in French and enjoyed conversing with his mother's family. During these moments in Paris, Kristoff began to comprehend his mother's joy while touring the city of lights. Her face beamed with contentment. Upon their return to Russia, he could sense changes in mood, not only with his mother, but also with Russians walking Moscow's streets. The differences were psychologically miles apart. His mother was a different person when they returned.

When Kristoff's father was promoted to the highest rank in the Soviet Army, life changed more dramatically. There were more privileges offered to the elite and Commander Rypchensky, a Ukrainian by birth, enjoyed a lifestyle reserved for a select few. Kristoff's opportunities expanded as well. New experiences were open to him, including travel and material comforts. His mother's deep French roots and artistic training highlighted her cultural deprivation in Russia. To compensate for this disparity, she frequently took advantage of privileged liberties that allowed her to share interests and freedoms with her relatives in France. Often, Kristoff thought of this paradox. The very establishment that was the defender of communism, was being corrupted by exotic comforts whose origin was often foreign. The Soviet Union, defender of monolithic communism, was being "corrupted" by material comforts and intellectual pursuits whose origins were not only foreign but also democratic and capitalist. In elite circles, this irony did not persist unnoticed.

Kristoff was aware and proud of his parent's intellectual and political interests. His father was a trained physicist whose military career was advanced toward the closing months of WW II, when his division captured several prominent German scientists, who were instrumental in establishing and promoting the Soviet Union's success with long range rockets, expanding the Soviet's military threat post war. Subsequently, rocket technology became a cornerstone for space exploration, leading to Russia's successful space program, culminating in Sputnik's success. These accomplishments advanced the world's view of communism.

Commander Rypchensky was reputed as the consummate professional. And he was. Tall and ruggedly handsome, he commanded respect from his subordinates and peers. It was only a matter of time before his leadership would replace an aging military hierarchy. The Soviet military had substantial political leverage, and, depending on leadership loyalties, could make unforeseen changes in the body politic. Military personnel's political preferences were unknown. Officers were promoted on the basis of professional skills. Many of the brightest were trained in math and science. Their understanding of communism's shortcomings was inescapable. Commander Rypchensky decided upon a military career rather than one in science because highly ranked military officers possessed more potential for political alternatives.

Commander Rypchensky's political views remained a mystery. His agenda may have been shared with loyal comrades. Being outspoken, however, was dangerous for him and other officers associated with intellectual provocateurs, especially when dissonant undercurrents circulated. Kristoff was kept uninformed intentionally. Protecting his son from political conflict was foremost. Kristoff believed his perception of reality was unmistaken. The status quo was unacceptable. He also knew better than to ask questions. Circumstances required silence. Within the Kremlin, a code of silence was mandatory for survival.

Kristoff's bond with his parents was strong. Having two loving parents was one of his most cherished possessions, followed by Nadia, a woman he met during an emergency snow delay at Boryspil International airport, east of Kiev. They made plans to meet again at Rasputin's, one of several popular discos in Moscow, where elite young professionals gathered to dance and commiserate. Nadia would alter Kristoff's future. Not only was she beautiful and smart, but she was also a member of the Bolshoi Ballet. Their relationship matured to the point where marriage was a definite possibility. He purchased a diamond ring to offer Nadia before introducing her to his parents. When she invited Kristoff to her apartment for dinner, the opportunity presented itself. Kristoff was unaware of Nadia's plan to defect during a future performance in New York City.

Chapter 2

Kristoff watched senior members of the Central Committee walk to their seats in a chamber at the Kremlin Palace of Congresses, a large complex built during the Khrushchev era. They were for the most part very old men and looked their age. The Central Committee was meeting to vote on two issues that party liberals and conservatives had deliberated for many weeks. Arranged in a semicircle, the older members led by Andrei Yermolov were seated at the right side of the chamber. Peter Yurov, an articulate spokesman for the loyal opposition within the Communist Party, was spokesman for the liberal wing. The speaker of the Central Committee began by reading the first proposal before voting occurred. He pounded his gavel, calling for their attention.

"We will vote on the following proposal." The speaker hammered his gavel again until silence prevailed.

"Shall the Communist Party liberalize its position concerning private ownership and free enterprise, including legal authority to decrease government control over decisions of commerce?"

Basically, this was an attempt to move the Soviet Union toward a market economy. The Chinese communist economy had made movements in this direction and it was believed that similar reforms might occur in the Soviet Union as well. Kristoff looked at his colleague Boris and smiled. They may have something interesting to write in their column after all.

Boris was not amused and his disinterest was apparent. He was a good example of what years of frustration can lead to for totalitarian journalists. At one time earlier in his career, journalism was an exciting profession until he was punished for writing the truth as he believed it to be. One year in Siberia highlighted fear only totalitarianism can generate. He was a "party writer" now and understood the implications of every word he wrote. He admired Kristoff who reminded him of years past when he too believed journalism had meaning and purpose for Mother Russia and beyond. Now, survival was most important, nothing more.

Boris still had some fire left in him but it was easily extinguished. This is why he enjoyed working with Kristoff who was determined to initiate some changes for writers. There also was the advantage in knowing someone whose father was a powerful broker in the Kremlin hierarchy. It was no accident that Kristoff was paired with Boris as journalistic team writers for Pravda. Boris was more than a friend and mentor for young Kristoff; he was a father figure whose role was to protect his protégé from indiscretions of youth. This was a personal and private request from the commander himself. Boris felt a strong loyalty to both father and son. He also believed both of these men would have prominent roles to play in future political changes as they unfolded. The commander left an indelible impression with Boris that conditions would improve. As an officer serving under Captain Rypchensky, Boris was reminded of inadequacies of communism, on more than one occasion. Boris also had his own reasons for not feeling optimistic about the future. Commander Rypchensky had personally revealed his disappointment with Communist bureaucrats who had little interest in reforming a system that provided them with advantages over an overwhelming majority of citizens. Their interest was self-interest, clear and simple. Reforming a system that made their lives comfortable was unlikely. The commander implied on more than one occasion, that abusive practices and entitlements would be addressed.

When the speaker used his gavel to quiet members of the Central Committee, Boris took notice. The second proposal read as follows:

"Shall the Soviet government rewrite laws pertaining to writers, journalists, filmmakers and performing artists? The new law will allow for more individual discretion and freedom in decision-making for these individuals and organizations within Soviet republics."

Kristoff smiled and felt a surge of joy. Boris inhaled on his cigarette and did not appear anxious, having experienced similar moments in the past.

"Enjoy the moment, Boris. We will have a story to write."

Boris winced. "A tragedy I can do without." Boris lowered his head in his hands. He had been there before and anticipated similar results.

The speaker asked for a vote on the first proposal concerning private ownership. "Those members in favor of proposal number one, please raise your hands." The votes were counted, with a total of 325 votes in favor. The speaker proceeded. "Those members against proposal number one, please raise your hands." The chamber housed 549 members in the Soviet of the Union and 526 in the Soviet of the Nationalities. The ballots were electronically tabulated.

"Proposal number one was defeated 750 no, 325 yes."

The liberal wing reacted with disgust. Shouts of anger disrupted the chamber until the Party Speaker regained order by pounding his gavel followed with his announcement of the second proposal on journalistic liberties, most important to Boris and Kristoff.

"We will now vote on proposal number two. Those members in favor of the second proposal, please raise your hands." The vote count was the same, 325 votes in favor.

"Those members against the second proposal, please raise your hands." The result was the same, 750 no, 325 yes.

The conservative majority applauded the results. The old men even managed to stand and applaud. Kristoff and Boris were frustrated and walked out of the chamber. Their walk to a parking lot behind the Kremlin was long enough to allow both men to vent their anger. "What will it take in order for these old men to see how much they are crippling our country? Are they blind? I cannot write what is not accurate and true anymore. I have reached my limits. Suppressed journalism is slowly killing me."

Boris lit another cigarette and responded in his raspy voice.

"You will write what you have to write. There is no other way."

Kristoff looked incredulous. "How can you continue to believe that anymore? Haven't you had enough? Our economy is bankrupt. We must buy wheat from Americans every year. There are lines at food markets. Meat is scarce. The people crave western clothing and music. Our brave Russian soldiers are being slaughtered in Afghanistan for almost a decade. What will it take, Boris? What will it take?" Cigarette smoke whirled around Boris who felt genuine anger and frustration but understood the repercussions of irrational behavior.

"You are talking dangerously. You are talking revolution. Keep quiet with such words. You will get us both killed." Boris felt he had to temper his young colleague's enthusiasm, realizing he would have reacted the same way when he was twenty-eight. Now he was tired, his youthful energy replaced by complacency and dejection. The system had destroyed his vigor. Boris understood Kristoff's feelings, but was concerned about his personal safety if he expressed his sentiments too vigorously. Even meaningful conversation was not prudent. Words had ways of finding public consumption and were easily twisted along the way. Totalitarian machinations run counter to reason. One cannot be too careful. Boris therefore tried to calm his young colleague. He turned on the car radio to lighten the mood with some music.

"I am trying to put you in a good mood with some music and what do I hear. Nothing but funeral music." He turned the dial. But all government channels were playing funeral hymns. Then Radio Moscow announced:

"We interrupt our musical program to announce the death of our beloved party chairman, Provenko." Boris turned off the radio and looked at Kristoff. Neither one had a word to say, but their minds were racing with mixed emotions. Political succession always presented Russians with mysterious undercurrents. Now with the death of Provenko, Boris feared a chain reaction that could lead to reactionary measures. Hardline communists who were out of touch with reality in the fifteen republics could make life even more miserable. However, the chairman's unexpected death created a window of opportunity for a network of communists waiting to revise the political framework. There were also several men competing for leadership who wanted to replace the deceased Provenko.

The struggle that followed was made more mysterious without a free and open press. Who can anyone really trust without accurate information?

When Boris and Kristoff entered the Kremlin the following day, throngs of citizens walked past Provenko's casket, most without expression of any kind. Among the long line of dignitaries were political suitors, waiting to fill the vacuum created by his untimely death. Two days after the funeral, Central Committee members ordered an emergency meeting. A struggle emerged between older and younger members. Yurov was the spokesman for the younger and more liberal wing of the party. Hundreds of party members were present. His voice was clear and to the point. All eyes and ears were focused on his every word and gesture. Yurov announced firmly, "The party must emerge from this sad moment equipped and prepared for the future of our nation. Youth is the order of the day. We must elect a man whose physical health is as vigorous as his intellect. That man is Kamir Mikoyanov."

There was a stir among the older members who were not prepared for this direct attack on their secured leadership and privileges. They whispered to one another and looked to their spokesman, Vladimir Lomov, who stood and slowly moved his aged frame toward the dais. Absolute silence rippled across the chamber. He made a brilliant call for the status quo.

"Comrades. Our wisdom will be judged by the decision we make in this hour. Continuity is the order of the day, not youth. This party has made great progress under the leadership of men whose beliefs have conformed with the principles of Marx and Lenin. We must not change that course unless we also relinquish our communist principles and heritage. The man who should lead this nation is present in this chamber. He is Stantin Rolanov." There was loud applause and approval from the committee.

Rolanov stood and acknowledged the warm recognition from his supporters. He raised both hands above his head and clasped them together as a sign of unity. Mikoyanov, nominee of the liberal wing, realized he could not win so he gestured to his committee supporters to rise and acknowledge the forthcoming election of Rolanov. Yurov whispered to his colleagues, "We must give the appearance of unity. Our turn will come in due course." The vote was unanimous for Rolanov. There was loud applause from the older party members. Journalists took copious notes as photographers snapped pictures. Stability and conservatism once again reigned over unknown liberal action and leadership. However, during his first year in office, there were several reports of Rolanov's ailing health. The media reported several accounts of his sudden disappearance. It was believed by some that his death was imminent. Headlines revealed his mysterious absence from the body politic. His whereabouts was a mystery. A series of disturbing political observations followed:

May 5, 1986, LONDON TIMES, "Rolanov is seen in public, reports of his illness divulged."

September 12, 1986, NEW YORK TIMES, "Rolanov makes appearance. The Soviet leader is seen in public but needs assistance walking to a podium. His voice is weak and he shows signs of shortness of breath."

January 30, 1987, WASHINGTON POST, "Stantin Rolanov disappears from public. Reports circulate that he has died."

February 10, 1987, BBC reports: "To quell reports of his death, Stantin Rolanov makes a public appearance, but looks gravely ill. His speech is slurred. He lost his breath on several occasions and had to discontinue. Officials standing near him helped him maintain his balance. Rolanov had to be assisted from the dais."

A week later, BBC reported Stantin Rolanov died in office. Once again the Soviet Union had an internal struggle for succession. With his death, the liberal wing of the Communist Party had an opportunity they had patiently and prudently waited for. Mikoyanov, along with his liberal colleagues, stood along the funeral procession with a somber expression. Hundreds of party members were also in attendance. An American journalist present wrote the following:

"This is the third funeral for a leader of the Soviet Union in recent years. Once again throngs of citizens walk past the casket looking even more incredulous. Their leader, third in just over three years, has died in office. The scene is very somber."

This was a turning point for a network that would now emerge under the cover of political uncertainty. In Mikoyanov's residence, under absolute privacy, several prominent network leaders gathered.

Among them was Commander Rypchensky and KGB Captain Orlov. Their discussion centered on the recent turn of events placing Mikoyanov center stage. The commander was pleased as he addressed his elite members, all men he knew and trusted. All were members of the Communist Party who wanted change.

"Gentlemen. We have been together for many years. Our success will depend upon faith and trust in each other. If we can replace the old regime with men of vision, integrity, and spirit, we will change the course of the Soviet Union forever." He understood threatening ramifications of his challenge to the status quo. His judgement was respected. He also understood the limits of his power. Reforms would be achieved by chipping away at oppressive doctrines of totalitarianism . Eventually, unrealistic ideals, based upon unattainable communist dogma, would be exposed for their failure to provide goods and services. Economic well-being was fundamental, followed by civil liberties and social justice. Communism was losing public support for these reasons. Replacing a failed status quo became the Network's goal. Up to this point, progressive policies were stalled or rejected. Patience was limited. Network leaders sensed their time had arrived.

Presenting his strategy, Commander Rypchensky informed network operatives of the importance of keeping the KGB preoccupied with diversions . The idea was clever. Implementation was a major concern. He began to explain his plan as follows:

"If the KGB is consumed with chasing spurious international threats, aka false leads, Network leaders and operatives will have more opportunity for expanding their domestic political agenda. If KGB agents are preoccupied with fake news assignments that divert their attention, Network policy alternatives will have more opportunity for success. We will have time to expose rigid communist economic and political failures, and by doing so, reveal their inability to address public demands. Basically this will involve fabricating and exploiting existing Cold War military and political threats as subterfuge. I repeat, if our enemies are preoccupied chasing false leads, our agenda will have more time for success. By diverting our enemies we are giving our policies valuable time for public consumption. Diversion of KGB operatives will act as cover. If they are consumed chasing false intelligence assignments, we will gain valuable time for our political agenda." He added: "However, it is only a matter of time before suspicions will arise. Our immediate goal is to explain our domestic reform agenda in order to increase our leverage in the next election. Political power in our hands can and will lead to reform." He turned and looked at Mikoyanov, whose face was flush, his gray white hair perfectly combed. Then he continued. "This strategy involves a peaceful transition of ideology from a failed communist system to a free market and democratic system. I want to emphasize peaceful transition." He paused and his tone became even more serious.

"But in the event we see imminent failure with our nonviolent approach, we can then move on to a more aggressive strategy which may necessitate military intervention. I am prepared for that eventuality as are my officers." Pausing again, he looked at Mikoyanov. "In either case, our legitimacy must include the election of our esteemed leader." Mikoyanov stood, paused, and finally spoke.

"I am honored by your trust, but suspicions of our political views run deep. We must determine whether our political opponents, who insist on maintaining hard line communist principles, will agree to some necessary changes. Their thinking and planning has smothered progress. Their strong arm tactics are spreading fear of retaliation. Communism is failing our nation. Our opponents refuse to accept this reality." He looked at the commander who responded.

"Word has it that Yermolov is suspicious of your leadership and motives. He has rallied his supporters in an effort to maintain control of the party. He is desperate, even suggesting the opposition may have poisoned Rolanov. Of course, this is not true."

Mikoyanov was angry. He despised Yermolov. "Those bastards will never change. They are not true Leninists. They see change as evil. Lenin saw change as survival. Our country is choking on its own spit and they will not change the status quo. I will never understand those selfish bastards. They make our work more difficult and dangerous." He paused, then asked, "How many members can we elect to the Central Committee in February?"

His assistant compared information with the commander, then responded.

"We estimate we can finally achieve a majority. This means a minimum of 538. It depends. Events can change minds. Yermolov has plans to increase his coalition. Maybe you should address the party and try to persuade some of the undecided members. Our succession crisis may change minds in our favor."

Mikoyanov disagreed. "No, that would be premature on my part. It will only serve to solidify the opposition. Moderate party members may become suspicious of any maneuvers on my part. I believe they may consider supporting us. We are better off maintaining a low profile." Then he motioned toward Commander Rypchensky.

"Have your son Kristoff write more articles critical of these bureaucrats. They are strangling us with their deceptions. They have been using lies and conspiracies as their diversion for decades. Now we can give them a taste of their own contempt for truth."

Commander Rypchensky inserted a new factor.

"You know the war in Afghanistan is very unpopular, especially here in the Russian Republic. Russians do not want to see their sons slaughtered in a winless struggle. This war has continued without end in sight for eight years. It's the equivalent of America's Vietnam nightmare. Our soldiers are dying as we are losing."

All present realized the commander was correct in his assessment. They understood how Soviet military strategy was outmaneuvered by introductions of American Stinger missiles that were shooting down Russian jets.

Mikoyanov listened to Commander Rypchensky and asked:

"What do you recommend?"

The commander stood and explained his well-thought-out plan.

"We can make the opposition look very bad by their refusal to withdraw our troops. A planned withdrawal from this war will be well received by our military. If we take this position, our military will support our efforts for policy changes. I believe they will support our network plans for the future. Field commanders have had enough. You must speak to the officer corps and let them know your true feelings. This will have tremendous political ramifications in our favor."

Mikoyanov was impressed. "That is an excellent idea. I will speak with them. Please Commander, make the necessary arrangements."

In the days that followed, events happened faster than expected. The Central Committee was meeting to select a new party chairman. Peter Yurov, spokesman and leader of the liberal faction, delivered a persuasive commentary and endorsement of his preferred choice. The elegant surroundings within the Kremlin's intimate chamber were impressive. Russian art and history embellished walls within the committee chamber, one of many lavish displays from an earlier era. Relics of czarist Russia were displayed. These masterpieces could appear to contradict orthodox communist ideals, however they were magnificent examples of Russian art and culture enjoyed during frequent public tours. Russians showcased their cultural heritage as superior to cultures of fourteen other republics. Their arrogance often caused resentment. By elevating their culture, they unwittingly stirred resentment among masses of non Russians. Elevating themselves for political gain frequently caused disturbances. The policy of expanding Russian culture by occupation began with Czars and continued with Stalin. Russians were forcibly assimilated throughout the European and Asian territory known as the Soviet Union, spreading their language and culture throughout the republics in order to mitigate influence of non Russians.

When Yurov spoke to assembled members, he was purposeful as well as emotional. Momentum had begun to shift. Cultural heritage beautifully displayed in the hall provided an impressive setting. When members were settled, Yurov began.

"Gentlemen. Once again we have gathered under tragic circumstances. Our recent history has been filled with unforeseen events. We must not repeat failures of past decades. My plea to you concerns the destiny of our great nation. I offer you the man who will meet our future with fresh ideas for success. That man is Andrei Mikoyanov." At first, there was no applause. Gradually, however, the liberal wing's enthusiasm dominated the room and cheerful support followed. Moderates peered at the conservative delegation, then gradually and steadily stood to support a new leader. A majority consensus had been achieved. When the vote was tabulated, the underground network had achieved political legitimacy. However, their pathway was perilous because traditional forces, deeply entrenched from years of patronage and corruption, would not easily relinquish power. Mikoyanov understood this more than any one because he had fought for years to reform totalitarian hypocrisy. He addressed the legislature, knowing that change would have to be framed carefully using conservative icons and ideology. He understood political undercurrents were in play. Therefore he was very selective with his choice of words that would not offend conservative opponents.

He stood tall and straight, projecting an image of strength and youth.

"Comrades, I am honored by your trust. Our nation must now heal its wounds. We have suffered together and we will triumph together. We can surpass expectations set for our nation by our predecessors. Our party must remain a symbol of Lenin and Marx. They are watching our movements and decisions as I speak." He pointed to large posters of Lenin and Marx on the walls of the chamber.

"If you observe them you will notice they are not taking their eyes off us." This was followed by loud laughter and applause. His words were well received. However, Mikoyanov realized that words alone would not appease the entrenched conservatives in the party. He was buying time for his underground network of reformers to finish the enormous task ahead. Both speed and patience were required. He did not want to bruise strong egos during a sensitive political succession. Posturing for influence and power during the succession was ill advised. The opposition must not be humiliated, at least not yet. They were still strong power brokers and could use their powerful connections to terminate reforms.

Mikoyanov feared totalitarian politics for that reason. It could be impulsive and erratic. He was careful not to inflame. His speech was well received and the transition to new leadership was formally announced for public consumption. Mikoyanov apparently had persuaded the body politic that survival required reconciliation and rational, long-overdue compromises and transformations of communist dogma.

Among elite Network members, precautions were taken to avoid indiscrete written or spoken words from being intercepted by enemy agents. At this stage, Kristoff was unaware of any underground movement. The network's most powerful leader was his father who chose to protect his son by isolating him from being involved as a participant. Now, with the election of Mikoyanov, the Commander was more confident for his son's safety. Therefore, at some point in the future, he would inform Kristoff of his leadership role and network operations in motion.

As time progressed, a policy of glasnost allowed Kristoff to assume more ownership of his critiques. He crafted editorials that would frame opposing political dialogues between old and new forces emerging from an unexpected political succession. He wanted to present to the public, choices that would stir debate, never before allowed in print. It was a risk worth taking, now with the election of Mikoyanov. Glasnost was emerging which allowed for more printed veracity. He was writing his editorial in the gallery above the chamber while below old bureaucrats used their remaining leverage to advance personal interests. This clearly meant the preservation of their privileges and power at the expense of public needs. For them it was still business as usual. In an attempt to expose their corrupt practices, Kristoff would include in his editorial a question for public dialogue.

"What public policies will advance our nation's political and economic freedom?" His editorial would contain arguments from each side taken directly from interviews with legislative members. He did not offer his opinion, but it was quite evident what the overwhelming majority of readers would conclude, leading to public demands. He wondered whether Pravda, the party newspaper, would even print his editorial uncensored or would screeners edit its content. He felt optimistic under evolving circumstances. However, Kristoff was not aware of network operatives in the legislature, reconstructing public policies. His father would eventually inform him but not until the movement was more advanced and secure.

Major life changes for his parents and all those involved in Network operations were possible. The Network was still operating as an underground movement. Members had to patiently wait and calculate opportune moments that would allow them to surface. It would be premature to identify themselves as advocates for change. Timing was key for successfully overwhelming their opponents. Totalitarian culture has deep roots.

Chapter 3

Kristoff was looking forward to spending time with Nadia, a woman he was certain would one day be his wife. After a year's time, he realized how important she was to his happiness. She was truly a beautiful woman inside and out. Her blue eyes, blond hair, high cheek bones, tall frame and curvaceous appearance were stunning. What really impressed Kristoff the most was her demeanor. She was level headed, intelligent and determined. Her apartment always cheered his spirits because Nadia had somehow managed to decorate it with beautiful and artistic trappings from her travels with the Bolshoi. She had friends in many special places, friends who loved her and showered her with unique gifts from all over the world of ballet.

While driving to her apartment, Kristoff noticed a car trailing him for blocks. It wasn't the first time he was followed. He always managed to lose pursuers in traffic because his car was faster than most and his driving skills were daring to say the least. Kristof was always fascinated with sport cars and speed. When visiting his relatives in France, he met Italian drivers who introduced him to racing. It was a passion unfulfilled. He even loved the challenge of outmaneuvering KGB agents, usually without difficulty. However, several blocks of sharp turns and dangerous weaving in and out of traffic did not work this time. The agent kept pace. Finally realizing the futility of his attempt, he pulled over, approached the man who parked directly behind him. He was smiling and appeared friendly. Kristoff was not amused.

"Who the hell are you? KGB!"

When the man responded, he smiled and said, "No, but you practically got us killed." He appeared to be in his early sixties and spoke in a friendly tone.

"So sorry to detain you, but I did not know which apartment was your girlfriend's. However, I recognized your Volvo and license number."

Kristoff's anger peaked.

"Why are you following me? And what does my girlfriend have to do with anything: Are you KGB?"

The man felt bad about what had happened.

"No, I know they are watching you, so be careful. I'm a friend of your father. He wants to see you this weekend at the Black Sea resort. Bring your girlfriend. Your parents want to meet her."

Kristoff was shaking his head in disbelief. "How do you know all about my personal life?"

His pursuer's response was straightforward. "It's my job. Your father's insistence!"

Kristoff was incredulous. "But why? What's going on?"

What Kristoff heard next really disturbed him.

"Your girlfriend is planning to defect during her next performance in New York. You must discourage her and let her know the danger in which she is placing her family."

It was difficult for Kristoff to fathom how his personal life and relationship was unraveling without his knowledge. He felt wounded by someone he loved, and yet he could understand and appreciate her motives. The stranger then provided him with more information.

"Reservations will be made for you and your girlfriend at the airport. My name is Trushin. I work for your father. He is very concerned about your safety as well as your happiness. Trust in his judgment. Now I must go." Kristoff took some comfort in Trushin's presence. For reasons he could not explain, he felt some kind of bond with this complete stranger.

When Trushin drove off, Kristoff waited a few minutes to collect his thoughts. His options were limited so he decided to continue his plans with Nadia and determine whether their relationship could be maintained with news of her defection plans. He drove to a florist and purchased a bouquet of roses, and combined with a bottle of French wine from his mother's collection, felt he was making every effort to create a romantic setting for his evening plans. While approaching her apartment, he noticed a pink ballet figurine attached to her door, just below the number. The figurine was a very special gift from her mother, purchased when Nadia was a young girl studying ballet. Her parents always encouraged her to train and discipline herself. They told her, it would change her life. They were right. She loved to perform and travel all over the world. After three knocks, a moment lapsed before the door opened. Her stunning beauty overwhelmed him, and he practically dropped everything. Her smile was followed by a warm kiss on his lips.

"Thank you for the beautiful flowers, and where did you ever find French wine?"

Kristoff prudently avoided Trushin's message. His response displayed hesitation. "My mother's friends have just returned from France. It should be chilled. Any ice?"

She walked toward the refrigerator.

"Absolutely! My refrigerator was made in West Germany, not here. I always have ice."

Kristoff felt no artificiality on Nadia's part, but he did feel very amorous. He could not withhold his attraction to her beauty and sexuality that overwhelmed his thoughts despite learning of her secret plans for defection. He approached her with outstretched arms. "That is not all you have."

After placing the bottle of wine into an ice bucket, he pulled Nadia into a passionate embrace. They practically disrobed while standing. Kristoff gently carried her off to the bedroom where their sexual encounter was both erotic and exhausting. They fell asleep for about an hour. Nadia then gingerly extracted herself from Kristoff's gentle grasp, slipped on her robe, and prepared the finishing touches for dinner. After she lit candles, she walked toward Kristoff, still resting, naked in bed, and gently rubbed his temples while kissing him with her warm lips. His eyes opened when he felt her blond hair tickle his chest. Her perfume enhanced the moment. Before he could react, Nadia effortlessly stood as though in a ballet and gently exposed a chair from the dining table, from which she brought a box wrapped with a purple ribbon and handed it to Kristoff. Inside, Kristoff found a beautiful evening robe purchased on her last trip abroad.

"I hope you like it. It's extra-large."

It was dark burgundy and Kristoff looked very handsome with it wrapped around his tall and shapely physique.

Kristoff was pleased with her selection.

"I do very much, " he said. He stroked the smooth, silky material.

"It's really nice. Thank you."

He tied his new robe in front. Kristoff felt everything was going well until her next comment.

"I purchased it at Saks Fifth Avenue in New York. Would you pour the wine?" Kristoff's mind raced with confusion. He thought it wise to avoid any mention of New York before dinner and hoped that after an exclusive bottle of wine, discussion would be easier.

Why ruin the beautiful moment and dinner Nadia had prepared? Nadia apparently wanted to set the stage for Kristoff when she commented:

"We should enjoy moments like this more often. That is why I love touring with the ballet. We dine in charming restaurants all over Western Europe and the United States. It is so wonderful." She paused, then added, "Will we ever live to experience that joy in our country, Kristoff?"

He noticed her eyes watering and embraced her warmly, holding her firm, shapely body as close as he could. "I love you, Nadia. Maybe our new leader, Mikoyanov, will move the Soviet Union in that direction."

Nadia stared at Kristoff. She could not accept his response and made him more aware of her frustration with life in Russia. The political climate debilitated her spirit.

"But I don't want to wait until I am an old woman. I want us to enjoy life now while we are young. We need more freedom, you as a writer and I as a performer. Why don't we leave? There is no future for us here. We need more than love, Kristoff."

He pondered her comment. Was this the perfect moment to reveal his knowledge of her planned defection? He preferred she reveal her secret. That would be a sign of her trust in him. Maybe Nadia would tell him outright.

He kissed her and through her lips he could feel her uneasiness.

"It is not that easy, Nadia. I am being watched." Her face tightened with fear. He quickly realized his remark was imprudent. She wanted to speak but held back. Kristoff had never seen Nadia appear so frightened. He embraced her until he felt her mood calm. The look in her eyes was one he had never seen before and would never forget. She was searching for a solution to her unhappiness, knowing the repercussions of her desires could jeopardize their relationship and mutual safety. Kristoff also understood her reasons for silence while living in a dwelling that could be wired for information. Enough had been said already. He placed his index finger over his lips to indicate that silence should prevail at the moment. He kissed her gently, poured more wine, sat her at the table, and asked her to pass the salad. A smile returned to her beautiful face. They enjoyed the moment.

After dinner, Kristoff felt the need to continue their conversation. They walked to their favorite rendezvous, Odessa, a nightclub several blocks from her apartment where conversation could be muted in social frivolity. There was a chill in the Moscow air as they walked in a light snowfall that covered them while dimming street lights. The café was crowded with cheerful clamor. Many patrons were standing or dancing to American rock and roll while they drank beer and vodka, losing their inhibitions as the night progressed. A friendly waitress motioned for them to follow her to their favorite table away from the bar. She knew Kristoff and Nadia and served them two cognacs. They stared at one another. Kristoff raised his glass to celebrate their love. "To our future together." His eyes focused on Nadia. Her smile was diminished by her emotions. She wanted to be cheerful but found it difficult. Kristoff could feel her anguish and hoped a few drinks would relax her mood. Apparently Nadia was thinking similar thoughts because she finished her cognac and asked for another. Her cheeks began to show some color. That was a good sign. She moved closer to Kristoff. Their eyes were inches apart. Kristoff whispered.

"Talk to me. Tell me what's inside."

Nadia's response was soft and appeared pensive. "I will." Kristoff anticipated her answer was forthcoming, but he gently nudged her. "When?" Her response was almost a whisper. "Soon."

Kristoff was pushing and he knew it. "Why not now?" Nadia's eyes began to tear. Kristoff held her hands and moved closer until his leg touched hers. He then revealed the engagement ring for this very moment. His proposal followed.

"I love you, Nadia. Will you marry me?" Nadia looked at the ring. She moved closer to Kristoff until her lips met his. She thanked him then whispered, "Yes I will, but you should know I am defecting Kristoff. Please join me."

Kristoff felt both joy and trepidation at her response. Without much effort, she had shared her secret with him. He felt a strong, warm connection based upon mutual love and trust. Now he felt obligated to respond. It wasn't easy for him because of what Trushin had told him. "When, Nadia? What about your family?"

Apparently her plan had been set in motion.

"My mother understands. I have her blessing. Our Bolshoi tour in New York is nineteen months from now. This will give us time to work out all the details. Are you with me, Kristoff?" She looked for some kind of encouragement but found little if any until Kristoff added:

"One way or another, I will join you."

Tears streaked down her face.

"Make plans soon. Please!" The desperation in her voice was genuine.

Then Kristoff informed her, "This weekend we are visiting my parents. They want to meet you. We will plan our strategy then, I promise."

His words were comforting. Nadia embraced Kristoff with a new sense of life and emotion she had never felt before. Her mind felt free at last. She had revealed her secret and now had something to look forward to. This alone altered her disposition and mood away from fear and uncertainty. Her lips pressed hard against Kristoff.

"I love you so much. You have made me the happiest woman in the world." Kristoff's heart pounded with mixed emotions.

Chapter 4

The next morning Kristoff's car barely started. The temperature was below zero and the air was dry and crisp. His father enjoyed bourbon in this cold weather so Kristoff was headed for a liquor store near Gorky Park. It was a long drive, which pleased Kristoff because his car would generate some warmth by the time he returned for Nadia. He thought of his father. Once again, his mind wandered to another episode of his youth when his father was stationed in East Germany. His rank of colonel involved more responsibilities throughout the Russian Republic and beyond. Kristoff missed not having his father at home. They were very close then as now. It was 1968. Kristoff was eight years old and just returned home from school.

"Hello Momma. When will Papa return from Germany?"

Speaking from his bedroom, his father's voice could be heard.

"Sooner than you think!"

Kristoff ran to his father's open arms. "Papa!" They embraced and love flowed strongly between them. Father and son could not be closer.

"Now about that game of chess we never finished."

Kristoff was pleased that his father did not forget their little moments together. "OK, but first may I tell you and Momma about something that happened in school today?" Kristoff was a very bright and well-informed young boy. His parents made sure he understood more than most other children his age. Now his parents wondered about their son's comment, but did not anticipate what followed.

His mother asked, "What happened that is so interesting?" Kristoff moved into a chair close to his parents who were seated on a sofa.

Kristoff's eyes appeared watery as he spoke. "Well, today at school, I spoke out."

His father sensed that something was wrong immediately. "Explain yourself." There was a strong sense of curiosity in his voice.

Kristoff hesitated. "Well, we were talking about fighting for our country and patriotism. The teacher said we should always fight for our country, right or wrong."

Kristoff paused and looked at his father, who asked, "And what did you say?"

Kristoff looked into his father's eyes. "I said, 'Why would you fight for your country, if your country was wrong." Kristoff hesitated, anticipating a comment from his father.

There was none, only a question. "And what did the teacher say?"

Kristoff hesitated and his father did not rush him.

"The teacher scolded me in front of everyone. I was embarrassed. She told me never to question my country, no matter what I think." The colonel remained silent.

"Should I ever question my country, Papa? You have always taught me to think for myself."

The colonel looked at Monique. His son waited for his reply, which was forthcoming.

"You are now ready for a very important lesson." Colonel Rypchensky lifted his son and placed him on the sofa between them. His wife Monique gently held his shoulders while her husband spoke. "Kristoff, you are now old enough for the truth." He paused.

"Remember what I tell you because it is very important." He lifted his son onto his lap and looked directly into his eyes.

"Are you ready to learn something important?" Monique appeared anxious for her son.

The seriousness of his father's tone was very clear to Kristoff and his mother.

"Yes, Papa."

The colonel continued looking directly at his son. He spoke with a soft and steady voice. He did not want to frighten his son any more than he already had.

"Our country is a great country but many times our leaders are cruel and not fair to our citizens. Many citizens have been arrested and tortured for their beliefs and for what they say. You were not wrong at all, but you were unwise." He pointed at his temple.

"You must never speak out and question your country in front of everyone."

Kristoff understood but then added, "But we were told by our teacher that we are free."

The colonel briefly looked at his wife, then emphasized his response while staring into his son's eyes.

"That is not true! Do not believe it!" Then he posed questions. "Are you free to work for the Communist Party? Yes. Free to fight for your country? Yes. Free to do what you are told? Yes. But not free to think, and never free to speak out." He paused again and looked at his son, then gently added. "You must never do that again! Understand!"

Kristoff had tears in his eyes when he responded. "Yes, Papa. Then we are not free, are we?"

The colonel held his son close to him. "No, son, we are not free."

The words echoed in Kristoff's mind as he parked his Volvo on a side street, a short walking distance from a liquor store. He occasionally thought of childhood episodes when he was about to visit his father. No republic in the Soviet Union, including Russia, was free from oppression. Kristoff learned at an early age that his fellow citizens were denied their dignity and human rights. One of several indelible moments of his childhood.

He was having difficulty locating a liquor store. The government had closed several in Moscow and also limited opening hours for business to discourage alcohol consumption. He was reluctant to leave his car because it was freezing outside. Two men suddenly approached. They appeared to be drunk.

"Hey friend, where the hell can I buy a bottle of vodka. The store used to be around the corner." He pointed in the general direction. Kristoff told them it was closed and that he was going to try the one two blocks down on the corner.

"You look familiar. Are you Alex Bracovic?" Kristoff asked the older drunk.

The man stumbled and smiled. "Yes, the drunken playwright who cannot express himself in this fucking country. Vodka gives me freedom of speech." Bracovic's companion laughed. He appeared young when he addressed Kristoff.

"Why is it not open? Usually opens at ten o'clock."

Kristoff then remembered. "Yes, I forgot. The government has ordered all liquor stores to open later each day. Their way of decreasing hours for purchases."

Bracovic slurped his words in anger. "What the hell they trying to do? We want vodka. Do you have vodka?" Like many other artists and writers, Bracovic drowned himself in alcohol to escape the pain of oppression.

Kristoff chimed in. "First of all, your young friend is not twenty-one. The new law means he cannot buy vodka or any other alcohol." When Kristoff approached the young man who appeared to be a teenager, he tried to encourage him to move on. It bothered Kristoff to see this young man who had a striking resemblance to his own youthful appearance. He leaned toward the young man's shoulder and whispered.

"You could be arrested."

Bracovic staggered forward. "Fuck the law. Come on. We will find a bottle somewhere. This goddamn country is slowly driving me insane. You cannot do this. You cannot do that. What the hell can you do? Huh!" Bracovic then unzipped his trousers and proceeded to urinate in the street. "Piss on them!"

Kristoff moved on, realizing the futility of his efforts, but he did share their frustration. The liquor store opened just in time for him to make his purchase of Kentucky bourbon, his father's favorite drink.

When Kristoff returned to Nadia's apartment, she was packed and the Volvo was warm enough for them to remove their heavy winter outer wear. When they left her apartment for the airport, her spirits were high because just the thought of traveling and the freedom attached to it were exciting. They were also happy about visiting his parents at their Black Sea resort. With Nadia by his side, the occasion was even more pleasant. Her mind was freed from the suspense of withholding her plans from Kristoff. In a teasing mood, she cuddled close to Kristoff and rubbed his legs and groin. Their lovemaking was exceptional the night before and she delighted in sexy moments. Kristoff became aroused and pulled over to a hidden area behind a line of evergreen trees. They were making passionate love within moments, consuming one another as expected from intense young lovers. His heart was pounding while his body's rhythm pulsated sexual power; the more he gave, the more she wanted. His heart continued pounding from the encounter while she displayed her feminine sexuality. She wanted more. Her warm lips consumed him. Their love and passion for each other was seemingly out of control. She whispered, "I love you." Their bodies compressed into one mass of human flesh, so close, they could feel their hearts pounding. Their grasp of one another slowly unfurled. Kristoff opened the car windows, which were covered with moisture. Refreshed by the rush of cold air streaming over their overheated bodies, they gazed into each other's eyes. When they arrived at the airport they realized their romantic love and relationship had crossed a new threshold. It was a wonderful feeling for both of them but submerged deep within his soul, Kristoff felt emotional uncertainty. His sense of unease did not subside.

While waiting for their flight to depart, Kristoff had time to reflect upon his relationship with Nadia. He knew she was not happy living in the Soviet Union. He could understand her reasons but he also felt that his country needed the very people who sought defection as a path to liberty. They were future entrepreneurs, teachers, artists and other creative citizens whose frustration with an ideology that confined them was unbearable. He loved Russia and thought of wonderful possibilities where Nadia's fulfillment could be experienced in the country he loved. What would it take to transform the Soviet Union? For Nadia, the answer was no where in sight, at least not in her life time. She wanted out and he would have to reconcile his expectations if their relationship was to move forward. His love for her was sincere, but he also loved his parents and realized his love for Nadia would eventually separate loving parents from his life. Being an only child can be difficult for several reasons. He would have loved having a brother or sister to share his personal feelings. Parents of one child may at times also feel that a second child would have been more fulfilling. He would never ask his parents and so would never know their explanation. He could only surmise their reason to be exactly what Nadia feels. Raising children in a police state can rob both parent and child from fulfilling their dreams. He understood why this reality was shared by millions of citizens who live behind the "iron curtain". Kristoff therefore had a choice that on the surface seemed apparent. But it was still a difficult choice. He would choose his love for Nadia over his love for country and family. He also realized that throughout the world there were citizens whose desire for liberty, no matter where they lived, were feeling similar emotional conflicts. He was not alone. For this he was certain.

Chapter 5

The airport was crowded with Muscovites scurrying to resorts on the Black Sea and anywhere warm. These were elite Russians whose status was elevated beyond the reach of over ninety percent of the population. Their dedication, loyalty, and service to one party provided them with many privileges causing quiet dissent among the masses, frustrated by a system that rewarded party loyalty instead of competence and hard work. Kristoff understood class distinctions within Russia, especially Moscow, where party members along with their families were part of what Russians called a comfortable elite, as long as you played by the rules. Kristoff was part of this privileged class and it bothered him because he believed prosperity and opportunity should be open to all citizens. His experience as a writer and journalist exposed him to economic and social disparities while touring a variety of ethnic communities from several republics. He realized he was taking advantage of privileges, which allowed him opportunities for travel where he could observe first-hand how his country's economy was imploding.

He believed the system was untenable and rigged. It was just a matter of time before economic forces would determine the Soviet Union's inevitable decline. The signs were everywhere. Shelves were empty, food was scarce, consumer goods could be purchased at outrageous prices on the black market. The economy did not produce the quantity or quality of consumer goods demanded. Citizens quietly complained. Privileged party members shopped in western Europe where goods were plentiful. Many well to do Russians preferred shopping in the United States. Some even used an American Express Card. What was missing? The answer is entrepreneurs. They are the dynamic force missing from the USSR.

Economic principles of communism were not models for cultivating entrepreneurship, and free market capitalism.

Most citizen's facial expressions said it all. Joy and levity were replaced with futility and despair. Nadia frequently pointed this out to Kristoff. Her international travel exposed her to many shortcomings of communist economies. Her observations increased Kristoff's awareness. She was clever with her persuasive commentaries of communism's failures.

With reservations in hand, Kristoff moved swiftly through the crowd. Once again, he was spared delays experienced by other travelers. The flight, however, was not an experience he looked forward to because Aeroflot was a commercial failure. Accommodating passenger comfort was not their strength. Without competition for domestic flights, citizens were at the mercy of socialist mediocrity at best. With the exception of military aircraft, which he would fly on occasion with his father, Kristoff, like many other citizens, endured failures of a defective command economy.

Odessa, a charming city on the Black Sea, was Commander Rypchensky's favorite getaway. Using his privileged status, the commander purchased a cottage. He and his wife, Monique , made it very charming, both inside and out. Wealthy areas of Odessa were lined with stately homes whose architecture was a mix of Greek, Turkish, and Russian styles. French and Italian-designed buildings were also part of the city architecture.

Post-war Odessa suffered the ramifications of occupation forces allied with Germany. Many natives suffered from collaboration with enemy occupiers. Over decades that followed, tension between Russians and Ukrainians continued, in part caused by bad blood during the war years. Russian and Jewish cultures were widespread and Russian/Ukrainian dialects were common. During purges before and after the Stalin era, many Jews emigrated from Ukraine to Israel, Western Europe, and the United States, motivated by strong antisemitism within Ukrainian culture. A large community of Ukrainians settled in Brighton Beach, Brooklyn, where their cultural footprint continues to flourish.

For years, Kristoff was interested in his Ukrainian roots. He had not been acquainted with Odessan politics, but when he experienced its beauty and studied its history and culture, his interest piqued. The taxi driver spoke Russian, with an accent that Kristoff noticed was common while walking along the concourse. The man assigned to drive him to his parent's cottage was unusually loquacious. He also provided car service for Kristoff's father.

"Are you familiar with Odessa? Your father always speaks of you and how proud he is of your achievements." He smoked Turkish cigarettes right down to nothing but ashes and continued with small talk.

"I have been driving for your father for over ten years. Special request! He has changed my life from destitution. I am indebted to him. He is a fine officer and leader of men, including me."

So it wasn't just small talk. Kristoff's father had cultivated a cadre of men and women to serve him for every possibility and eventuality. This taxi driver was one of dozens that Kristoff had knowledge of in the past three months. His father's vast political arm stretched throughout the Soviet Union. Similar experiences explained why his father's reputation was widely respected. He had cultivated a large number and variety of patriots willing to serve him. Their admiration went beyond loyalty. This influence had tremendous potential if his father ever planned a political future. His father's awareness and understanding of power politics had been expanded by utilizing his authority and ability to persuade. The commander was also very kind and generous to his subordinates. He paid them well and treated them with respect. He remembered their names and asked about their families. On many occasions, Kristoff observed his genuine social grace and how he turned it into soft power.

When Kristoff asked the driver about the Ukraine, he received an earful of information.

"Russians are angry because Khrushchev transferred Crimea to us. It belongs to the Ukraine now. Russians want it back." Then he continued. "The Russians are backward. They know little about business, unlike Ukrainians. Communism has made them lazy and dependent on the state. Ukrainians are entrepreneurs. We want more trade and business but the Russians are too stupid to see opportunity. If they let us be free, we could make them rich too." Then he added: "Your father will change everything one day. He is a leader; he is smart and wants to stop this communist bullshit. Please excuse my language. Nothing works under communism. It's a joke, but people are afraid to question authority because the police will arrest you. Ask your father; he knows what to do and some day he will change the mess we're in." Kristoff and Nadia could not believe what was being said. Then the driver continued. "That is why the communists pushed Khrushchev out of power. He wanted to change communism so it would work for the people. More freedom for business and commerce. They stopped him and silenced him. Now we all suffer in silence. It's terrible what they are doing to us. We are bankrupt. Everyone knows it. Communism does not work. It favors only Communist Party members who have privileges. The rest of us pick up the crumbs. It's that simple."

His anger was controlled, but it managed to illicit a whisper from Nadia.

"You see, Kristoff. This is why we must leave Russia. It's dying."

The commander and his wife observed the taxi's arrival from a room overlooking their driveway entrance. Upon noticing the taxi, Kristoff's parents moved closer to welcome their son. The driver noticed the commander and his wife waiting so he pulled as close to the entrance as possible, and moved quickly to open the car doors for his two passengers. Nadia observed his parents' joy and love immediately upon greeting Kristoff. Their only child was their treasure. Their bond for one another was strong. With a big smile, Kristoff's father approached the taxi. "Welcome, my son." He warmly embraced Kristoff who barely exited the taxi. Kristoff's mother then approached and he embraced and kissed her warmly. He loved his parents and the three of them wrapped arms around one another as Nadia looked on. She could now connect the wonderful parents who made Kristoff the man in her life. His parents meant everything to him. Now she understood his concerns and reservations while discussing her defection plans.

Commander Rypchensky peered into the cab, then asked Kristoff:

"Please introduce us to your charming companion." His voice was clear and mellow to Nadia who smiled and immediately felt a warmness emanating from both parents.

"Mama and Papa, this is Nadia, the love of my life."

Both parents extended a warm welcome and Nadia responded. "I am very honored to meet you, Commander and Madame Rypchensky." Nadia felt a good connection, especially after Kristoff's loving introduction. Nadia's stunning beauty and remarkable poise were obvious to both parents. Her training in ballet taught her social grace, good posture and familiarity with cultural amenities. Now his parents understood their son's attraction. Nadia had much more than beauty. She had charisma, impeccable language skills. Her friendly demeanor was evident. Exposure to international cultures enhanced her confidence. When they reached for her hand, Nadia sensed a gentle and genuine feeling of parental love.

Kristoff smiled while staring into Nadia's eyes. Their love communicated a message of confirmation and finality. He felt comfortable with their plans for marriage. Monique offered her arm to Nadia and walked with her through flower gardens, housed in a glass enclosure adjacent to the cottage. Kristoff was directed by his father to his herb garden adjacent to the flowers. Southern exposure allowed herbs and flowers to grow during the colder months. Parsley, shallots, dill, chervil, French tarragon, and garlic were neatly arranged, surrounded by large stones. Flowers were arranged along the perimeter, especially Camomile and other daisy varieties. The cottage was rustic, yet made more charming by his mother, who managed to decorate it tastefully with pieces of antique furniture and art. Her expensive taste beautifully displayed her skill in interior decorating. She was a gracious woman who maintained her poise despite her displeasure with communism's many shortcomings. She was not alone. The vast majority of Ukrainians, Russians, and other ethnic communities had even more antipathy for the system. Kristoff's extensive travel abroad made him sensitive to faces and body language that projected joy and contentment, both absent from citizens throughout the Soviet Union.

His father's garden provided relaxation from stress, stemming from pressures of being the army's highest ranking officer and now a major leader in an underground movement. Discussions with his father among herbs and flowers would soon involve more substance than any previous time together. His father realized it was time to finally be straightforward with Kristoff. It was time for his son to be informed of future plans, extraordinary plans. At first, he hesitated. For a brief moment, Kristoff felt like the parent. Their roles seemed reversed. What was on his father's mind? Kristoff was prepared to ask but decided to wait until his father was ready to speak. He could see signs of stress and aging.

Finally, after thoughtful silence, Commander Rypchensky began with:

"Kristoff, I have enjoyed reading your editorials in Pravda. It is remarkable how you walk the line between what is permissible and what is not. Very clever!"

Kristoff felt his comment was more than a compliment. He was disguising something deeper. His gut instincts told him his father had something to reveal. He remained silent while his father pulled weeds growing between herbs and flowers. Finally Kristoff reacted.

"It took me many months to learn how to walk that line. I am very disappointed at the lack of progress being made for journalistic freedom." His father did not respond to his comment. Kristoff continued, this time with a personal edge in his tone, hoping to elicit a reaction. "I feel too inhibited by our system. Nadia feels the same way."

His father stood up and dusted off his hands. Kristoff was hoping that now, at age twenty seven, his father would not disguise or withhold information. Kristoff was prepared for and expected straight talk. He had many questions that his father could answer. He waited in silence. His father's reluctance to speak was in part explained out of concern for his family's security. Protecting his family was a priority. Kristoff understood family loyalty. However he also understood that his extended "family of friends" and colleagues were also important. Included were men and women who were politically connected and dependent. His father's relationship with them, in a police state, was problematic. Privileges and power possessed by his father were occasionally utilized to protect individuals from vagarious indiscretions. The Commander personally warned individuals not to speak out too vigorously. His ability to protect his "family of friends" had its limits. The commander could not abuse his authority to correct every indiscretion. He also realized it was time to inform his son of looming danger. Kristoff finally heard his father's long withheld strategy. He began with his political connections.

" Kristoff, I have withheld what I am about to tell you for obvious reasons. To protect our family. But it is time for you to know what is happening. I am working closely with Mikoyanov to change the balance of power in the Central Committee before our meeting in February. We have a network of contacts who will work with us from every republic. They include laborers, artists, writers, police, teachers, government and party officials. We even have powerful members of the KGB and high-ranking military personnel. These people are dedicated to bringing about some radical changes to our system. Our goal is a peaceful transition of power, if that's possible. I trust you will also work with our network."

Kristoff could not believe what he just heard. His father, a leading force in a major political movement, was not only informing him, he was inviting him into the struggle. Now he understood the hesitancy in his father's past behavior. His instincts were confirmed. He felt excitement and joy because now he could finally work for a cause he believed was long overdue. He also knew his skills were important for their cause. However, his father warned him, liabilities were very real for dissidents. Many were detained, followed by sentences to gulags. Sons and daughters of powerful men were among them. Kristoff finally inquired:

"This is obviously an underground operation." He felt that question was necessary. With so much at stake for him personally, it wasn't a stupid question. He had to hear the answer directly from his father. His insecurity and fear for his parents were obvious.

His father understood and sensed his son's doubts.

"Absolutely. We have to remain underground. Otherwise our opponents will move to expose us as traitors and destroy us in the process. Remember, their decision-making has remained firm. They still control our legislature."

Kristoff's heart was beating with mixed emotions. He underestimated the power his father could generate. He also sensed determination from his father, potentially a strong and prominent force in Russian politics. His father's tone was very serious. Drastic change was logical as well for his parents. They were both very well-educated and cultured citizens. Communism was suffocating them. Kristoff wanted to know more.

"You are undertaking a very dangerous task. Why?" What Kristoff was about to hear were words he had longed for but never expected.

"I have reached a point of no return, Kristoff."

His father continued his explanation to settle any doubts in Kristoff's mind.

"Why? How have I raised you? Surely not to be a robot of the state. Our country is hurting badly on many fronts. Our bureaucracy is sitting on their asses because they have a good life. They will not change our economic policies. Lenin would. He was no fool. His only mistake was having any trust in Stalin. Our people are suffering under a heavy blanket of incompetent bureaucracies. The old men refuse to change, but we must. In democracies, problems such as these are resolved through free and open debate and elections. We do not enjoy those options."

Finally Kristoff heard what he had been waiting to hear for years. It was no longer a family secret. He wished Nadia was standing next to him this very moment so she might reconsider her plans. Her forthcoming defection frightened Kristoff because he loved her and feared losing her. He felt torn between his parents and the woman he loved. Also, for the first time in his life, he feared for his parents.

They were always his protectors and moral teachers. Now their lives were being placed in serious peril. He shared his fear with his father.

"I am afraid for you and mama. How sealed is this operation? There have been several occasions where agents have followed me. Could there be a leak somewhere?"

Kristoff could tell that his father was disturbed when hearing this from his son. Network operations would be more difficult and dangerous for him now with his son's knowledge and involvement.

"I will have our network agents investigate. They will be observing us along with the KGB. You must for the time being maintain a low profile. Nothing out of the ordinary. Understood?"

Kristoff responded with a firm, "Absolutely!" Kristoff used the occasion to inquire about Trushin. "Who is this fellow, Trushin?"

The commander smiled because he knew his son would ask sooner or later. It amused him to tell the story of Trushin.

"He, my son, is your godfather. Yes, you were baptized in this atheistic state. Trushin insisted. He will be at your service on rare occasions. A very trusted friend."

Kristoff had a good feeling about Trushin. He wanted to know more.

"How did you meet Trushin? Where does he fit in?"

His father expected these questions. "We served together during the war years; on the German front. I saved his life more than once. He is a very noble and humble man. He's also a powerful link in our network. He's KGB. I need him and he has great connections. If you can believe it, he went to seminary to become a priest, but realized he could change nothing there. His brilliance in the KGB is well known by party officials. He wants change as much as we do, real change. He is the conscience of our movement. The ethical component."

Desperate for information, Kristoff pursued his line of questioning.

"What about Mikoyanov? How does he fit into this operation? He does seem more open minded."

His father stared at his son. "I understand you are nervous about this operation, but I assure you, it's under control. Party chairman Mikoyanov is supporting our cause. However, his name will never be mentioned. We have to protect him until the very end; until our victory is secured. As far as we are concerned, he's an insider; part of the established conservative power until the right moment when he will emerge as our new president with a truly democratic constitution. He is a silent partner, but a partner nevertheless. There is no other way for him to be involved without political turmoil."

Kristoff was not satisfied. "And if you don't succeed? Then what?"

The commander was clear: "I do not plan on failure."

Kristoff walked to the rose bush, which was covered with dark red roses. He smelled their fragrance from a distance and Nadia came to mind. Should he discuss Nadia's plans with his father? He decided not to say anything at this time. Instead, he continued with his questions.

"How do you propose to keep the KGB from interfering with your network? They must be suspicious."

The commander responded confidently. "There is always suspicion in a police state. We have several plans for that. First, we have powerful KGB men in our network. Trushin and I have designed some diversions. The KGB will be preoccupied with them."

Kristoff was curious and asked, "For example?"

His father explained: "Well, some diversions are based upon information that is completely false. However, more diversions are based upon real challenges to party authority throughout several republics. Eastern European states under Russian hegemony, despise being trapped behind an iron curtain. You know there are credible anti-communist sentiments and movements in Poland, for example, and here in Ukraine. Even Russians are sensing glasnost, a concept we have made popular. They want change and soon. Our strategies conform with these sentiments. We have network KGB authorities who assign agents to investigate existing dissident activities and contrived activities. By overloading agents with investigations, some fabricated, we believe they will have less time to direct their manpower toward probes of our network."

Kristoff did not appear satisfied with his explanation.

"Is it really that simple? How can you be assured these distractions will not be detected? What if they are traced back to your network? Without credibility, your schemes will not work. It won't be long before they're on to your plans. Then what?"

The commander smiled because his son was raising good questions. Questions whose answers better be persuasive to those being asked to risk their lives and security. Totalitarian cultures heighten feelings of paranoia. Conspirators could never be too cautious, even with trusted friends and family. The commander was silent. Kristoff's argument was logical and critical. His father then commented, "Well, if you have a better plan, please share it with me. We believe there is no perfect plan, however, ours has a chance. It's all timing; we know that. And we also know that we have a window of opportunity for success. That time is now. There's no turning back. The overwhelming majority of network members agree. I hope you are with us. You and Nadia."

The commander could sense that his son was thinking about past years when their communication had been incomplete, stifled by design by his father, in order to protect his family. The commander always believed family comes first. Family security was still paramount, but their personal liberty and dignity now had become priorities as well. His father had reached a new stage in his life and career. He felt it was time to sacrifice some of his security in order to achieve his goal. It was time to leverage his power and influence for a noble cause.

Kristoff had more questions. "What about diversions that are not totally false?

I don't understand."

His father lit a cigarette. "I will explain. There are very real anti-Soviet sentiments and movements in Poland, the Baltic States, Czechoslovakia, and Hungary. We simply create rumors based on this dissidence. The KGB is currently chasing a story that is a creation of ours concerning dissident protests in Prague."

Kristoff finished his father's thought. "And when the KGB chases these stories, they have less time for investigating your network activities."

His father drew on his cigarette. "Exactly. They are too busy for us, following situations that are mostly genuine and organic. We add fabricated stories to complicate and mislead them. But our time is precious and limited. We can't fool them forever. Our window of opportunity is now. Many factors are aligned with our timing for change. Failures with our economy, war in Afghanistan, dissidence in Berlin and eastern Europe, glasnost and perestroika. We can also add the fact that our nation is bankrupt. These are their pressure points. They are issues that will pull and tear communism apart. Their confidence to secure their power is waning." Kristoff felt his father had carefully thought about his decision to move forward. His uncertainty diminished after listening to his father's explanation. He extended his hand.

"I am with you one hundred percent."

Embracing his father was assuring but his feelings of anxiety persisted.

They walked to the cottage where his mother and Nadia were comparing their experiences in Paris. They were very engrossed with each other due to their shared interests in cultural activities. Monique's fondness for Nadia was very apparent.

"Where did you find this sophisticated lady? She is so charming. I just adore her."

Nadia smiled and looked at Kristoff, who placed his arm around her and informed his parents of their plans for marriage in the future. An exact date was not established.

"I met Nadia at the airport where, thanks to a storm delay, we became acquainted. It was my lucky day." Nadia beamed with happiness. She felt a warm connection with both parents. A confirmation of their approval. Their only child would be her husband. Nadia was also an only child. She understood fear of losing family. But her feelings for freedom and her urge to escape the confines of totalitarianism were as determined as ever.

The table was beautifully set for dinner. Political conversation was discouraged. The occasion called for family sharing, especially plans for their future wedding. Nadia shared her joy of being part of the Bolshoi. Monique was impressed with loving envy. It was a beautiful moment appreciated by all. Their preoccupation with celebration was intentional. Relevant and useful political information was not shared, including Nadia's plan for defection. This was an unfortunate omission.

Chapter 6

Moscow was cold in November, usually an indication of a forthcoming brutal winter. The Kremlin office of Mikoyanov included a view of beautiful buildings displaying a rainbow of colors. The view from the southern exposure was a large parking area filled with black sedans and several security vehicles. Alex Orlov, vice chairman of the KGB, had his office one floor below and when he walked in at 9:00 am, his secretary and wife, Alicia Bankers Orlov, informed him of Mikoyanov's meeting at 9:15. Alicia was Latvian, whose marriage to a Russian officer of occupation was frowned upon by her parents and community. But she genuinely loved Alex even though she despised the Soviet Union's hegemony in the Baltic States. Because of her husband's influence, she was not classified a security risk. Her two sons were raised in Russia and were on their way to becoming citizens of the republic.

Alicia had a natural sense for clandestine activity, learned after years of occupation by Russians, who were despised for their boorish and arrogant behavior. From incoming correspondence received in her office, she calculated that orders currently being processed for dozens of KGB agents were excessive. Something didn't seem right. She was especially upset when she read that agents were working in Riga, the capital of her beloved homeland.

Latvia is located along the eastern coast of the Baltic, bordering Russia. Independent for years, however its proximity to Russia made it logistically strategic for the Soviet Union during WWII. Their language is Indo-European. Russian is a Slavic language that is mandatory in schools throughout Soviet republics. Latvia's economy exports lumber, metal, machinery, textiles and equipment. They were not pleased with Russia's permanent occupation during and after

World War II because their wealth was being drained by Russian bureaucrats who recognized Latvian's commercial success. Alicia despised Russians because they stifled their economic growth by manipulating the free market. She knew her history and was proud that Latvia's ancestors were Vikings, not Russians. Many Latvians were married to Russians as a result of occupation after the second world war. Alicia convinced her Russian husband that Latvia's future must be independent. His conversion made it possible for him to be recruited by network agents who were spreading their political connections in every republic for the purpose of encouraging all republics to announce their independence from the Soviet Union when the opportunity presented itself. Alicia was also actively involved in the underground. Motivated by her contempt for communist ideology, her behind the scenes participation was critical for spreading the movement into Baltic republics. Because of her Russian husband's status as second in command at KGB, and Latvia's contempt for communist policies, Alicia's influence with other Baltic states was instrumental in providing financial support for network operations. Because of the tireless efforts of this dedicated woman, network support was solid and spreading in the Baltic states.

Alicia Bankers was a woman who knew her Latvian roots and was very proud of her heritage. As a child of five, she experienced the invasion of Nazi Germany . Her parents were tortured and enslaved. Her older sister was raped by SS thugs. To add even more trauma to her life, when the Nazi's retreated, Latvia was overtaken by communists who pillaged whatever assets remained. When asked by an American journalist after the war, who was worst her response was: the Nazis shoot and kill first, then ask questions. The communists ask questions, then shoot and kill civilians. Either way both were terrorists she detested and swore to never cease to resist any form of totalitarianism.

The three Baltic nations, Estonia, Lithuania and Latvia all wanted their national sovereignty reinstated. They experienced economic progress, despite being burdened by communist ideology. Entrepreneurial skills were an important reason for their success. They managed to utilize their natural and limited capital resources because their human resources valued education which emboldened self preservation. They survived with limited assets. Their economies managed to produce goods and services that could be marketed in post war-torn economies. These experiences shaped Alicia Bankers life, making her determined to overcome obstacles by utilizing her intelligence and education. Early on she realized her occupied nation was trapped by terror and duplicity. Rather than concede defeat, Alicia endured her misery by embracing subterfuge for survival. When she fell in love with a Russian officer of occupation, her remaining family members and several friends encouraged her to reject his offer of marriage. When she decided to marry, many believed she sold her soul to the devil. But she knew their love for one another was genuine as was her contempt for occupation. Her husband, Captain Orlov, was a brilliant attorney who she believed, over time would assess totalitarian shortcomings. Within ten years of marriage, two sons were born. They were educated in Riga and Alicia assured her husband they would learn their national heritage. Over time, Captain Orlov learned the Latvian culture, language and history. He admired Latvians for their tenacity, hard work and value for education, at all levels. Just to qualify for carpentry, his eldest son had to study advanced mathematics and apprentice with a master tradesman for over five years. He was proud of his oldest son who became a master carpenter just before Captain Orlov was promoted to KGB headquarters in Moscow, second in command. Alicia and her two sons became Russian citizens. His son's high level carpentry was in demand and provided him and his younger brother with comfortable lives. Their strong work ethic was responsible. As

Latvians, they could see for themselves how communism managed to destroy incentives and motivation within Russia. They believed Russians were too dependent on the state for survival.

Living in Moscow, Captain Orlov could observe and evaluate an inefficient communist bureaucracy. Alicia made a point of comparing the two republics, one inspired by ideas, the other trapped by archaic ideology. Husband and wife became silent dissidents, and upon meeting Commander Rypchensky, joined the Soviet Network. The art of subterfuge was second nature to Alicia. Her husband, realizing her natural instincts for intelligence work, appointed her secretary, where she could monitor KGB and Network activities. Although their lives were comfortable, contempt for communism altered their world view. Both experienced a paradigm shift. Communism's patriotic appeal vanished because they viewed it as disingenuous. Communism's many shortcomings were obvious. Men and women who followed intellectual pursuits, filled with reason, education and science, could no longer embrace a false ideology. Their determination to destroy it became an obsession.

Alicia's familiarity with the Baltic culture and language was used affectively by the network. Captain Orlov assigned her to travel throughout the region for the purpose of monitoring surreptitious activities for the KGB. In reality she was working for Commander Rypchensky who provided her with lists of network operatives. The communist party's control in Baltic States had a different configuration. Real power rested with tradesmen, manufacturers and commercial interests who were masked as Communists. In order to please party ideologues, Communism's fascade was manipulated, specifically for optics. Communism appeared to be something it wasn't, namely progressive and for the masses. Every politician knew the entire system was rigged. By projecting communism in a positive light, party hardliners were satisfied. By transforming Communism's image, reprisals from hardline party members were avoided. The entire system was a sham, but it kept revenue coming in so corrupt phony bureaucrats could extort their share, just as mobsters who intimidate businesses for a piece of the action. Extortion payments by communist party hacks were made possible by a code of silence. This is how the system was greased. Basically an underground economy. A Russian version of the Mafia. At some point, network operatives believed, communism would fade away for one simple reason. It didn't work. It was an economic failure. Network strategy was to hasten the transition from underground economy to a genuine and honest free market, where hiding behind a corrupt bureaucracy was no longer accepted.

A major problem that resulted from this corrupt system was it harbored and encouraged criminal activity. How can free markets flourish under these circumstances? Network agents did not anticipate these problems. And if KGB thugs who have no moral compass are reconstituted from the ashes of totalitarianism, a future economic business world of fascist criminals is created. Alicia Bankers' goal was to stop this progression from communist incompetence to crony capitalism. Because Baltic states had some experience with entrepreneurship, their chances for transitioning communism to market capitalism was feasible. The Baltic States would be a model for all to emulate. Not an easy task.

When Alex Orlov arrived at Mikoyanov's office, he could expect a cordial greeting but brevity as well. Mikoyanov always shifted to his business agenda; he was not inclined to waste time with small talk and moved efficiently to complete a long list of daily tasks. He was a workaholic of the first order, which added immense strength to the growing network under his command. He realized his dream of leading the Communist Party and was now in a position where his every move was being scrutinized. Conservatives in the party were not pleased with his style of leadership, based on consensus; it was perceived as weak. To counter this perception, network leaders encouraged him to highlight strong conservative sentiments on matters of little significance, just to appease hardliners. This included paying lip service to Communist slogans used in a multitude of public policies. His disingenuous comments appeared to satisfy hard line conservatives whose main concerns involved promoting ideological propaganda, not necessary reforms and matters of substance. Overcoming skepticism from his opponents was crucial to Mikoyanov, during what was now considered a transition stage of their under-the-radar power grab. He was not comfortable with political maneuvers that conflicted with his genuine democratic instincts, but he had to maintain an image of autocratic leadership to appease his opponents. He had to constantly remind himself that he must appear and act like an autocrat, not a democrat.

When Orlov walked into the chairman's office, he was pleasantly surprised to see Commander Rypchensky drinking a cup of coffee along with several other military officers, and three of his closest aides in the KGB. After a warm greeting, Mikoyanov turned on an electronic device that prevented eavesdropping; a gift from Orlov. Mikoyanov initiated their discussion.

"Gentlemen, we have been together for many years. Our success will depend upon absolute faith and trust in each other. We are a human chain that will pull our nation out of its paralysis. Our network is growing. It frightens me. So many people want a piece of the future. No one seems to realize that we are still a political minority. We must be cautious." He paused and sat at his large desk with photos of his wife and children facing him.

"Any news from our agents?" He then glanced at Orlov, who appeared hesitant to speak, but then clearly and emphatically stated:

"Careful as we have been, there is a chance we may have a problem in our midst."

Mikoyanov was very upset with this news. "How certain are you?"

Orlov noticed that he may have been too earnest with his comment. He softened his next comment. "Not certain at all. Fortunately, nothing critical to our immediate security. It's just that…"

Commander Rypchensky cut him off because he anticipated what was about to be said and preferred to divulge this information himself.

"My son's fiancé is planning to defect in the future, when the Bolshoi visits New York. This does not breach our security. However, I realize that because it indirectly involves Kristoff, the appearance of a security risk is apparent. My son assures me he will not defect. He is one of us. This information has not been shared with his fiancé; however, she is being encouraged to wait. I think she will comply. They have announced their plans to be married."

Orlov poured himself another cup of coffee, showing his satisfaction with the Commander's explanation. "Actually that was not the news I am concerned with. In fact, a defection rumor may be a good distraction because it signifies rejection of life in the Soviet Union, being expressed by many young citizens. Defections may work in our favor." However, he acknowledged, this defection, being that it involved personal connections, could pose problems. Orlov then voiced concerns about new information discovered by his agents.

"There is, I'm afraid, another development that must be handled immediately. There are agents among us who could be saboteurs. They must be found immediately. These three men are prime suspects." Orlov reached into his lapel and handed the names of three prime suspects to three agents sitting adjacent to him. He then excused himself when his secretary interrupted the meeting with a written note. For matters of security, Alicia was instructed to only deliver messages in person. Before leaving, Orlov shook hands with Mikoyanov and asked to be excused and would explain when he returned. Three agents followed him to his office. The written message was in code, and after Orlov translated it, he realized immediate action was required. His agents sensed this as well but remained silent. Orlov began instructing them as he lit a cigarette.

"There are agents in our network who may be traitors. They must be found immediately. These three men are prime suspects." He then handed agents a photo of each suspect.

"After you locate them, bring them to me for questioning. Say nothing about their loyalty. Inform them of an important review to be held in my office and escort them. Do not allow anyone to escape. I will expect you here by 6:00 o'clock this evening. Find them!"

As the three agents walked away they briefly looked at each other and instinctively understood Orlov's behavior had become unsettled. Orlov may have concluded a breach in security had occurred. He trusted his agents and had nothing to fear from their assigned tasks. He did however become anxious over matters where he lost control. He believed time was working against him. Revolutions have many moving parts, some unpredictable and dangerous. Strategy and timing were extremely critical components. He anticipated several more similar episodes as network operations moved forward.

Through a series of phone calls, each agent determined the location of their suspect. It was through network cooperation that all three suspects were located within four hours. At 6:00 pm, as ordered, agents returned to Orlov's office but only two returned with their assigned suspects. The third, Smansky, appeared without anyone. Orlov was walking to his office and saw Smansky in the hallway. Smansky's gesture forced an immediate question from Orlov. "Well, what happened?"

Smansky looked around to make sure no one was listening or watching. They entered Orlov's office. "I have him, sir."

Orlov looked around his office. "Where?"

Smansky's response was the surprise Orlov did not want to hear.

"In the trunk of my car. He tried to kill me on the way here."

Orlov did not want to hear that. "Is he dead?" When Orlov heard, "Yes sir, " he shook his head in disbelief. "Wait in the secretary's office until I speak with the others."

The urgency of the situation was compounded by this mishap. Orlov had to move quickly and would need accurate information before determining his course of action. In an adjacent room where two other agents were waiting, Orlov walked in and without hesitation ordered staff assistants to medicate each suspect, and when the drug's effect was certain, interrogate them with questions Orlov had written down.

"Record all their statements." He then returned to Smansky who was smoking his fourth cigarette. He realized his error in procedure, but his reaction with his captive was unavoidable.

Orlov admired Smansky, but he had to determine whether his trust in him was justified. Nevertheless, Smansky knew what to expect from his boss.

"You know what I must do to find out the truth."

Smansky shook his head. "Sir, I thought you knew me better than that."

Orlov felt awkward but insisted. "We cannot take any chances."

Smansky was upset and sat in complete silence. Injection with truth serum was not a fun experience. "Make it quick; I have a lovely woman in waiting this evening." One hour later, Smansky and two other agents were drugged and questioned.

Orlov returned to his office from the interrogation room. He felt bad for Smansky but under the circumstances he had no choice. He then called his secretary.

"Have Bostia accompanied to my office when he comes around."

Agent Bostia was tall and thin. His eyes were red from the administered drug. He wobbled into a chair. His eyes were now wet with tears. His head was down and he sobbed. Orlov spoke loudly and clearly.

"I humiliated poor Smansky. I never suspected you. Smansky had to kill an agent on the way here. What was Kurrin planning?"

Bostia could barely talk. "Nothing. He was a desperate man, just like me."

Orlov was angry. "What are you talking about? Why would he try to kill Smansky?"

Bostia was slowly awakening from his drug hangover.

"Because he was going to defect and thought Smansky would divulge his plans. Kurrin's lover lives in West Germany."

Orlov treated his agents well and could not tolerate behavior that was dangerous for network operations. He always attempted to accommodate his men with whatever lifestyle they preferred, homosexuality included. "Defect! When?"

Bostia was sobbing. "We both had weekend assignments in Berlin. From there we would cross into Holland. We have friends and family in the west."

Orlov understood family and friend loyalties and if they could be arranged, he would move agents close by. This procedure was used by KGB to assimilate agents more easily into foreign communities. The problem for Orlov was network operations being compromised. In this instance, defections were red flags. Attention would be focused on his agent's activities by other departments who constantly monitored one another for security reasons. His fear was that one careless event would lead to another, raising suspicions and probable investigations. His agents should know better. They obviously placed their personal lives above their professional responsibilities, which infuriated Orlov.

Exposure to western culture created discontent and frustration among agents. Requests to leave the Soviet Union made by ordinary citizens had increased. There were KGB agents who had similar plans. Their problem for defecting was more complicated and dangerous because KGB culture would make defection almost impossible. It was known that agents who defected had mysteriously been found dead, victims of radio active poison or other means used by KGB death squads specifically assigned for that purpose. Defection for freedom can be contagious for ordinary citizens. For KGB agents it can be a futile endeavor.

Orlov understood Bostia's sentiments. Fortunately, he did not betray the network, but his actions stirred internal tension within Network KGB operations. Orlov could make Bostia's life miserable but decided to use his misguided actions to his advantage.

"Who have you spoken to about our Network?"

By this time, Bostia was stable and in control of his behavior. "No one. I have not betrayed you. I wrote you a letter requesting reassignment. I am desperate. My wife and children are in Britain. I want to be with them." KGB agents sometimes married citizens from abroad. It enhanced their social acceptance, mobility and effectiveness.

Orlov was concerned about leaks. "Does anyone know about our operation?"

Bostia was regaining his composure. He was an attractive man who had high marks as an agent. "Only that I am available for information. Otherwise KGB know nothing."

Orlov inquired why Bostia did not reveal information.

"And why did you choose not to inform them? You had a chance. Or are you lying to me?"

Bostia shook his head. He sounded sincere.

"No! The truth is I was confident that my letter to you requesting a foreign station would be well received."

Orlov stared at Bostia and emphasized his remark.

"Well, here is my response to your letter. Listen carefully because your life will depend upon cooperating with us. Understood?"

Bostia nodded. "Yes sir."

Orlov's experience in twenty-five years of intelligence taught him how to read his agents. He had Bostia in a vulnerable position and now was the opportune moment to utilize his power over him. He also happened to trust Bostia.

"The KGB expects information from you, correct?"

Bostia nodded. "Yes sir."

Orlov then snapped, "Then you will give them information, as expected, misinformation really. You understand my order?" Bosnia nodded his head.

"Yes sir, I understand and can assure you of my cooperation." Orlov then asked.

"Can you identify them?"

Bostia took a deep breath. "Only by code. We correspond once a week."

Orlov was very pleased.

"Wonderful. I have plenty of information for you to give them. If you do not cooperate, you will never see your family again. If you work with us and we succeed, I promise you a permanent station in London." Orlov had a way with his agents and Bostia knew his boss always kept his word. When Bostia was dismissed, he left with more confidence in Orlov and himself. He was determined to make things work. His life and family would be his reward.

Orlov immediately returned to Mikoyanov and Commander Rypchensky to explain details of what happened. Both agreed that having network agents feeding misinformation to the KGB was critical at this time. Monitoring the situation however was equally important to determine whether agents could be trusted. All agreed that what motivated these men was freedom from their totalitarian prison. For KGB professionals, the irony was unmistakable.

KGB officers were recruited from different levels of society and from several republics. Most were highly educated in police state culture. That did not mean they believed in totalitarian culture with all its nefarious characteristics. Some came from well educated families, others were more inclined to be thugs and had strong criminal tendencies. This variety made the KGB a powerful instrument for implementing and enforcing Communist ideology. Commander Rypchensky, over years of experience and contact with hundreds of KGB officers, knew exactly what he was looking for and he found many that he gradually introduced to his network of like minded professionals. He would gather them for social and professional conversation and could sense their current views when he offered opportunities for them to express political views and philosophy. There was no political agenda associated with these sessions. However it was a forum where ideas diametrically opposed to totalitarian beliefs were shared. These men and women were very keen observers. Some believed they were being tested for their ideological convictions but gradually all understood and appreciated similarities of those in attendance. There were no thugs among them. There were no extreme ideologies among them. As a result their comfort level at these gatherings increased over time.

As insurmountable problems in the Soviet Union increased, caused by communism's failures to address economic and social issues, their discussions became even more revealing. At some point they realized what Commander Rypchensky was promoting. When he concluded the time had arrived to clarify his intentions, he addressed them as follows.

"Gentlemen, welcome to our gathering of like minds." They smiled while holding their glasses of vodka. In fact they clicked their glasses as a salute to the Commander. He continued.

"We have these gathering for several reasons. First to show our appreciation for your professional contribution. But as you may have concluded, there are other reasons. Our great country is at a crossroad in history. You know and understand our problems. There are many. For example we have to import much of our food and merchandise. You are smart enough to understand the reasons for these problems. You also know that our citizens live in fear of persecution for being outspoken, as many of us have been at our gatherings." They nodded, laughed and looked at one another. Their faces revealed their bond with their Commander. He continued.

"You know where I am going with my explanation.' He paused and looked at them.

"Your services are needed by our country. We have an opportunity to correct many shortcomings of our system of government and economics. Many of you know first hand from your experience in Europe and America that our system is failing our nation and citizens. We have an opportunity to make some changes but it will not be easy. Can I rely on you for assistance?" Their response was unanimous and quite boisterous. He continued.

"It is very important for us not to reveal our purpose at this time. You obviously understand. We have many powerful men who disagree with our convictions. First of all it will jeopardize your safety. At some point we will be forthright with our intentions. Now is not the time. Captain Orlov will speak with you and will ask you to sign your name as a promise of your cooperation to help us make the Soviet Union a nation we can all be proud of. Thank you for your friendship and loyalty." Applause followed.

It was now Captain Orlov, second in command of KGB who explained the Soviet Network to all those present. These meetings were held in all republics for several years with similar results. Networks were also organized by young communist party members whose political frustration led them to secretly organize citizens with similar beliefs. Secrecy was paramount. An underground press originated by dissidents, circulated articles written and passed on for others to read. This was a Russian version of freedom of the press. Demands for liberty were spreading, especially after glasnost was announced, . Citizens were encouraged to test communism's tolerance for opposing views. In Europe, the "iron curtain" was being torn apart. Euphoria spread east into Soviet Republics where dissidents were encouraged to speak out. For all republics, this would not be an easy transition. What was not expected was an elite circle of KGB members would become prominent agents for change.

Chapter 7

Russians loved book fairs. There was always a chance that satirical or even controversial books could pass by censorship before they were banned. The Communist Party did not encourage literary controversy that could undermine party discipline. Kristoff was waiting in line with hundreds of Moscow natives who shared a common love of reading. He recognized someone he thought was a KGB agent and concluded he was being followed. In an attempt to appear less conspicuous, he began to chat with a woman in line. His Pravda badge was on his lapel and with notebook in hand, he began asking her questions as they waited to enter. She seemed very pleasant when he asked:

"How long have you been waiting?"

She was impressed when Kristoff told her that he was a writer for Pravda and she appeared very willing to respond.

"About two hours, but I am used to this. They don't make it easy for us to read. We have no choice. We wait for food at the markets and we wait for new books just the same. Our system fails us. Why not write that?"

Kristoff concurred and thanked her. He was, however, more focused on the person following him. When the KGB agent was looking the other way, he discretely vanished into the crowd, walking behind a truck where he hid and waited. He noticed the agent frantically looking for him. Kristoff remained still, while the agent scurried toward the end of the crowd to determine where his suspect had disappeared. At that moment, Kristoff stepped toward the entrance of the Book Fair, displayed his Pravda card and was admitted without question.

Western books amazed Muscovites. Everything from Rock and Roll to the Sears catalog. Jane Fonda's exercise album was getting attention. Crowds moved slowly as they perused hundreds of books. The organizers forced them to move forward due to the masses of people waiting to enter. Within the hour, Kristoff was about to leave when he noticed a special section on poetry. The guest poet, Yevgeny Yevtushenko, appeared out of nowhere. He was referred to in Russian circles as the "angry man" of the 1950s. Kristoff approached him. "I read your recent poem critical of bureaucrats. Well done."

Yevtushenko stared at Kristoff, skeptical at first, but then could sense a connection.

"Thank you. I hope Chairman Mikoyanov's promise to reduce the inefficiency of our fat and corrupt bureaucracy is sincere." Kristoff felt a kinship with this man right away.

"Is it safe for you to be quoted in Pravda?"

Yevtushenko smiled. "Well, that will be one way to test the sincerity of the chairman. Real change will have to be tested on a regular basis, wouldn't you agree?"

Kristoff wrote everything down and acknowledged his agreement, thanked him for his contribution, then furtively peered out, checking his exit surroundings, before advancing to his car. His appreciation for Russians' love for reading inspired him with a topic for his next editorial. He noted the following in his pad.

Desire for literature and free expression can overshadow the obstacles of living in a police state.

Kristoff planned his next editorial, and would make reference to those he interviewed. He wanted to determine whether a reform policy known as glasnost was genuine and sustainable.

Darkness spread over the streets of Moscow. Kristoff had a long walk to his car. He chose a shorter route through several narrow alleys. He sensed someone following him. A chill overcame him. Just as he thought of running, he was attacked by several agents, blindfolded, and dragged to a truck. One agent was twisting his arm while another began interrogating him. "What do you know about a network?"

Kristoff couldn't believe his ears. They knew. So much for secrecy. He responded to their shouts. "Nothing!" One agent twisted his arm beyond a painful threshold.

"You're lying, Rypchensky. Can't expect your father to save you this time. Just tell us and we will let you go. What do you know about a network?"

Kristoff was angry and frightened. "I told you, I know nothing about a network."

The agent then screamed, "Then let me tell you, Rypchensky. Maybe you will live to print my story in Pravda for all to read. Is that fair?"

The second agent who said nothing at this point spoke out.

"Rypchensky, maybe you should tell us." A gun was pointed at Kristoff's temple.

Kristoff feared for his life; he had to say something.

"How can I tell you something that I know nothing about?"

The more aggressive agent then responded with deep conviction.

"Then maybe you will print what I tell you."

"That can be arranged, " Kristoff responded. "Tell me; I am a reporter and writer."

The agent grabbed him by the throat.

"You are also a liar. But we have ways to make you speak the truth."

The truck began to move and Kristoff was roughed up by several agents trying to break his silence. Unknown to the abductors, the truck was being followed and monitored by network agents under Orlov's command. Moments later the truck came to a stop. Nearby, a van carrying network agents recorded the following conversation, monitored by Orlov.

"Take this lying son of a bitch into that dark alley and make him talk. If he refuses, drug him and dump his body when you're through."

Orlov immediately ordered his men into action to protect Kristoff. "Move quickly, before it's too late." Two cars then positioned themselves. One blocked the abductors from advancing forward, the other stopped directly behind while network agents stormed into the truck. Kristoff was being roughed up. Network agents smothered the abductors, knocking them out with clubs to the head. Kristoff's blindfold was removed. Orlov's flashlight glared into his face. "Are you hurt?"

Kristoff could not see but recognized a different voice. He grimaced as the pressure from handcuffs loosened from his wrists.

"No, thank you, your timing was perfect."

Three unconscious KGB agents were lying on the street. Orlov then ordered his agents, "Load them into their truck. I will meet you in one hour as planned." He then introduced himself to Kristoff.

"I work for your father. He wants to see you immediately. He's very concerned about your safety."

Orlov raced his sedan through Moscow's streets in a heavy rain. Commander Rypchensky was nervously waiting for his son on a side street. He had been informed that enemy agents were going after his son. The commander had predicted his enemies would use Kristoff as a warning, knowing it would force a response. Now his family's safety was being threatened. His thinking and response would have to change. Network operations would have to adjust to more aggressive action. Plans had to be altered not only for his family's safety, but for the success of the network. With events moving faster than anticipated, the commander had to act accordingly, knowing his options were being limited.

Orlov raced by a parked car that flashed its lights several times. He came to a screeching stop when he realized those flashing lights were from Commander Rypchensky's car. In pouring rain the commander opened his door as Orlov and Kristoff approached. He noticed a bruise and blood on his son's forehead.

"How bad is that cut? They will pay for this." He handed Kristoff his handkerchief from his shirt pocket. "They will continue to stalk you, trying to get me to react. I will, and soon, but when they least expect it."

Orlov observed fear and anger, rarely seen in his commander's voice. The commander concluded that he had to take steps to protect his son. He stared directly at Kristoff when he said, "If you are willing, I can arrange for you and Nadia to have diplomatic status in Britain."

Kristoff removed his handkerchief and wiped blood from his brow.

"I feel I can be useful here with you. Are you ordering me to leave?"

His father lit a cigarette.

"I would like to if I was certain it would protect you, but even that is questionable."

Kristoff didn't understand. "You mean I wouldn't be any safer there than here?"

His father nodded. "That's exactly what I'm saying. Our agents have mysteriously disappeared from our foreign stations as well."

"Then I am staying here with you, " Kristoff said. "I can contribute. It's my struggle too." He held the handkerchief to his head and continued.

"You should know what they said. They asked if I knew anything about a network. Your secrecy has been breached." Upon hearing this from Kristoff, Orlov and the Commander realized future operations would have to be altered. This meant acts of violence. They were prepared for this eventuality. It just happened sooner than they expected. The commander's comments could not be misunderstood.

"We will respond with an iron fist. They will pay for this and much more. Our plans will be adjusted to deal with their attempts to destroy us. We're prepared."

The Commander grimaced. His son's life, his only child, was so important to him. He preferred him close by where he could have a better chance of protecting him. "Kristoff, what about Nadia? Wouldn't you prefer to be with her?"

It appeared to Kristoff that his father was trying to decide what was best under the circumstances. If he left with Nadia, not only was his safety still in doubt but he would create even more suspicion for his parents. This was not an option he preferred. Kristoff understood their security was threatened. For the first time, he experienced his father's emotions being expressed and wanted to appease him.

"Nadia is currently touring with the Bolshoi. Our country makes her very depressed. When she travels in the west, her spirits are uplifted through comforts produced by freedoms. Freedom is lacking here. She has expressed an interest in defecting if I join her. I told her I would."

The commander knew how much his son loved Nadia. Their previous conversations revealed their commitment to one another.

"If our network succeeds, you and Nadia will not have to defect." Those words from his father were not delivered with conviction. Fear of losing his only child had altered his thinking. After he heard the terrifying exchange on his car monitor when his son was minutes away from serious injury or death, his confidence was shaken.

"Maybe you and Nadia should leave together. Your mother and I will join you when this operation is over."

But Kristoff assured his father that his commitment was strong and he preferred not to leave at this time. He was more secure close by and his emigration would appear too suspicious; his father reluctantly agreed.

The commander motioned Orlov to his car where they could communicate privately.

"What happened tonight must not be repeated. I want twenty-four-hour protection for my son. He's a target. You will have to take extreme measures to protect him. Take no prisoners. Is that clear?"

Orlov responded with conviction, "Yes sir. We will have to use all of our darkest instincts from this point forward."

The commander nodded in agreement.

"That's exactly true. If we don't, our enemies will have the upper hand. We have no choice." When the commander returned to his car, he handed his son writing material. His mood had dramatically changed.

"We have uncovered some important news at the Kremlin. Our enemies are taking action to solidify their political base. They fear losing their privileged status. They are proposing changes in party membership rules that would inhibit expansion of the liberal wing. You must write a scathing attack of this proposal in Pravda."

Kristoff was taking notes. "I will work on this immediately. Anything else?"

The commander did not hesitate.

"Yes! In China it was reported that older party members from all levels of government are being forced to retire so that younger men and women can assume positions of power and leadership. We must endorse this idea with a strong and persuasive editorial. That is top priority for you. I have arranged for this story to be broadcast on radio and television stations regularly for the next forty-eight hours without censorship. We must act swiftly on all fronts. Events are moving faster than I anticipated."

Kristoff was excited and very pleased with his father's assignment and candor. Their relationship had crossed a new threshold. Kristoff was committed to his family and country. His role as a journalist for Pravda was now more relevant and meaningful.

He realized his life was in danger. But he was motivated as never before. He refused to allow totalitarian thugs to debilitate his spirit. Recent events energized him. He assured his father that his writing would target key issues.

"Consider it done. Nothing would give me more pleasure." Russia was in the midst of a major coup and he knew it. His father was leading the network so he realized that both of their lives would be primary targets from opponents.

His father approached him.

"Here, strap this revolver to your body and learn how to use it. Wear this vest. Orlov will take you to a range for practice." Kristoff was shocked. He did however heed his father's advice and planned to learn how to effectively use his weapon while wondering whether he would ever find that necessary. From that day forward, the pistol was strapped to his body and he made a habit of wearing a protective vest

Events suddenly generated serious consequences for both father and son. Every action now had meaning attached. Kristoff's thoughts of his future with the woman he adored were now altered by his father's trepidation about their survival. Revolutions disrupt personal lives. Sacrifices had to be expected. There was no going back. Father and son knew that change was better than the status quo. Discussing failure or anything short of success would be counter-productive. Neither father nor son wished to reveal emotions that could expose, even weaken their nerves and will. The commander was especially aware of the importance of detaching his personal life from his mission. Years of military life had disciplined his emotions. This was the ultimate test for a military leader, husband, and father. His next comment to Kristoff demonstrated his focus.

"Have you heard that the prime minister of Britain has expelled twenty-five Russian officials? Most of them are network KGB agents stationed in Britain under my direction. They are creating all types of distractions in Western Europe. Our efforts to confuse enemy agents must continue. It's effective, partly because our stories are authentic. We have overloaded them with truth, mixed with fabrications."

The commander lit a cigarette. Protecting his son meant informing him of life and death scenarios. Information had to be shared with Kristoff until and unless he decided upon reassigning him to a foreign station, possibly in America. Nadia performed in New York on a regular basis. He raised the possibility.

"Did you know we also have American agents working for us?" He was baiting his son, hoping he could convince him of his usefulness in the United States.

Kristoff's reply was encouraging.

"I have always wanted to visit America." His father thought at that very instant, his son was destined for assignment there. The

Commander had to find the proper opportunity. Recent events forced his father to act expeditiously.

"When the time is right, that will be arranged. In America, you could be very useful to our network. You can be part of our propaganda machine. Remember, our real enemies are party bureaucrats who refuse to reform our system. Unlike China, where revision of economic policies is taking hold, here we are stuck with archaic dogma."

Then Kristoff startled his father.

"What if you fail? Will you and Momma defect?" His father stepped out of his car onto the pavement where he crushed his cigarette as he looked at his son.

"I will never defect, nor do I intend to fail in this mission. Lenin took over this country with a handful of dedicated Bolshevik revolutionaries. We can do the same with the power we hold. Your job is to write our narrative for the masses to follow."

The rain stopped as they walked toward Kristoff's car. The commander inspected his car for wired explosives. He knew what to look for; Kristoff paid attention as his father explained. There was some comfort in knowing that the men who attacked Kristoff earlier would be eliminated. But their enemy was in no way diminished. KGB operatives who replace those eliminated would be more determined and dangerous. Extreme Machiavellian behavior was now in play.

Orlov was ordered to assure twenty-four-hour protection for Kristoff. Before the commander drove off he warned his son: "Always inspect your car before you open it, or start it." It was an important lesson that could save his life. His father's commitment to his son was now a question of life or death, kill or be killed. A totally shocking and unexpected realization took hold of Kristoff.

Chapter 8

Viktor and Zelensky, two network agents stationed in Glen Cove, Long Island, New York, were puzzled by orders received via electronic code. The Kremlin was flooded with mysterious political machinations, which made their work challenging. Messages were wired by network KGB agents in Kiev, and translated with devices used by CIA agents in New York, working with the Soviet underground. Experienced network agents were having difficulty determining their assigned tasks. Some tasks were based on legitimate events while others were fabricated. Verification was problematic. This was intentional in order to make detection of network operatives more difficult. To add to the confusion, some network operatives worked as double agents. Again, they could cover their tracks by working both sides. Their true mission was the overthrow of the Communist Party currently in power in the Kremlin. To add even more confusion, many fabricated schemes planted were based upon actual events that made them more credible. Clever intelligence machinations are never black and white, rather somewhere in between. There were codes that would determine pro and anti soviet operatives. Therefore suspicion and tension was constant. Adding even more confusion was the fact that many soviet agents stationed in New York metropolitan area wanted to defect. They weren't blind to the distinctions between two ideologies worlds apart. Temptation was constant and omnipresent. New York was very appealing. You could compare the situation to East Berliners who risked their lives to live in an environment that allowed liberty and opportunity. How many East Berliner's crashed through the Berlin Wall for a better life. It was ironic how those sworn to uphold communist ideology altered their fundamental beliefs.

There's even more irony. A faction of KGB agents who initiated intelligence operations in New York did so to disguise and assist criminal minds who in fact, wanted to defect from day one. Compensation for recruiting skilled criminal agents originated from Russian drug lords. The KGB was in part a training ground for agents with skilled criminal propensities. Payoffs were highly lucrative. Agents used code words and numbers programmed to change periodically to maintain secrecy. Sounds confusing and it was. For this reason, KGB operatives were recalled to Moscow to preempt potential defections. Some of these agents disappeared upon their return to Russia. It is also important to point out, the borough of Queens, on Long Island, where thousands of Russian nationals reside, maintains strong cultural ties. The availability of goods and services is incredible in contrast with the drab commercialism of Moscow. This was the appealing environment surrounding network agents Viktor and Zelensky..

Viktor, an attractive man, was overwhelmed by the availability of women in and around New York City. Viktor's life history, and the mind-set it fostered, made him a candidate for defection. He and his partner, Zelensky, realized their lives were made very comfortable living in metropolitan Long Island, New York. Many of their morning conversations were enjoyed in a Sea Cliff diner where their native language was part of the social mix. Viktor would often verbalize his pleasure in Russian and felt very comfortable.

"We are fortunate to be assigned here in the United States. Long Island has much to offer. There are women everywhere. Living here is so much better than life in Russia. Don't you agree?"

Zelensky, unlike Viktor, was a native of the Ukraine. He wanted to smile at his friend's comment but his thoughts and concerns were elsewhere. Recent intelligence made him nervous about completing assignments on schedule. As network operatives, their assigned tasks had strict timetables attached.

"Maybe our stay here will be shorter than the time we need to accomplish our mission. The State Department is threatening to remove Soviet personnel. We far outnumber American personnel back home."

Viktor sensed his partner's serious tone.

"What are the Americans worried about? Aren't we . . ."

Zelensky interrupted with scolding language. "Russian spies! In Britain and Germany, agents have been deported! Our days may be numbered!" He then lowered his voice to almost a whisper. "It is imperative we complete our work. Maybe we can avert deportation if we prove our worth. The KGB are constantly monitoring all personnel stationed here, waiting for us to make a mistake. Agents are always under suspicion. We have to be vigilant."

Viktor's personality type accepted situations as they unfolded more so than Zelensky, who as a Ukrainian was suspicious of Russian authoritarianism. He wanted his republic to free itself from police crackdowns. His sense was that Russian autocrats had little knowledge of the entrepreneurship required for economic growth to occur. For Zelensky, more market economics would stimulate changes, unlike command theories that were totally out of sync with free enterprise. Zelensky kept asking himself, "What is it they don't understand?"

Now that Viktor was experiencing free enterprise culture, there were indications he understood and appreciated his Ukrainian counterpart. However, he chose to take the long view. He was willing to wait for the Russian economy to implode. In that regard Viktor's thinking was on the mark. Don't make things happen, allow them to happen, organically, not by force. With this approach, there was less fear of retaliation directed against network agents. Maybe it was also Viktor's composure that made Zelensky nervous. Viktor's behavior appeared detached. His attempts to calm his partner usually failed. He tried unsuccessfully to explain himself.

"We are just following orders. They do not realize anything different about our work." Zelensky's response was direct.

"Don't assume that to be correct."

Zelensky found Viktor's response unsatisfactory.

"Remember one thing. We are being watched by the FBI, CIA, and KGB. We must be careful and not dismiss unknown factors if we are to control our future." Viktor recognized his partner's unsettled nature, but also realized their differences made them a good team.

Viktor feared their attempts to control and manipulate events would expose them to perilous outcomes. He was confident the Soviet Union was in decline. Network agents' assignments were designed to cause reactions that would hasten this downward process. Forcing the inevitable, was for Viktor, unwise and unwarranted. He was convinced, in its current state, the Soviet Union was doomed for collapse in less than a decade. Network leaders were hastening the process forward. Viktor was willing to wait it out. However at this point, he had few options. Disobeying orders was not one of them. One future possibility was defection. That would have to wait not only because it was dangerous, it was also very complicated. He therefore complied, knowing their assignments were made unnecessarily dangerous. What he feared most was being caught.

Zelensky asked the waitress for more coffee, then, speaking softly, said:

"Our orders are very clear. Create scenarios that distract our KGB opponents. We must keep them busy chasing false leads. All types of reasonable misinformation." He lit a cigarette. "I have a list of projects that have been decoded. Memorize this because they are not to be recorded in any way." Zelensky waited for the waitress to pour coffee. As she walked away he proceeded to explain four schemes for network agents to implement in New York. He stared at Viktor with intense eye contact. Then, speaking softly but with intensity, he said, "First scheme. Mikoyanov's life is in danger. Assassination attempt during summit with American president in Moscow. Suspect is a terrorist under orders of Central Committee." Zelensky explained the purpose of this scheme was to create suspicion among party members. Mikoyanov was their silent political leader whose association with network operations was top secret. The assassination plot was a ruse to mislead their enemies. Zelensky continued, maintaining his eye contact with Viktor. The next scheme involved United Nations Soviet headquarters. American agents wanted to wire it with sensitive devices for tracking messages. If successful, agents could compromise diplomatic maneuvers. This would require having the entire office inspected and rewired by electricians approved by Soviet officials. Zelensky added: "Of course those officials and technicians will be network affiliates. This will provide our network with access to all conversations within UN headquarters."

Viktor smiled with approval.

Zelensky then spoke of Russia's war in Afghanistan, which was very unpopular with Russians whose sons were being slaughtered by mujahideen extremists.

"We must claim the CIA has infiltrated military operations in Afghanistan, endangering Soviet officers and other personnel. We are not sure whether this is true or not. In fact, that makes it more realistic and credible. So you see, our techniques can involve information that is not always false. This increases our credibility." Zelensky had one last scheme to present to Viktor. "Finally, we want it known that NATO commanders are intercepting military intelligence from our Warsaw Pact allies. As a result, military maneuvers have been compromised. The source of this information is from an agent stationed in Berlin."

Zelensky paused, and observed Viktor light a cigarette before asking:

"Is that all of it, or is there more?"

"Yes, one more thing, " Zelensky said and then paused. He always introduced the element of fear last. "Don't get caught or you will mysteriously surface in the Hudson River."

Viktor was not amused.

Zelensky was serious as he continued. "Plant one scheme and then wait for a reaction. Create as much paperwork as you can for the KGB office. Get them totally immersed in these schemes. If we have them preoccupied with misinformation, we can succeed in our mission. Our leaders need valuable time for internal network operations to overpower and destroy our opponents in government. With our enemies chasing our fabrications, our network can conceal their plans for a coup. This is critical." Zelensky managed to unsettle Viktor's confidence for the first time since arriving in America as a KGB network operative. It was true that agents disappeared. Zelensky reasoned that instilling fear in Viktor would encourage vigilance.

"When do I start?"

Zelensky looked at his watch. "Immediately! Keep me informed." Viktor finished his coffee and left the diner. His gut feelings were filled with trepidation. His partner's warnings had hit their mark.

Chapter 9

CIA Director William Sullivan was a political appointee who didn't concern himself with political correctness. As a result, some decisions he made stirred controversy among members of congress who were conventional in their approach to American-Soviet relations. Sullivan was his own man and took chances and was willing to face the consequences. He was now presented with a scenario that from the beginning was very questionable, but his faith in agent Quinn made his decision-making less stressful. Quinn was highly regarded within CIA circles as a reliable professional. Sullivan trusted him.

When Quinn entered Sullivan's office, his boss was reading a report on Russian agents deported from Britain. He presented his two-page plan to Sullivan and waited to speak.

"What's this about?" Sullivan asked.

Quinn poured himself a cup of coffee and began to explain:

"Our task is to camouflage the network's movement by creating diversions in intelligence."

Sullivan was listening but was not very impressed.

"What kind of diversions?" The notion involving the CIA assisting a coup within the Soviet Union seemed far-fetched.

Quinn explained the plan. "Through contacts with KGB agents, using coded electronic language, we are sending messages that are designed to create misinformation."

Sullivan shot back, "So what? We've done that many times and in fact are currently. What's so special about this tactic?" Sullivan was not prepared for the explanation Quinn was about to offer.

"We have opposing factions of the KGB operating here in the States, each with their own agenda. We must allow network KGB agents to access bona fide technical information that can be shared with the old guard KGB. This will instill confidence and credibility for network operatives who are also creating misinformation to thwart KGB operations here in America and within the Soviet Union. Network agents are requesting our assistance to confuse intelligence operations within the KGB. It is strongly believed this will divert their attention away from a plot to overthrow the communist regime. If we provide network agents access to this technology, they will appear more credible before rank and file members. Suspicion of their loyalty and competence must not become an issue. Their goal is to maintain majority coalitions within the Communist Party. The liberal wing now has a majority but conservatives are still entrenched in powerful bureaucracies. If network KGB operatives are successful with their espionage, that translates into more power for reformers who want to change the system. If network spies outmaneuver the KGB, communist hardliners will suffer losses. An intelligence victory for the network translates into a political victory for agents of change. We must not jeopardize their ultimate goal of maintaining support of moderates who now hold the balance of power in the Duma."

Sullivan listened with keen interest. He asked what kind of data would be requested. He was not thrilled with Quinn's reply:

"High tech computer systems. We must. This will advance their credibility."

Sullivan was not convinced. "What if this network is a hoax? I can't imagine them pulling off a coup. We cannot compromise our high tech for a possible hoax."

Quinn did not back down. "We have convincing evidence this network is for real, including the involvement of major power brokers. This is no hoax."

Sullivan wanted to believe the whole scenario. He had good instincts and believed Quinn was on to something. "I want the names of the so-called power brokers. When can you have this information? Confirmed by British SIS."

"Within twenty-four hours, " Quinn responded.

Sullivan walked back and forth mulling the plan while staring at Quinn.

"Request assistance from British intelligence. Have them monitor their activities in the Soviet Union. Maybe then we can determine whether this network is for real before giving our technology away."

This sounded reasonable but Quinn disagreed vehemently.

"Any delay will blow their cover. It's absolutely essential we act within twenty-four hours and maintain a low profile."

Sullivan was very uncomfortable with his options.

"Can we delay the release of high tech systems?"

Quinn held firm. "Not without endangering their success. Their time schedule is limited. Currently, KGB agents are chasing false leads. They can only be fooled up to a point. Stealing this technology would give them the credibility they need and make them less vulnerable to surveillance. It's a price we have to pay. We have to act now if we are to act at all. If this network is successful, the Soviet Union will be turned upside down. And besides, IBM has informed me that next year they will introduce new technology that will neutralize any losses. They can implant chips that will disable these computers with viruses."

Sullivan was feeling pressure. He wasn't worried about political fallout; he was, however, worried about failure. "What if the State Department moves to have Soviet personnel expelled? Look what the British government did recently."

Quinn had an answer for that. "The president would not allow that to happen. There's a summit meeting in December."

There were other political considerations Sullivan had to take into account, even though he dismissed most politicians from his decision-making.

"Some members of congress may demand some expulsions. Then what?"

When Quinn smiled, Sullivan knew what was coming next.

"So what? You've dealt with lightweight politicians ready to scream before they know the facts. When you inform the president and chairmen of intelligence committees, the details will be convincing."

Sullivan rubbed his forehead, then wiped his brow with a tissue. He believed Quinn's intelligence data was correct. It was also complicated and dangerous. He deferred to his most competent operative.

"OK, pending the president's approval, let's go with it. I'll see him momentarily. Hope I don't live to regret this decision."

The president met with Sullivan in the next hour. He was concerned with the situation but since his term of office was ending in less than a year, political damage was not a concern. His feeling was basic. If the Soviet Union experienced major political and economic changes, instigated by liberal forces within the Communist Party, that would break their hold on Eastern Europe.

Chapter 10

Over a period of twenty-four hours, Viktor and Zelensky made several contacts with CIA agents. The forthcoming results motivated Zelensky to move as fast as possible with orders received by network agents whose names remained anonymous. He was reviewing notes at his desk when he spoke to Viktor who was smoking a cigarette.

"Long Island industries have high tech secrets we must find ways to access. There is tremendous pressure from the Kremlin for us to intercept this technology. CIA agents have recently arranged for us to locate this data, via an agent that you are to meet in Huntington."

Appearing tired, Viktor yawned. "And who is this agent?"

One of Zelensky's few smiles crossed his face. "I have her resume. It's very impressive."

"She is a beautiful brunette who speaks fluent Russian and Italian. You will just adore her." He placed a picture of Yolanda Spieler in front of Viktor. She was indeed a beauty. Zelensky read a report with specific details.

"Her parents met while studying medicine in Europe. Her Jewish/Russian father and Italian-born mother were married in Florence and began practicing medicine in Milan. Her mother is a pediatrician, her father, a neurosurgeon. They immigrated to the United States ten years ago." Viktor would learn more details from documents, including photos of her ancestry. She inherited the beauty of both grandmothers, tall, slender, blue eyes, dark brown hair, beautiful skin and a body to match. A graduate of Georgetown, she worked for her U.S. senator before attending Cornell, receiving her PH.D. in international law. She had been recruited by the CIA, where she was currently employed and had been for two years.

Later that same day, Viktor was driving on the Northern State Parkway, heading east to Park Avenue, where he would meet agent Spieler at her residence in Dix Hills. He parked his car in a circular driveway and approached her front door, when he heard a voice from his far left. "Yes, may I help you? I hope you're not a salesman."

Viktor was stunned, as he approached Yolanda Spieler. Sunlight made her beauty even more spectacular. He responded humorously:

"Hardly! But I am buying you lunch if you are interested."

"Please identify yourself, " Yolanda said, smiling pleasantly.

Viktor was pleased that he had worn his new suit and tie for the occasion. He looked and felt handsome. "Viktor. I hope you weren't expecting someone else."

Yolanda noticed his slight Russian accent as she graciously stood from her front porch chair and greeted her expected visitor. "Yolanda Spieler. Please wait, I'll get my coat and purse." While in her bedroom, she dialed a code into her phone and within one minute, she confirmed that Viktor was the agent assigned to her.

She drove to a highly recommended Afghan restaurant on Main Street in Huntington. Viktor followed, driving his Ford rental. At her request, they were seated by the restauranteur, adjacent to a window where they could observe pedestrians. The natural light enhanced their appearance. Viktor was experiencing difficulty focusing on his assignment. He found it inconceivable that such a beautiful woman worked for the CIA. They were a very attractive couple. Within a half hour, he felt their personalities were compatible. When an attractive man meets an attractive woman, it's not unusual for them to observe each other's body language. Although both maintained their composure while making every effort to appear professional, Viktor did experience a stronger than expected attraction and wondered if she felt similar pulsations.

He was impressed by her charm. Yolanda sensed this when she commented. "I don't know if you can tell, but I'm new at this line of work."

She was equally unsettled and impressed with his personality. She realized her mutual attraction when his stare went right through her. An exciting connection flowed between them. Both were pondering, was this really happening?

Her orders were to review and determine plans established by the CIA and network collaborators. His orders were to assess the viability and cooperation leading to a workable transaction concerning IBM technology. But instead of discussing intelligence assignments, they persisted with personal dialogue.

Viktor continued with: "To tell you the truth, I am amazed that a beautiful woman like you has been spared matrimony and children, to be a spy. In time you may have second thoughts. Am I missing something?"

Yolanda was startled by Viktor's directness. She countered with:

"Until that time, I am what I am." She redirected the conversation and countered with a sly remark: "KGB agents must live a much better life here on Long Island, rather than in your totalitarian prison. Or am I missing something?"

Viktor smiled. He actually appreciated her clever retort and immediately decided not to appear presumptuous. Instead, he agreed with her assessment.

"Yes, very true, especially when stationed in metropolitan New York."

Their exchange didn't qualify as small talk but Yolanda found her comfort level acceptable and increasing as she responded.

"And why is that?" She smiled, sensing her retort had casually disarmed his discomfort.

Viktor hated the Soviet Union and enjoyed revealing its pitfalls.

"Because you Americans have so much to offer. You are filthy rich in consumer goods of all kinds. I just love to go shopping. My country is bankrupt. Totalitarian socialism is a failure. The whole system is crumbling. It's just a matter of time." Viktor felt his criticism of the Soviet Union was justified. Neither one expected their conversation would lead them to an expose of communism's negativity

Yolanda was surprised by his direct exposure of conditions attributed to failures of Soviet socialism. She was more interested in his personal life. There was no indication Viktor was married.

"What about your family back home? Don't you miss them?"

Viktor's response clarified his status.

"I have no family to speak of. No ties whatsoever. I was raised by the state and recently have learned my parents, sister, and brother were victims of Stalin's pogroms. I believe my father was targeted because he was a Jew. Those who cared for me were kind and loving caretakers. It was through their love and guidance that I managed to work my way into political favors. They played the system well and long enough for me to qualify for foreign service. So here I am, working for a network that wants to overthrow our government. For me this is a form of poetic justice." Yolanda identified and sympathized with Viktor but decided not to share her father's similar history.

"Then America can be a garden of paradise. You better be careful. It will grow on you. Our freedoms are very addictive and contagious."

They stared at each other with a look that both understood meant there was more to their relationship than intelligence work.

Yolanda's eyes looked down at her menu but she could sense Viktor's hold on her when he asked:

"You understand the purpose of our first rendezvous?" He didn't have to choose the word rendezvous. She felt his choice of that word was indicative of other possibilities. For a moment, she lost her focus.

"Absolutely, but let's enjoy our lunch. The open buffet looks great."

Viktor looked at his watch. "Unfortunately, I have to leave in one hour. A bowl of lentil soup is all I have time for." What followed was a brief discussion of their personal history where they discovered a unique connection. Both had Russian, Jewish ancestry. Their knowledge of Russian history concerning Jews made their assignment more relevant and personal, not exclusively professional. They managed to postpone discussion of their personal histories for the time being.

Awkward as it was, for a beautiful woman and handsome man to defy natural chemistry, they maintained their composure. Both sensed their first meeting should be cordial, but nothing more. When Viktor's schedule required his departure, he made sure to pay for lunch. He waited for her to complete her meal before politely excusing himself.

"Sorry, but I must leave. It was a pleasure meeting you. We'll communicate in the near future to resolve our professional assignment."

Her response was delivered with a warm smile.

"Thank you for lunch. Until we meet again." Their rendezvous was pleasant. Was it successful? He sensed good vibrations from her as he walked to his car while she observed him through the window. Viktor could not stop thinking of her. His mind felt trapped by her feminine charm, beauty, and wit. He felt an obsession overcame him. Now, in addition, he sensed their Jewish link as well. While returning to Manhattan, he could not concentrate on his mission and wondered if she was experiencing similar feelings.

Viktor's emotions had been frozen for years. His childhood was far from ordinary, but that was the case for thousands of other Russian Jews whose families were disrupted by pogroms initiated throughout Russia for centuries. Normalcy was not part of his frame of reference. He was fortunate to have been embraced by a childless married couple who knew his family. His life and childhood were spared by their love and concern for his future. He sometimes felt that God was looking after him but he also experienced feelings of agitation from psychological baggage that lingered in his subconscious. He remembered his parents, especially the nurturing of his loving mother. This was embossed into his memory and as loving as his new parents were, his connection with them was incomplete. However, he owed them his success and made a point of sending them gifts with notes of appreciation. They were "his family" and he was thankful for their act of love that rescued him from a life of destitution. He was aware of other children whose Jewish heritage had been stolen by similar circumstances. Although totalitarian Russia had destroyed his heritage, it did not obliterate his will to restore what was lost. For this reason, his attraction to Yolanda Spieler captivated him, as though she appeared out of nowhere. He felt a strong connection that made him want to restore his lost heritage. He also realized his preoccupation with past emotions might jeopardize his security. KGB operatives faced many risks. Viktor's work was even more dangerous because he was part of a network whose goal was the destruction of a government that systematically destroyed human rights. He had to remain focused. Yolanda Spieler became an untimely distraction. He found it incredible that this very attractive Jewish woman, with Russian ancestry, walked into his life. Their rendezvous had just begun.

When Yolanda and her parents moved to America, she was ten years old. She had studied English at a private school in Milan and her accent was apparent. Her American childhood friends would sometimes imitate her and laugh but she understood. It wasn't long until her accent disappeared and her assimilation was complete.

She was accepted at Choate Rosemary Hall in Wallingford, Connecticut, for three years. Choate is a prestigious prep school with a list of prominent graduates including movie stars and politicians. One in particular was John Kennedy. Her roommate was from Washington, D.C. On occasion she would visit her and found the nation's capital offered young women many opportunities. For her, Washington was an exciting city. Upon graduation from Choate, she accepted her offer from Georgetown University, where she majored in international law.

Life in the nation's capital was exciting because she met students from all over the world who, like her, became U.S. citizens. Her ability to speak several European languages was an asset as well. In particular, her fluency in Russian exposed her to several peers whose parents lived and worked at the Russian Embassy. Over several years, their friendship was an important part of her leisure activities. She learned first hand how life in the Soviet Union was a world apart. Russian students shared private information with her during vacations, skiing in Vermont and beaching on Caribbean islands.

One of her Russian friends, a woman her age, informed Yolanda that her parents wanted to defect and relocate in America. One evening, her friend overheard a discussion between her parents and an American couple, both scientists, who worked at Brookhaven National Lab on Long Island. She shared this discussion with Yolanda involving the American couple who endured a horrible and unforgettable experience in Moscow. After hearing the story, Yolanda's emotions displayed fear as well as curiosity. The story began when the American couple, who were nuclear physicists, attended a conference in Moscow. The Russian scientist who greeted them at the airport informed them of what to expect during their five day seminar at the Academy of Science. He warned all attendees that a KGB agent would be watching them every step possible, in fact, he discretely identified the man who was within sight. All foreign scientists were given advance warning, particularly Americans. The following story made Yolanda take notice. It occurred in the hotel where American scientists and their spouses were residing for a week.

On the fourth evening, the American couple were getting dressed for dinner. The American scientist said to her husband: "I hope our dinner is something different. They served us the same meat stew for three nights. I would love a fresh fish fillet or something other than meat." Her husband agreed. When seated at their magnificent round table, after drinks were offered, the waiter began serving their party of eight, the same meat stew. However when another waiter presented her with a fillet of fish, beautifully prepared, she became sick to her stomach. Horrified, she looked at her husband. Her emotions could not be contained. She excused herself from the table and returned to her room where she swallowed a tranquilizer and fearfully cried herself to sleep. Her husband, before excusing himself, explained to all present what had transpired. All scientists and spouses at their table realized the horror and drama manifested before them. They barely ate their dinner and quietly excused themselves, dreadful of returning to their rooms, wired for information.

Upon the day of departure, the American couple joined a large entourage of Americans at the Pan Am terminal for their return flight. When the the plane took off and gradually rose above the ground, passengers applauded spontaneously. It was as though they were escaping from a totalitarian nightmare. Several passengers had tears of joy in their eyes. Upon landing several hours later at JFK, they hugged one another, sharing their emotions of safely returning to their loving homeland. When Yolanda heard this story, goosebumps ran up her arms. It frightened her but also managed to trip her curiosity about intelligence work.

After graduation from Georgetown, she spent one year to investigate careers. While working as a congressional aide, she decided her options improved if she pursued a PH.D. After three years at Cornell, she completed her doctorate in Diplomatic Law. A male colleague, employed as an intelligence officer, suggested she apply for employment at the CIA. She was twenty five years old when her training began. Her desire for intrigue, inspired by a story she would never forget, had finally begun.

Chapter 11

Tourists have described Moscow's beauty and delight, overshadowed by grim faces of citizens living under tyranny. With its beautiful architecture and culture, Moscow could have been a city of joy, but years of absolute and totalitarian rule, combined with secret police tactics, had destroyed its soul and elation. Compared to Paris or Rome, the faces of Moscow's citizenry were somber. The city's atmosphere revealed a social malaise devoid of human spirit and freedom. Energy was absent.

KGB headquarters personified this environment, a perversity of human normality. Andre Chekov, head of the KGB, portrayed the stereotypical version of a psychopathic leader whose suspicion of others is obsessive. These characteristics made him a very effective bureaucrat. No agent dared to sidestep his orders. He was a consummate professional even though he was psychologically unbalanced. Those who knew him, claimed reasons for his disturbed personality could be attributed to his unfortunate childhood, cultivated during periods of excessive terror and death. Estimates of those who suffered from extreme exposure to national paranoia are difficult to calculate. The Stalin era destroyed many citizens both physically and psychologically. Chekov was one of millions who suffered during widespread turmoil; he was a mental casualty of Russia's reign of terror.

Some survive emotional onslaughts intact. Some have nervous breakdowns and are permanently institutionalized. Chekov survived by employing the most sinister defense mechanisms imaginable. Now at age fifty-six, his evil personality handicapped his mental health, making close or intimate relationships difficult. Although there were a few exceptions with particular women, his abrasiveness was a liability. Because he rarely experienced normalcy, he did not understand or even expect it from others. But he was clever enough to learn how to remain under the radar of extreme paranoia.

His agents understood his shortcomings, both from personal experience and from other agents. They were careful to always leave correct impressions. In fact, Chekov could sense evil motives and used his intuitive sensitivity to enhance control and terror over his subordinates. His most trusted agents were also victims of Stalinist purges. They were hardened emotionally and understood firsthand what terror can accomplish. He took these craven men under his wing. Their loyalty to Chekov displayed an unbridled cult of personality. His followers were brainwashed by violent experiences and therefore embraced malice. There was no room for failure or compromise. So when Chekov was informed of three KGB agents who disappeared while investigating a suspicious underground, he became furious. When he finished reading a report of the incident he had several questions for his officers who were summoned to his office.

"What was the nature of this investigation?" he demanded. "KGB agents disappear! Did they defect? What the hell is going on here? Get Orlov in this office immediately."

His secretary was an attractive woman who attended most of his meetings. She provided Chekov with some important relief: outstanding sexual encounters, but she also feared him. She scurried out of his office to find Orlov, who was nowhere to be found. Knowing Chekov wanted immediate answers, she located a senior agent, a subordinate of Orlov, and directed him to Chekov's office. When he arrived, and before he could say anything, Chekov abruptly shouted another question:

"When was the last time you saw these men?"

The agent understood he had to look directly at his boss while responding with sparse information. "Two nights ago. They were working on an investigation. The way they acted made it seem urgent, and they left before I could discuss anything with them. They always report back within two hours, but I never heard from them. Lately we have been swamped with a variety of inquiries, much more than usual. Every agent is working long hours."

Chekov was furious. "Did you have them followed?"

The agent responded quickly: "I did. But it was the third agent who also disappeared. There was no one left at my post at that time."

Chekov was still not satisfied. "Then why didn't you follow immediately?"

The agent felt trapped and swallowed hard.

"I was ordered to always have someone in our office at all times. I also had to finish a great deal of paperwork that Captain Orlov wanted the next morning. Like I said, we have been swamped lately; it's more than we can handle."

Chekov smelled a rat. He had a keen sense for subterfuge and his instincts kicked in with all types of emotions. He screamed.

"Does Orlov know about their disappearance?"

The agent was practically quivering.

"Not sure. He hasn't mentioned anything."

Chekov's secretary finally made contact with Orlov by phone.

"Orlov speaking."

Her voice was breathless and filled with anxiety. She liked Orlov and was not about to see him humiliated. Maybe an advance warning would help.

"Sir, the chairman is furious about recent events involving three missing agents. Wants to see you immediately in the front office. Sounds very urgent."

Orlov appreciated her warning and realized Natasha was overstepping her role as secretary.

"Thank you, Natasha. I am on my way." Natasha respected Orlov because he had human qualities that could be felt by his words, such as thank you, you're so kind, etc. Her boss lacked these interpersonal qualities. Orlov sensed this kinship with her and held it in abeyance; there might be a future time when his kindness could be useful. He rushed to the front office and used every spare minute offered by Natasha for cover. It was enough time to plan his response knowing he would be queried by Chekov.

When he arrived at the front office, he greeted his boss.

"Good morning Mr. Secretary."

Chekov looked into Orlov's eyes and stared at him for several seconds before speaking. Orlov did not flinch under the pressure.

"Are you aware of three agents who have disappeared?"

Orlov was prepared.

"Yes I am. They were investigating an assassination conspiracy directed against Party Chairman Mikoyanov."

Chekov was furious. He screamed.

"Why am I not aware of this?"

Orlov kept his composure.

"This information was just received moments ago, just before I walked to your office."

Chekov took a deep breath.

"What happened to those agents who disappeared?"

Orlov looked at his notebook, then directly into Chekov's eyes. He knew Chekov would study his body language and was not about to divulge any suspicious gestures or movements.

"Sir, their bodies were found early this morning, badly burned in their vehicle. No survivors."

Chekov remained quiet and very still. As expected, he studied Orlov and sat at his desk waiting for the slightest miscue. Orlov passed the test. Then Chekov asked, "What do you know about this assassination conspiracy? Is it for real?"

Orlov had what he thought was a convincing response.

"The murder of three KGB agents makes it real to me. Unfortunately these men died leaving us limited information. Before they were killed, early morning hours, they dispatched a message, indicating the assassination plot was in motion. We must alert Mikoyanov."

Chekov stood, walked to his huge window overlooking the Kremlin and ordered Orlov to proceed.

"I want an investigation started immediately. All agents are to stop their current work and begin work on this emergency. Understood?"

Orlov did not like to bow his head to anyone but he learned this mode of deference to egomaniacs was useful, so he bowed his head and said, "Yes Mr. Secretary. I will get to work on this immediately." He paused, carefully observing Chekov.

"Is there anything else, sir?"

Chekov glared at Orlov and firmly responded. "No, keep me informed."

Orlov left the central office and walked down a long hallway. Inside the walls of his office he was careful not to smile or make any gestures that might be recorded. He dialed his secretary and ordered her to inform all available agents of an emergency meeting at 11:00 that morning. His voice was firm.

"I want all available agents to report to my office in one hour."

Events were moving along. Orlov's concern was that maybe it was more than their network could handle. Events could backfire when they aroused suspicion, making his work more dangerous. Chekov would have to be handled very carefully. Instincts were often his primary source for action under perilous circumstances. Orlov would have to incorporate his instincts as well, before time ran out. Chekov was a ruthless bureaucrat. Orlov had to maintain his poise and focus on his mission, remembering to offset Chekov by anticipating his next move.

From early in his childhood, Orlov learned how to adapt. He was a man whose childhood was altered for survival by his Jewish parents who converted to Christianity. The safety of their only child could be made more secure if he was not labeled as a Ukrainian Jew. Anti semitism was expanding throughout the republic in the waning years of World War II. Their rabbi suggested the idea after speaking with a Ukrainian, educated in a Jesuit seminary in Switzerland, now an ordained Russian Orthodox priest. For young Mikhail Orlov, it was drama he could not comprehend. He was baptized, received his first holy communion, followed several years later by confirmation. His parents made sure he attended service every week and young Mikhail eventually made friends with other Christian boys growing up in Kiev. His successful academic experience while attending university made it possible for him to qualify for officer training in the soviet army where he achieved the rank of Captain.

His military assignment in Latvia was to weaken resistance to Russian authority. Promoting Russian culture and language was also part of his responsibility. Mixing with Latvians and learning their language improved his ability for relaxing tension between Russian and native Latvian cultures. He made effective use of his interpersonal communication skills whenever clashes flared. His techniques proved successful. Having Ukrainian roots made him sensitive and sympathetic to Latvian concerns. He knew first hand how Russians used intimidation with Ukrainians. He also remembered his Jewish roots, held deep within his soul and realized now as an adult, why his childhood experience was altered by his loving parents who suffered a life of hardship. He recalled his parents who wanted to leave the Soviet Union but were too poor to make an attempt. When they both died on the same day, only hours apart, he was left distraught. Their passing altered his attitude, perception and loyalty to his superiors. He was bitter and filled with contempt. It was during this emotional state of sadness when he met a beautiful Latvian woman, Alicia Bankers. Latvians had contempt for Russians so it was strange how they managed to set aside their cultural animosity. Alicia respected Mikhail because he demonstrated his respect for her culture. He learned to fluently speak their language and did not display arrogance associated with Russians. When she learned his parents had died on the same day, she expressed her humanity to comfort him for his loss, despite being scorned by locals who disapproved. Her expression of sympathy was deeply appreciated by Mikhail. He realized at that moment a strong attraction to Alicia, not only for her beauty, but for her compassion. She could also see and feel his goodness. Over time, they fell in love and were married the following year. Natives also began to realize that Captain Orlov was not typical of Russian occupiers. His beliefs in human rights were discretely shared with Alicia and community leaders. The basis for changing politics in the Baltic states had begun by the marriage of a Latvian to a Ukrainian. One year after their first son was born, they met Commander Rypchensky. Two brilliant and determined minds joined the leadership of the Soviet Network.

Orlov and his wife Alicia moved to Moscow for the purpose of transforming totalitarian politics as prominent KBG operatives.

Andre Chekov's life history is a horror story that needs to be portrayed with all its tragic moments. He was the son of two alcoholic parents who abused their son when he came home from school, for no reason, other than their extreme insanity induced by alcohol addiction. At age nine he was sent to an orphanage filled with children who experienced similar acts of violence directed at them by their parents, uncles, aunts or any other abusive family member. This form of malpractice left thousands of children exposed to incredible torture and abuse without any significant intervention. Surrounded by evil in his environment, Andre, who was an intelligent young boy, learned how lying, cheating, stealing and fighting could help him survive another day. The men in charge, who were also borderline psychopaths were amused and impressed with Andre. They observed his cunning ways and even encouraged his malevolent behavior directed toward the weakest of the lot. The Darwinian principle of "survival of the fittest" was a common mantra of these depraved men. Young boys were encouraged to preempt their hostility toward others before they were targeted for attack. This mind twisting mentality inspired paranoid and impulsive behavior that consumed him.

When Russia was invaded by Nazi Germany in 1940, Andre's mental health was spared and redirected by military training. The Army emphasized survival by collective security, not survival of the strongest.. This concept was absorbed and mastered by Andre during the Nazis invasion. Now his focus was defeating invaders, not fighting his countrymen. He may have endured the German invasion due to his high capacity for survival learned while living in an orphanage where paranoia enlightened his ability to outwit opponents. His remarkable leadership defending the western front of Russia was observed by the Russian High Command and he was promoted to rank of captain.

He did however retain his display of paranoia. Several of his peers reported signs of his malady to their superiors, including Colonel Rypchensky. However, when the war ended, Chekov's interview for the secret police actually utilized his paranoid tendencies to his advantage. His relationship with women could not extend beyond his limited social amenities. Several relationships ended due to his abusive conduct toward women. He scored the highest grade ever recorded for the secret police. After training in the Cheka during the post war, his keen sense for subterfuge was recognized and he was appointed to the new State Security, aka, KGB, shortly after its inception in 1954. After ten years of successful maneuvers, he was considered the smartest agent in the agency and was made KGB Chairman in 1965. He was highly praised for leading the agency during the Cold War. His ability for identifying and undermining enemies, both foreign or domestic, made Andre Chekov a man everyone learned to fear.

Chapter 12

As Viktor drove west on the Long Island Expressway, he could not stop thinking about his connection with Yolanda Spieler. After saying goodbye, he wished they had never met. It affected his ability to concentrate on his mission. She was the most attractive and intelligent woman he had ever met—a wonderful combination. They made plans to meet again. Intelligence strategies had to be reaffirmed before they moved forward. Zelensky had strongly recommended avoiding unnecessary contact with her. Viktor's personal feelings would have to wait, however his strong attraction to her might weaken his discipline. He wondered if the CIA planted her to exploit his vulnerability. Viktor realized a professional calamity was potentially in store if he allowed his desire to overpower sound judgment. He was being disarmed by a beautiful women but decided there was something special between them that made pursuing her worth the risk.

Meanwhile he realized how important his forthcoming United Nations mission was for creating a series of events that were critical for network operations to succeed. He drove to UN Soviet Delegation Headquarters in Manhattan, parked his car in a nearby garage and hailed a taxi uptown to a public telephone hidden in an alcove, adjacent to a pub on East 84th St. Zelensky was waiting at a restaurant where he frequently dined. While sitting in a phone booth, he looked at his watch; it was 4:15 in the afternoon when he answered a call after one ring. "Hello, it's me."

Zelensky cupped his hand over the phone as he spoke.

"Now would be a perfect time to implement scheme two. Use another phone. Wait fifteen minutes."

Viktor walked two blocks away to another public phone hidden on a side entrance to an office building, out of sight of pedestrian traffic. After dialing a seven-digit number, he placed a small electronic code transmitter over the telephone and pushed a button. A high frequency code was transmitted to Soviet UN headquarters. A green light flashed indicating message transmitted.

Instead of waiting for another taxi, Viktor decided that a long walk to UN headquarters was something he would enjoy. Walking would allow him time to think about his latest personal contact. He wanted to believe Spieler was being honest with him. Even though their initial meeting had been arranged by CIA and Network operatives, he thought she could be a plant. Was he being set up? He could not understand why and began to doubt himself. He finally allowed his instincts to conclude she was genuine. Not to worry. When he arrived at the UN, he passed through security, entered an elevator, exited at the eighth floor, and walked to a central office where other agents were waiting for Burkov, head of Soviet UN intelligence. The room was filled with cigarette smoke.

When all personnel were seated, Burkov entered, stood at a podium and began with: "Moments ago, we received a coded message indicating that Warsaw allies are leaking our intelligence to NATO command. We also are finding that our workload has been increasing lately. We must determine the reasons for this activity." Viktor remained absolutely still. He was surprised that his coded message was announced so soon. Usually there was a procedure involving analysis of data to confirm coded messages.

One agent asked, "Was the code traced? Could be CIA operatives at work."

Burkov's response unnerved Viktor.

"I am not certain. Our technical experts will let us know if, where, and when." Soviet UN headquarters in Manhattan had all personnel working phones, making calls to agents in metropolitan areas from Boston to Washington. The nature and purpose of these calls was to ascertain whether investigations were being assigned to agents based on expertise. Agents with specific knowledge or experience were preferred. Some agents were familiar with relevant historical information. Others possessed more technical skills for deciphering information. Ironically, even Viktor made calls and, to his pleasant surprise, the misinformation schemes had made a significant impact. Soviet intelligence was experiencing a constant barrage of inquiries. Viktor was concerned that maybe network agents had spread too much misinformation at once. He would have to inform Zelensky as soon as possible. Burkov was very perceptive; he knew past communication breakdowns were caused by moles within their system. He watched all his agents making phone calls. Viktor noticed him staring, but maintained his composure. It appeared Burkov was suspicious of his behavior. When Viktor walked into the smoke filled room, he noticed Burkov immediately wrote a notation.

It was early morning, the following day. Viktor showered, dressed and left his apartment at 7:00. He stopped in his office to review contact information concerning Yolanda Spieler. He was looking for specific details that would provide some insight about her past assignments in the CIA. Was she in fact assigned to him? There was nothing in his file. He asked his secretary and she had no new information about Yolanda Spieler. There was, however, a letter informing him that U.S. State Department officials ordered reductions in Soviet personnel at UN headquarters. Their numbers had more than doubled. This meant some Russian spies would be deported for security reasons. After meeting with Burkov to review and discuss his contact with Spieler, Viktor realized he was not listening to a word. Instead, he found himself thinking about her. His obsession with Yolanda Spieler had taken hold. Later while driving east on the expressway, he wondered if Burkov sensed his preoccupation. If Viktor's body language and eye contact were scrutinized, he failed the test.

Before he approached her residence in Dix Hills, Viktor stopped at a deli for two large coffees and two buttered croissants. His desire to share a discussion with her about their personal history consumed him. He discovered feelings for a woman he had never experienced before. His attraction deepened when he learned both of their fathers were Russian Jews. Ancestry was always elusive for Viktor whose youthful past was lost without knowledge of his parental heritage. Something so important and unknown altered his outlook. He also wanted to determine whether their relationship would extend beyond intelligence exchanges. Was their mutual attraction worthy of pursuit or should they remain strictly professional? When he arrived at her home around nine-thirty Saturday morning, she appeared pleased to see him again. He handed her a bag containing his purchase. "I have coffee and croissants."

She smiled and directed him to her kitchen table.

"So what brings you here so early?" Her voice was as pleasant as her appearance.

He didn't hesitate. "You. I wanted to see you again." His direct response made her pause. He watched her eyes for clues. They welcomed his warmth, but he maintained his poise when she responded.

"You know, we have to be careful. Mixing our professional and personal feelings may have serious consequences." They stared at one another. Their attraction was mutual but still controlled.

Viktor did not hold back. His impulses overpowered him. He wanted her feelings revealed. "Under our circumstances, I realize my behavior is not professional, but I feel very attracted to you and would like to know if your feelings are mutual." There, he said what was on his mind without hesitation. They sat quietly and sipped hot coffee while continuing to stare at one another. Yolanda was poised but remained silent. Since he initiated this contact, she reserved her right to remain silent, wanting to hear more. Viktor understood her reticence, so he continued.

"Maybe if I place our meeting under different circumstances, would that help sort your feelings?" He paused. "If, for example, we met at a cocktail party and had mutual friends with normal social relationships, would that change things?"

Yolanda realized his sincerity and responded, "The scenario you describe is quite normal. Our reality is, however, very different. It would be imprudent for us to succumb to our emotions. I'm sure you see that."

Viktor was not disappointed with her response. She did not reject him. He realized and appreciated her ability to separate two very different realities.

"I know exactly what you mean. Your assessment is correct. But that does not change how I feel. My future is not in Russia, it's here in America. I am waiting for the right moment to request political asylum. I want a normal life. I want marriage and children. Currently, my life is not my own. I want to take ownership, and soon. Believe me, I am not using you for that purpose. I am being sincere when I tell you I am very attracted to you. I plan to make our current mission my last, before it's too late to escape."

Yolanda's compassion and sympathy emerged.

"If that is true, I will inform my superiors of your intentions, if you think that would help."

Viktor understood and respected her position. He did not want to come on too strong, but his heart throbbed with passion. He had never felt such strong emotions and feared losing his chances with her. He decided her offer was a beginning step.

"I accept your offer of assistance. Where do we begin?"

Yolanda was processing her own feelings. She was very attracted to Viktor but she would place both of their lives in danger if she allowed emotions to trump her judgment. They sat, drank coffee, and enjoyed croissants, using their time together to share personal life histories.

For the time being Viktor felt like a normal human being, in love with a beautiful and exciting woman. He then made reference to their Jewish heritage.

"Your father and my father were Russian Jews. We have that common link."

Her response was pleasant and positive. "Yes, how unique is that? My parents have shared their history with me. I can understand your desire to know more about your past. It must be difficult for you."

Viktor thought about her comments before responding.

"The only thing I can remember about my parents is through two wonderful adults who raised me. They had no children of their own so when the opportunity came for them to have a 'son' of their own, they moved quickly. I was only four years old. Believe me, I was very fortunate. Many children my age were lost to famine and despair. My adopted parents had only been married two or three years when they took me in. They knew and loved my mother because she was very kind to them and apparently asked them if they would take me in if anything happened to her. My older brother and sister disappeared along with my mother and father. For whatever reason, I was allowed to remain with my adopted parents who informed me about my parents many years later, before I left for university and beyond. I had asked them from the beginning and they told me, in due time, they would have an answer for me. And true to their word they told me just before I left. I was just eighteen. I learned that my mother was a nurse from Ukraine. When she met my father it was love at first sight. He was an attorney. When the secret police discovered their political views, everything changed." He paused with emotions barely under control. He cleared his throat and took a deep breath. She could sense his anguish as he continued. "They were sent to labor camps when I was a child. I never saw them again. My older brother and sister also disappeared in gulags."

Yolanda listened with compassion. As his humanity became more pronounced, her emotions swelled. The morning progressed. They gradually relished their time together. He did not want to leave and she sensed his mood. When he reached out for her hand, she complied and he looked into her eyes and said, "This is the most wonderful moment in my life of thirty-two years. Your presence and friendship give me hope. My current life is not one I chose. My loving guardians coached me toward intelligence work because they knew it offered foreign assignments. Their recommendation that I master English was most important. With their guidance, my education was a priority because opportunities for escape were in foreign service or intelligence. They were loving and caring people whose compassion for my loss was sincere. There are many good people in Russia who suffer in silence for their beliefs. I lost my entire family. My guardians understood. They wanted me to survive the onslaught of totalitarian life. I owe them so much. Because of their love and guidance, I am here in America." His emotions stirred but he wasn't finished. As difficult as it was for him to continue, he persisted. "Now maybe I have a chance. I want to share my future with someone special, here with freedom and opportunity. You probably don't think of that because you never lived without freedom. It's difficult for me to explain my feelings. Do you understand what I am saying?"

Yolanda did not expect what she just heard. Her emotions stirred. She remained still and silent. Her silence beckoned him to continue.

"Please forgive me for sharing my personal feelings so soon. I have learned not to take anything for granted. Life in a police state terrifies me. You are so fortunate to live in America. Something for you to think about."

Yolanda remained silent, incapable of responding.

He looked at his watch. "It's best if I leave now but I would enjoy seeing you again." He looked into her eyes. "If you would allow me this."

Yolanda's emotions peaked.. Her instincts told her this man was for real. Her attraction to him could not be withheld much longer.

She waited for him to say goodbye. When he finally did, he reached out to her and she responded with an embrace. He held her close. His heart was beating fast. He looked into her eyes again and they kissed with feeling.

"Please believe me. I want to know you and share more time with you. This is just a beginning. Will you see me through?"

She held him close; her response was measured.

"We must not create emotions that cannot be fulfilled. Be focused on your mission. I care about you. When our mission is complete we will continue where we left off. That's all I can say at this time."

For Viktor, that was good enough. He was more inspired to complete his mission knowing there was a remote possibility she could be part of his future. His personal life had all of a sudden found purpose through the loving arms of a woman he hardly knew.

Chapter 13

Viktor's careless disregard for his professional well being was not intentional. Walking away from agent Spieler's embrace was difficult. His fragile personal needs caused him to make unforced errors along the way. Mistakes in his judgment were mounting. Intelligence work required focus to detail, concern for perception by others. There was no other line of work where absolute regard for discipline and focus was most important. He failed on all counts. He realized that without delivering proof of his competence to his superiors, especially Burkov, personal life ambitions would be impossible. Meeting Yolanda Spieler had altered his judgment. She filled a large void in his life. As much as he wanted her to be part of his future, he concluded there would be no future unless he backed off. Then he asked himself: Am I being realistic?

When a man unexpectedly falls in love, his thinking can miscalculate reality. One reality he knew for sure. Intelligence work would have to be phased out; the question was how? It meant betraying his native country and in particular KGB culture. Other agents had done so but with unforeseen consequences. Leaving the KGB was not a simple matter. He was confident Yolanda sensed his sincerity and desperation. His opportunity to extricate himself from the grasp of KGB culture was filled with obstacles. Viktor felt trapped.

Now he was stuck on the Long Island Expressway. The traffic was backed up due to an accident that shut down all lanes for almost an hour. Tardiness was not something that would improve his status with Burkov. Being late for his meeting at the UN was problematic. He drove as fast as he could once traffic opened up. When he arrived at the UN, the conference room was filled. Soviet UN staff were all present, including nameless agents. His late entry was not unnoticed as he quietly rushed toward a seat in front of Burkov, who did not hesitate to comment.

"Are you having a good time with your American feline friend?" Burkov resented Viktor. This was partly because Viktor was a cut above most agents and could be a possible replacement for Burkov, whose abrasiveness stood out in American culture. Viktor's training as an intelligence officer ranked him at the top of his class. Because of his Jewish heritage, he believed, his advancement was stifled. In the United States, Viktor had also assimilated. This quality would not elapse unnoticed when promotions were scheduled each year. KGB higher-ups preferred polished, Americanized agents. They were a better fit for assignment in the States and were often promoted. Burkov understood Viktor's advantages and resented him intensely. The contrast between them was unmistakable. Ironically, promotion may have been a good cover for Viktor but it was the last thing on his mind. He wanted out.

When Viktor rushed to the front of the meeting taking place, he was twenty minutes late. Burkov made a point of scolding him.

"Why are you late?" Viktor was apologetic.

"Sorry sir, there was an accident on the expressway."

Burkov was not satisfied. Once again, Viktor realized his carelessness provided another reason for Burkov's resentment and distrust. Those present remained still, expecting a comment, which, after a spiteful glare, Burkov delivered with a boorish, condescending tone.

"For your information, Viktor, all KGB activities have been suspended until we settle some important matters. You better stay away from that bitch until further notice. We have been inundated with all kinds of activity. Top security matters. Zelensky will inform you." Then in a spiteful tone he continued.

"Don't forget who you work for! That is all." Burkov humiliated Viktor, who cringed with fear and contempt. All in front of several administrators in order to portray Viktor as incompetent.

Always efficient with his meetings, maybe too efficient, Burkov adjourned the gathering of Russian employees. He did not conduct open meetings where agents could inject pertinent information or ask questions. Viktor welcomed his brevity, but his comfort level with his superior had deteriorated substantially. His gut instincts told him his life was in danger.

Zelensky and Viktor received their orders and left the building. They walked into a pouring rain and quickly waved for a cab. Zelensky was annoyed with his partner.

"Why do you have to make yourself a suspect during these tense moments? Keep it in your pants. Your personal life is crossing a dangerous line." Viktor was silent and calm. Zelensky was agitated.

"We have totally shocked the system. We must get our hands on that new technology promised by the CIA. That should convince headquarters, especially Burkov, that we are competent and doing our job. You must get this information to save your ass."

Viktor didn't appreciate his partner's pessimism.

"Yolanda will have that information in a few days, if not sooner."

Zelensky always lit a cigarette when he was nervous.

"Tell her it's urgent. We have to establish our worth as spies; it will take some pressure off."

Viktor became slightly annoyed. "Yes, OK! You worry too much."

Zelensky shot back, "And you do not worry enough."

That was not true. Viktor was filled with fear and uncertainty.

Later that afternoon, Viktor returned to Long Island. He was under pressure to deliver computer technology with Yolanda's assistance. Usually he handled pressure well. Now, however, his anxiety level made him tense. He attributed one source of anxiety to Burkov. He feared retribution. The other source of his anxiety was Yolanda, who embodied his passionate and loving side. He had to find a way to ameliorate both relationships, one with a man he detested, the other with a woman he loved. Was it beyond his reach, like a frustrating dream where one grasps for emotions inexplicably blocked by an unknown force?

Viktor longed for normality. Living on Long Island would fulfill that desire. He wanted to experience American life more than anything else. All his dreams centered on having a wife and family. The contrasts of living in a free and open society compared with a police state were never more pronounced. This realization accentuated his growing fear of failure. He observed family life in America and wanted to fulfill that dream before it was too late.

His gut instincts told him that his cover was being unveiled. Burkov made him think negative thoughts every time they met. Visiting agent Spieler was now crucial for his peace of mind. If Yolanda came through with critical high tech data arranged through CIA director Sullivan, his situation would be improved dramatically. He forced himself to be optimistic. Viktor did not relish feeling anxious. It was not his style. His was a free-spirited personality. His best results were achieved when he maintained a relaxed frame of mind, which allowed him to work through his tasks effortlessly.

He thought of calling her first when he arrived at Huntington Station. He wanted to see her; he couldn't wait. Then he changed his mind. When he finally did call, he was not himself. Yolanda sensed his uneasiness. He was about to speak when she asked.

"Where are you?" She recognized the train announcement in the background.

"I will be there in ten minutes. Wait along the main road." When she arrived, he was comforted by her warm embrace, something he did not expect.

He held her close while releasing his emotions.

"I never want to lose you. You're too precious."

Yolanda could sense fear in his bright blue eyes. He was unable to disguise his confused state of mind. She noticed this right away.

"You seem very upset. Tell me what happened today. Please, Viktor, tell me." She wanted to ask more but thought it best to remain silent as she drove Viktor to her home.

Her neighbor's children were playing in their front yard with their father. Their fun and laughter made Viktor smile. His lost childhood flashed before him. He had a brief glimpse of his parents but it soon faded. He looked at Yolanda. Then he looked out her living room window.

"See them playing. That is something I long for." Yolanda remained silent but sensed a man whose mind was somewhere else. She tenderly held his hand. His gaze was that of a man lost in time. When he finally spoke, she could barely understand what he was saying, as if he was only talking to himself.

"Today was nerve wracking for me. My KGB supervisor suspects me of something. I can sense his lack of trust in me." He looked at Yolanda.

"I am also concerned about your safety in case they have evil intentions."

Yolanda wanted to assure him otherwise.

"Listen to me, my cover is protected, concealed by a regular job at Grumman. I report to work every day. If the KGB is watching me they know my entire work schedule. My contacts with intelligence are transmitted at my office where electronic security is in place. Nothing to worry about. In fact, the KGB should be impressed with you, knowing you are seeing a Grumman employee. Relax, Viktor."

Her explanation made sense. For the time being, his concern for her safety was appeased. It was Burkov's disposition that was bothering him.

"It's Burkov. He's an evil man."

Yolanda attempted to assure him.

"I'll have that high tech information for you tomorrow. That should please your boss. Bring it to him personally. Let him see your competence and loyalty." Excited, she stood up, wanting to distract him from his anxiety.

"Let's celebrate. I know a great seafood restaurant."

Viktor made an attempt to feel relaxed as he stood next to her. He took a deep breath. "Thank you for your concern. You are so kind. As soon as this nightmare is over, I would like to spend some special time with you." She turned away as if to say, let's be professionals and get the job done. Her body language directed him to divert his thoughts elsewhere, something he found difficult. Then he added.

"You must know I never sought this line of work. Ironic how my friends in Russia realized how intelligence work was a way for me to escape. Now I have to figure out how. All I want is a normal life with someone as kind and beautiful as you. Am I asking for too much? At some point our lives must become more meaningful for us personally." Then he smiled. "Interested?"

She pretended not to know what he was referring to.

"And what might that be?"

He smiled and remained silent, thinking she understood what he had in mind. They remained silent, allowing the moment to consume their thoughts. Viktor stood up and walked to the window. Watching children playing catch with their father made him think of their current place in time. His thoughts led him to his next comment.

"You know we would have never met had either one of us made different choices at some point in the past. Isn't it amazing how two people's past choices have delivered them to the present. I thought my experience as a KGB agent was my ticket out of a totalitarian state. Working as a spy was not what I had in mind. I forced myself to move in this direction for eventual freedom. Your experience was very different. Why did you decide to become a CIA operative?" Yolanda had not really thought of this before. She started with: "Well, for starters, I lived in Washington where international intrigue is everywhere, under the radar. One of my colleagues at Georgetown, worked for the CIA and persuaded me to apply. With my PH.D. in international diplomacy, recently completed, my prospects were excellent. I thought it would be exciting. Totally different from your experience." Viktor understood and appreciated her response when he said.

"Maybe now we can more clearly understand our current state of mind. Our motives and experiences are very different. I am 32 years old and would like to be pro active with my future choices. I am afraid I may not have control over the outcome. What is it I want? A wife and family of my own who I can grow old with. You do have more control over your future. However I think you would agree we share common ambitions and goals. Happiness may be an illusion. I will settle for contentment. For me that means surrounding ourselves with people we care for. Having children. Just being normal like most people."

She wasn't surprised by his comments because she believed he was sincere. But she also knew the reality of their situation. How does a KGB agent stationed in America, who is emotionally involved with a woman in the CIA, defect? She feared for his life but tried not to reveal her concern. "It sounds like a plan. It would be wise to place these goals on hold for the time being."

Yolanda allowed Viktor to release emotions that were causing him angst. This had a calming effect on his disposition. Her response and assessment were realistic. Under their circumstances, she would not allow her emotions to complicate a man's feelings for her.

Viktor, preferring caution over desire, decided to return to Manhattan. Exposing Yolanda to more surveillance made him uncomfortable. As he knew from experience, the KGB could make accidents happen.

"I am sorry, but I think it would be best for me to return to Manhattan. We must not continue to target ourselves. The KGB have ways to make accidents happen. Hopefully by tomorrow, your technical data will become available. As you suggested, I will personally deliver those documents to Burkov."

She nodded her agreement. Deep in her heart, Yolanda realized she was falling in love with this man. She wanted to demonstrate just how far she was willing to go, short of marriage.

Feeling unsettled about his future, Viktor returned to Manhattan. Seeing her did calm his state of mind. He wasn't sure if he was falling into a trap. He recalled KGB agents who were relieved from duty and returned to Russia. They were charged with treason, tried without legal counsel and sentenced to labor camps, without any publicity. Basically they disappeared from circulation without any contacts with family, friends, or government bureaucrats. Burkov was capable of resorting to similar disciplinary action, even for a slight infraction. However, if Viktor could demonstrate his worth as an intelligence officer, he could mitigate this possibility. The one man who could assist him was Orlov, but communicating with him was off limits. Exposing a network leader, third in command, was too dangerous. Viktor had to practice caution in his surroundings for the next twenty-four hours. Rather than return to his apartment, which he feared would be cased, he decided to spend the night in a hotel. After parking his car, he rode a subway uptown and made several changes in an attempt to lose anyone following. Then he flagged a taxi to 94th street where he walked four blocks to the Flemington Hotel on Central Park West. He requested a room that overlooked the park. Fortunately he had packed a small suitcase. He locked the door and wedged a chair under the door handle, kept the bathroom door open while he showered so as not to obstruct his view. His pistol, equipped with silencer, was within reach.

The only person he could contact was Zelensky. He called at 5:15 pm from a public phone in the hotel lobby, adjacent to a cocktail lounge. After three rings, Zelensky answered. "Zelensky here." Viktor did not respond. "Zelensky here." When his name was repeated twice it was code for "all clear." Their communication schedule was to talk every day at 5:15, from different public phones located in diners or restaurants. Viktor had memorized all five locations and numbers. They changed periodically.

Zelensky was waiting for a table in one of his favorite Italian restaurants when Viktor informed him, "I am staying in a hotel tonight. Following my instincts. Will see Yolanda tomorrow morning. Call me tomorrow, early." Viktor walked into the lounge, sat at the bar and ordered a dry vodka martini, up, with olives. Two of them usually were enough to bring on sleep. But he asked the bartender to mix him another, just in case. When he left for his room, third martini in hand, he was thinking of the woman he loved. If everything went as planned he would celebrate tomorrow night with Yolanda Spieler.

Chapter 14

The following morning, Viktor learned the transfer of technical intelligence data was completed. Zelensky called and informed him of their success. He was ordered to retrieve the information immediately. This meant another ride to Long Island. Viktor called Yolanda to request she meet him at Huntington Station. She agreed to wait for him in her car with the long-sought-after computer technical data. Viktor believed his successful accomplishment would persuade his KGB superiors that he was competent. This he believed would convince Russian intelligence that he was a reliable and loyal agent; he hoped it would take some pressure off and increase his credibility. When the train arrived, Yolanda was waiting in her car. When he opened the envelope with documents in numerical order, he was pleased, as was Yolanda. She knew the information was old technology that would be obsolete within six months. Viktor thanked her and confirmed he would hand deliver the package to Burkov upon his return. Then he gathered the nerve to ask, "Can you join me in the city? I have a hotel room on Central Park West. We could have dinner and go to a club."

She looked pleased. "That sounds nice. Yes. What time?"

He was thrilled with her acceptance. "Say around five o'clock. It would be best if you take the train. I will be on the corner of 7th and 34th, outside Macy's main entrance." He was feeling better after she kissed him on the cheek.

"I must get this package to Burkov. I'll see you around five o'clock." They embraced. As much as he wanted to remain with her, he pulled himself away and reboarded the train.

He arrived at Penn Station sooner than expected and flagged a taxi for his ride to UN headquarters. He knew Burkov would be in his office, knowing he was a workaholic. Sure enough, he was there smoking a cigarette, overwhelmed with more piles of intelligence reports than he had ever experienced before. Viktor knocked to get his attention. He turned to face him. "Yes Viktor. What are you doing here?"

Viktor held out the envelope packed with intelligence documents.

"This is for you. I just received this from Yolanda Spieler. She's an engineer at Grumman. I hope you will be satisfied with the contents."

Burkov opened the envelope and studied the contents; he was pleased. Viktor lit a cigarette, sat, and waited. After several minutes had passed, Burkov commented, "Well done. We need this information to upgrade our computers." Unfortunately at this moment, Burkov's phone rang which diverted his attention. He covered the speaker with his hand and said to Viktor, "Our intelligence is being bombarded with one crisis after another. Something is not right. You'll have to excuse me. I have to take this call." He looked at Viktor when he said that. It was apparent that Viktor's attempt to reset his relationship with Burkov at this time was not going to happen. Viktor waited, hoping for another opening to mend fences with Burkov, but unfortunately, was ignored. Burkov nodded and motioned to Viktor as he turned to speak, suggesting that he could not talk at this time. Reluctantly, Viktor decided to leave. He did feel somewhat relieved that he had personally delivered intelligence to him, however he still believed his life was in danger. He didn't trust Burkov, nor did Burkov give him any reason to believe otherwise. For the time being, his thoughts of meeting Yolanda managed to change his mood.

Yolanda looked beautiful when he saw her walk out of Penn Station, carrying a shoulder bag. She noticed him waving from the front entrance of Macy's. As she approached, Viktor could appreciate her beauty in the bright sunshine that lit up her face. They walked uptown, stopped in a pub, held hands and stared into each other's eyes, sipping a Compari and soda. Both sensed what the evening had in store. Walking uptown on 7th Avenue was exciting for Viktor. He felt like a free man living his dream.

In comparison, Moscow was quite a contrast, for several reasons. Residents had somber faces, looked burdened by their environment and lacked the energy of Manhattanites. When Yolanda looked at him she thought of his preoccupation with his life in Russia, filled with painful memories. She gently squeezed his arm to indicate she was with him, not distant. He appreciated her gesture when looking at her.

"Thank you for your love and concern. It's so important to me. I need your assurance now more than ever." She wanted to assist him with his defection plans but was not sure what action should be taken. She looked at him, leaned closer and kissed his lips. "You're very welcome."

The romantic moment did not escape Yolanda. Here she was, falling in love with a Russian spy whose future was unclear. She felt a strong connection to a man whose family were victims of genocide. Now his desire was to restore his life with traditional family values, plain and simple. She thought of their Jewish connection and possibilities that would offer. It had to count for something. Besides, she was very attracted to him and felt genuine compassion to comfort his loss. At age twenty sevem, she was ready for an intimate relationship. For the moment, she blocked out her reservations and maintained a positive attitude.

His mood suddenly changed and she could feel his exuberance when he said, "Let's take a cab to Tavern on the Green. I think you will like it." Funny, how she never managed to go there for any occasion but had heard of its appealing atmosphere. "We can have a few drinks, have dinner at a nearby restaurant, then walk to my hotel."

In the Tavern, they were seated at a quiet setting with banquet seats where their bodies and hands could explore one another. She looked beautiful with her dark hair and blue eyes sparkling. She thought how handsome he was, and was learning more about him every moment, enjoying his tender masculinity. His sense of humor did not surface but she believed his anxiety had denied him levity. She used her feminine body language effectively, and he gradually responded by kissing her gently. After a prolonged moment of quiet romantic gestures, he finally broke their silence.

"Yolanda, we have to talk about us. Where do you want our relationship to go? You know my feelings."

Before responding, she looked at him while tenderly holding his hands.

"I hope my actions speak more clearly than my words." She paused.

"We are in a difficult place. Your situation is dangerous and our relationship could make it worse. Let's be in the moment until we know what your future has in store. Please don't interpret this as negative. I'm just trying to protect both of us."

His response was not expected.

"That sounds like a death sentence."

For a moment, she lost her composure.

"No!" Her voice carried and some patrons looked toward them, causing her to whisper:

"Please Viktor. Be in the moment. Can't you tell my feelings are strong? But our situation is uncertain. How does a KGB agent leave his post in America? Do you have an answer? I'm caught in the middle. Our relationship is not exactly the norm. I'm as conflicted as are you."

Viktor was silent, then nodded his affirmation. He smiled while assuring her.

"You're right. I must learn to enjoy our time together no matter what the future holds. I must allow myself to live in a world of fantasy. Please interpret that to mean a wonderful, joyous, spectacular and loving relationship, with a woman who has swept me off my feet." Then he quietly laughed. "This really is a fantasy for me. I'm residing in a country where freedom reigns, with all the comforts one can imagine, but most of all, I am with the woman of my dreams." He kissed her lips softly, then continued.

"You are right. Let's not waste our precious time together. From now on, I am in the moment, for however long that may be."

Her eyes looked glassy. Then a tear appeared. She knew his commentary was sincere but also filled with unknown drama. Silence followed, filled with emotions transmitted through their eyes and lips; nonverbal, dramatic romance where words were unnecessary. Their behavior revealed how their minds focused on similar thoughts and feelings. They were connected. Their romantic minds slowly drifted to whether they should have dinner, then make love, or make love, then enjoy dinner. The answer was forthcoming. They laughed out loud when the pulse of their body desires motivated them to abruptly leave. Chemistry was definitely speaking to them. Hand in hand, they walked to his hotel room where for over two hours, his moment of fantasy continued. During their love fest, the bond between them grew stronger, while undercurrents swirled.

After lying in bed in restful sleep, they felt each others bodies touching one another. They turned facing each other and smiled. Both seemed to realize their lives had crossed a path taking them toward an uncertain outcome. Viktor felt liberated in one sense because he was no longer confused and he wanted to share his liberation with Yolanda. He turned and faced her.

"I know our lovemaking speaks for us. It was beautiful and I will always cherish our first experience together. I am being in the moment now but if you wouldn't mind, I would like to share with you my dream. It's very simple really and not necessarily in any particular order, except for one part and that is you. You are definitely part of my dream. But there are other parts that are worth sharing as well. I would like to teach in a liberal arts college. I observed a class last year at Columbia and enjoyed every minute. I could see myself teaching young adults beginning their life long search for their place at the table. What do you think? Do I appear professorial?" Yolanda's smile revealed a twinkle in her eye. She felt his genuine love for life with all its possibilities. He wanted to imagine a future filled with meaningful purpose. Her instincts told her not to go there but her heart was touched by his simple request. "Yes, you would be a great teacher. I would sign up for your class. What are you teaching?" He responded with:

"That's a good question. I'm not sure. Maybe psychology or art history. I also enjoy literature."

She played along with his dream. "Follow your passion. That will help you decide." She then asked him another question. "What else do you dream about?" His response was immediately clear. "I would like to become an American citizen, marry the women I love, buy a beautiful home, raise at least three children, have dogs and cats and a garden. That's it. Simple really. Nothing complicated about my dreams." She moved close to him and kissed him with feeling. At that moment she realized this man was genuine. Someone she wanted to spend the rest of her life with.

Chapter 15

Commander Rypchensky's office was beautifully decorated by his wife Monique. The elegance was noticed by everyone who entered, including Orlov, who had scheduled a meeting at 9:00 am. Orlov walked around the office observing tastefully placed artifacts Monique had purchased throughout Europe. It made him think how wonderful Russia could be if it was free to trade with European and American markets. He knew the Commander, being Ukrainian, looked west to Europe for his cultural replenishment, as did many other natives. Orlov justified working for the Network because he could visualize the results if they were successful. Russians, and citizens from fourteen other republics, had experienced massive deterioration under communism. Their standard of living was crimped by an economy hampered by lack of incentives. Profit motives remained politically incorrect. Persecution and censorship had not subsided despite several attempts by a handful of liberals in the party who focused public attention toward glasnost. While the commander was speaking on the telephone, he observed Orlov admiring his fine collection of art and paintings. Markets in Western Europe highlighted many inadequacies of a regime out of touch with citizens demands.

Leaders of the network were men who served their country with distinction for nearly forty years. Both of these men were driven by similar desires and there were thousands more who quietly expressed their frustration, but were powerless. Two powerful men were risking their lives, and the lives of their families, to create a free and open society. The end result was uncertain. It was a gamble they were willing to take.

When the commander had completed his telephone conversation, he welcomed Orlov, who gestured with his index finger in front of his lips. The commander understood Orlov's concern. "It is safe to talk. I have personally inspected everything in this office and have my own surveillance system in place."

Orlov was not convinced; he preferred talking elsewhere. He motioned quietly.

"I prefer not talking here. Let's walk to the dining room and chat on the way." For a senior KGB officer to feel this insecure in his military commander's office, indicated how paranoid the atmosphere had become. The commander was somewhat surprised but respected Orlov's concern. They walked along a grand hallway that was a reminder of Czarist Russia. Beautiful Persian carpeting, French impressionist paintings in gold leaf frames, pottery from the Ottoman Empire, and elegant Italian furniture highlighted with fresh cut flowers. Orlov observed how this opulence displayed standards not representative of citizens craving basic necessities.

Orlov preferred their discussion begin with positive news. "The KGB is bogged down chasing false intelligence reports. So far everything is moving in the right direction for us."

Orlov was about to continue when the commander cut him off.

"Mikoyanov will meet the American president in two weeks. We must intensify our security with our assassination hoax in motion. Maintaining our credibility is important. This is also an opportune moment to expose our bureaucratic opponents as conspirators. After we destroy them, we can appoint our allies to the Central Committee."

Orlov was pleased with the idea of acting boldly and swiftly. He preferred more direct action. The commander was not about to disappoint him. Orlov inquired, "Let's review your plan."

The commander responded with confidence, "Yes, we will plant explosives, guns, maps, and printed material in their residences. This information will reveal their plans for assassinating Mikoyanov. Once this is done, we have our network agents and KGB investigate. Our enemies will be arrested with all that planted evidence used to prove their guilt as conspirators."

Orlov nodded his approval and inquired, "Sounds like good old-fashioned police state procedures. How many members should we implicate?"

The commander smiled, reached into his jacket, and removed a piece of paper. "Here is a list. There are twenty-five names. These men have been our most bitter enemies in the Politburo and Central Committee. They must be destroyed. I will arrange for printed materials and weapons to be stolen and traced to them. Study this list carefully. You may want to add a few names; let me know where you think my plan needs your input."

Orlov was silent for a moment before he asked, "How can we break into their homes to plant evidence without creating suspicion?"

The commander had anticipated this question but his response did not convince Orlov, who sensed there was something wrong or missing with his plan. The commander continued, "Chairman Mikoyanov has invited all members and their families to participate in a party rally on Saturday before the soccer game. Everyone listed will be there with their families."

Orlov offered this suggestion: "Instead of breaking into all twenty-five residences, why not plant incriminating evidence in some of their cars and places of employment? This will make our investigation more convincing and will also make it safer for our agents."

The commander was impressed with Orlov's analytical mind. "Yes, you are correct. Good idea. Just let me know the final details as soon as possible."

Orlov was pleased that his modification was accepted. Planning with Commander Rypchensky was gratifying because Orlov's KGB experience and logic was respected. Orlov had one more question. "When do we begin?"

He was pleased with the commander's response:

"As soon as we complete these important details; we must not delay. Once we agree on our final plan, we will move, and move fast. Two of my men will meet you at the airport warehouse to review specific details and required items. Call them at this number. Leave no trace of that list or any written plan. Understood?"

Orlov motioned his response. "Understood! Now let's have lunch."

The commander then made an unexpected comment:

"Living in a totalitarian culture gives us options democracies do not allow. I regret our use of violence is necessary. I also realize our enemies would not hesitate to execute us for what is about to occur." They entered an elegant dining hall reserved for communist party members where they could enjoy meals and drinks at taxpayers' expense.

While enjoying lunch together, these two network leaders discussed future capabilities a free nation could enjoy. The commander continued. "Imagine our citizens no longer living with fear of expressing their views. Imagine a free press and real justice in our courts. Imagine an economy where our shelves are filled with all types of food and merchandise. We have to remind ourselves. This is what we are fighting for and what many of us will die for." Orlov realized the commander was projecting his dissonance for what was about to happen. He refrained from adding his views. In fact, his many years of KGB experience conditioned him never to look back. Orlov's thoughts were expressed as follows. "Our enemies created generations of terror, murder, and economic depravity inflicted upon millions of our citizens. Soon many will die for their evil deeds." He realized at that moment, there was no turning back. He raised his glass and said, "To our success for liberty!" Cold beer never tasted so good.

Chapter 16

As planned, on Friday night a box truck with CITY POLICE written on both sides appeared at their rendezvous point, a large warehouse located adjacent to the airport. Equipment and personnel for sabotaging reputations of over twenty-five conservative/ hardline members of the Politburo, were gathered to prepare for the operation. The Soviet Union's elite political body was their main target. Orlov was there to explain and review details. He preferred meeting with each agent to emphasize how the future of their country depended upon actions they were about to undertake. The Moscow police chief was also present. His loyalty to Commander Rypchensky was critical for a successful outcome. Local policing was preferred to maintain control by Moscow authorities, who could cover up any unforeseen errors in the operation. In a large trailer, Orlov reviewed every possible flaw of their plan. He had several documents that would implicate guilt of every party member. Charges would include treason, fraud, bribery, and theft of services. Large caches of weapons, documents revealing collusion and bundles of rubles would be hidden in their cars, residences or workplace.

When Orlov began speaking, there was absolute silence.

"I want you all to know and believe our actions tonight are for securing our future. Our personal liberties and those of all citizens who believe in freedom are relying on our actions. It's very important we succeed. It's also important that you believe in what we are doing." Then he paused and took time to study his loyal comrades.

"Are there any questions at this important time?" He waited while maintaining his serious gaze, then continued. "I have uniforms and schedules for all of you. Your individual schedule must be memorized. I will destroy all paperwork. Make sure your pockets are empty of any information that could implicate you. These uniforms will identify you as police officers. Use these helmets to protect your identity. I have been assured that no one will notice anything different about your presence in the area we will occupy. Any questions?"

One agent in the rear asked, "What if a member of the family is present when we visit their homes tomorrow?"

Orlov had discussed this possibility with his commander.

"I have been assured that all family members have been invited to the festivities at the stadium. If anyone is home, avoid that residence. We will have to make other plans for those individuals. Remember to inform me if this should happen." Orlov was confident this possibility would not present itself. He emphasized the importance of working diligently.

"Don't rush. Work methodically. No mistakes." He paused and looked at his men.

"If there are no further questions, our operation will begin this evening. All vehicles that are targets have been identified for you. Conceal all weapons and printed material in these vehicles. Avoid the chance of having these items detected. We will break into them the following day while they are moving from their residences or vehicles. For whatever reason, we may not be able to target every vehicle or residence today. If that should happen, we will have to avoid those targets until a time that works for us. Understood?" Orlov paused, then saluted his troops and made a triumphant gesture with his fist.

The Friday night operation began when cars owned by party members were broken into without any damage. Items were hidden under seats that were removed. The planted material clearly implicated party member involvement with corruption and the assassination of Mikoyanov. Car seats were then reinstalled. Some items were cleverly hidden in trunks as well.

The next morning, Orlov was pleased with Friday night's operation. Could they be as successful in a daytime operation? His men were outfitted with a variety of uniforms used by Moscow city employees. Mail carriers, utility crews, and policeman were involved when entering designated homes. Some residents adjacent to targets were informed their gas or electric service had to be temporarily shut down in order to repair a main line. It was done with precision and every residence was successfully visited. Orlov was proud of his agents. The difficult part would follow. He knew there would be casualties. Unfortunately that was also part of the plan.

The soccer stadium was filled to capacity. In a room for dignitaries in the upper decks of the stadium, families of privileged party members gathered for a luncheon. The roar of the crowd could be heard as two competing Soviet soccer teams were being introduced. A subordinate of Orlov confirmed that all targets were in attendance. The festivities and levity enjoyed by a select elite would momentarily turn to violence. The contrast of events would be stark.

The interesting aspect of this bold operation was it relied on common tactics used by totalitarian states: violation of civil and human rights. It was conceived as an event where the ends justified the means. Very totalitarian. Network agents would violate civil liberties to achieve noble goals. Their means were practical, efficient, and despotic, including murder and callous disregard for legal and ethical conduct. An understanding of Russian history, devoid of democratic traditions and civil rights, for centuries, can explain the methodology. Ironically, in this revolution, a plethora of maneuvers frequently used by the Communist Party, would now be employed for eliminating them, leading all factions into a state of panic. The rationale of network leaders was, democratic tactics were not suited for this operation. A successful outcome would necessitate brutal gestapo force. After several long discussions and debates, Network operatives decided it was time to kill or be killed. There was no other way.

There were plenty of risks for all involved. Network leaders and agents realized their exposure would result in swift and contemptuous retaliation by their enemies. There was no room for error or timidity. Psychologically, they were required to detach themselves from prior obligations to protect powerful elites of the Communist Party. Now the establishment was portrayed as demonized enemies. The network accepted Machiavellian principles of power politics. The end would justify the means. There was no more efficient way of dealing with an entrenched oligarchy. Violence was therefore a foregone conclusion. Seventy years of Communist rule was a long time to wait for radical change that would improve the lives of millions of citizens.

When Rypchensky discussed strategy with his subordinates, he had to disavow many of his moral beliefs. Telling his son was most difficult, but he could not mislead Kristoff. His personal safety would be compromised by not knowing what to expect.

He arranged to meet Kristoff three days before violence would commence. They met in a park, not too far from the Kremlin. The commander expected Kristoff would find his briefing incredible. His value system would be challenged by events about to unfold. Preparing him for the worst was important, because as a journalist, his writing had to frame the event. Swift and extreme action would be justified and written for public consumption. When the Commander met his son he was direct and to the point.

"Good morning, Kristoff." He paused and lit a cigarette. "It all begins in three days. I want you to know that a number of people will die. It's either us or the opposition. We choose not to die.

Our tactics necessitate swift action. Hopefully our revolution will purge our republics of communist failures. You must realize and understand for years we made attempts to persuade our opponents. They were ideologically driven to maintain hardcore principles that were unattainable. You can judge for yourself how their twisted ideology has destroyed our country."

Kristoff remained silent. He had just heard his father make statements he never could have imagined. For a brief moment, he was shocked. Then his father continued.

"You know, Kristoff, my true beliefs run contrary to all the violence that is about to take place. However, if we are to remedy our national malaise, we must not be timid. You must understand, this is war. All rules change."

Kristoff maintained his silence. He understood his cravings for political reform were unattainable under the status quo. His father waited for his son to respond. Kristoff knew where he stood.

"I understand. I just never imagined that violence would be so widespread and vicious."

His father assured him it could be worse than imagined.

"Violence may be an understatement for what is about to happen. Before you leave for America, we need you to write a persuasive summary of events. We must keep the public informed. Your writing must identify enemies within our corrupt bureaucracy whose life of privilege and power diminish the lives of all who are struggling. Eventually citizens will embrace our movement for justice."

Kristoff realized his written accounts had to comport with expectations of journalism found exclusively in police states. This meant lies and exaggerations had to be woven into his essays. He had to compose several persuasive accounts of what happened. Mixed feelings ensued. He wondered if he was capable of writing reports that were totally fabricated. Revolutions require propaganda. There was no point in questioning his father's request.

In six days he would be departing for New York. His emotions were stirring, especially for his parents safety, but he realized revolutions can tear families apart. Dismissing his father's concern for his safety was not an option. His father's words stated earlier that morning rang loud and clear. "One of us must survive this ordeal."

His father explained his UN assignment.

"I am assigning you liaison to the United Nations in New York. We can use you at the UN office where a major part of this operation is currently diverting our enemies' focus. You will be safe there. In this envelope, I have your visa, passport, flight schedule and other pertinent information, including your contacts in New York. Report to the airport Wednesday afternoon. Your flight departs at 10am."

Kristoff wanted to stay in Russia. He felt an obligation even though he wanted to be with Nadia. He was disappointed and wanted to let his father know.

"Why are you doing this? I thought I was here to assist your cause with my writing."

His father could sense his disappointment.

"As I said earlier this morning, one of us must survive this ordeal. It is impossible for me or your mother to leave. Besides, you can be useful in New York. I have included a list of assignments where your skills apply. We also have friends who will look after you."

Kristoff noticed skepticism in his father's voice. He wanted more information.

"You must have reasons for your uncertainties. What are they?" His father responded.

"The Central Committee will appoint new members to replace the twenty-five caught in the conspiracy. The old regime will be severely threatened by this action since all new members are more liberal and a threat to their power. They will not sit idle and wait to be outmaneuvered. Something is going to explode before too long. You will be safer out of the country."

Kristoff expressed concern for his father's safety.

"But your life is in danger!"

His father looked directly into Kristoff's eyes.

"When you live in a police state, your life is always in danger, especially when your luck runs out."

His comment unnerved Kristoff. Why was his father gambling with his life? Risks no longer appeared calculated.

"Is this all luck? I thought your network had control of our destiny."

The commander became even more foreboding. He was familiar with American history which he enjoyed reading for many years. He envied leadership qualities of America's first six presidents, especially their concerns for future generations.

"I am not too sure of that anymore. What we are attempting is a rapid overhaul of an entrenched oligarchy. We thought of a slower approach but that has always failed miserably in the past. We have stopped thinking small. As Americans would say: 'go for broke'. Over a century ago, Americans referred to their vision as manifest destiny. Its meaning was interpreted in several ways. We must decide what our vision entails. Americans were bold with their democratic experimentation. We must also be bold. In the end, our destiny will be manifested by factors beyond our control."

His father looked at his watch.

"I must leave. We will meet again, when our situation is more certain. Pray for our family and country."

His father kissed his son on the cheek. Kristoff took a deep breath. He wrapped his arms around his father. Would he see him again? He never imagined this moment could be their last. They embraced in silence.

Chapter 17

The KGB, under Orlov's direction, made plans to protect president Mikoyanov. The first stage of their deception, leaking the story, had been implemented by network agents for the purpose of misleading KGB intelligence. Chekov had been informed at KGB headquarters, but he insisted upon another meeting with Orlov before any action was taken. The atmosphere in the Kremlin, usually subdued, became frantic as more reports revealed evidence of a planned assassination. Liberal-conservative factions within the Communist Party added credibility to these reports. Divisions among Communist Party members were not reported publicly but insiders understood animosity was strong. Politics had become personal and spiteful as well.

Orlov arrived at Chekov's office holding a folder. He immediately addressed Chekov, whose piercing stare was foreboding.

"Here is a list of conspirators gathered by agents. Their names are revealed in a conversation that we monitored. I have a partial tape of that conversation. They plan to assassinate Mikoyanov and blame their political enemies." Orlov could once again feel Chekov's glare. He maintained his poise and remembered that Chekov's behavior was very typical of his paranoia. Orlov was told to play the tape, purportedly received from an agent earlier that morning. The voice on the tape was that of a network agent, speaking the part of the agent who died from a head blow. Although the quality of the tape was poor, it verified crucial information about the planned assassination.

When Chekov stopped the tape, there was silence among the small group of agents present who had quietly assembled in his office waiting for their orders. He addressed them:

"We have just listened to a conspiracy in the making. Here is a list of names of those involved. We have information that requires immediate action. Arrest these traitors before it is too late." Then, looking at Orlov, he continued.

"Captain Orlov will supervise this operation."

Orlov, who was seated, stood, then addressed his agents . "You will work in pairs. These individuals must be arrested. Their residences and vehicles must be searched for any pertinent evidence. We must move quickly and efficiently before time is lost and evidence destroyed. Be prepared for violence. These are desperate men." Network KGB agents present, were teamed with nonmembers to maintain control over the desired outcome. Several enemy targets would be murdered. Those who survived would be scapegoats for the deaths of agents during the operation. Orlov handed each team photographs of their targets. Without delay, the next stage of the coup was being implemented.

Later that afternoon, Commander Rypchensky met with criminal investigators, including three forensic inspectors. Specific details were explained. They had been briefed by Orlov, but the commander wanted to make sure everyone understood their critical part in the operation. The Commander's serious tone was matched by his direct eye contact. "Unfortunately, we have to sacrifice some good men to add more credibility to our plan. You understand the importance of this action. Forensics in this situation is extremely critical. Evidence must confirm they were murdered by conspirators. You must destroy any evidence that could be used against us. Understood!" He waited for their response. "Yes sir." Then, looking at his marksmen, he reminded them, "Be careful. We do not want our network agents shot by mistake." His insistence for perfection was repeated. Then he emphasized, "Have I made myself clear?" He asked all present to respond individually. Each firmly responded,

"Yes sir, I understand." Each marksman was assigned a KGB agent for elimination. The commander understood how assigned murder, a critical necessity of their plan, could fall apart under pressure. He therefore reiterated to network agents, that years of totalitarian executions and torture of innocent civilians was finally culminating with revenge. He walked around the room and made eye contact with every operative present. Then he addressed them with some personal history.

"In 1938 when I was sixteen years old, I felt anger and sadness for the persecution and murder of innocent parents of children who were my friends. They disappeared from their families and friends, never to return. That was 50 years ago to this day." He paused again, raising his volume as he continued.

"Now we have an opportunity to rid ourselves of men who have perpetuated torture and misery for our nation. Men who are unwilling to allow freedom to determine our personal destiny. Freedom that will unleash our ability to grow our economy and improve our lives. Freedom that will allow us to govern ourselves. We have tried our best for over two decades to address the Communist party of our misery through peaceful dialogue and deliberation. That method has failed miserably. Our opponents have continued to abuse their power to silence us by imprisonment, persecution, and murder. Our only remaining option involves eliminating our opponents. We have no alternatives. We must strike with deadly force before they can react. They will not hesitate to kill us if they get the chance. They will direct extreme retaliation against you and your families if we do not act first. At this stage of our revolution, our enemies are most dangerous. If you don't kill them, they will certainly find a way to kill you. As your commander, I cannot allow that possibility. Therefore we must strike first. Our survival will depend on swift and precise action that will place our enemies at a disadvantage." He paused and looked at each agent directly.

"Men, it's important to know what you are fighting for." His persuasive presentation made its mark.

A massive police and military presence was organized to prepare for any unknown contingencies. The network operation began with the sound of sirens and thunderous movement of military police vehicles throughout Moscow's streets. Citizens were curious while watching rarely observed activity. Suddenly, pedestrians ran for cover when gunfire was heard and several cars exploded. Hundreds of troops and police suddenly deployed from military transports. Observers concluded this activity meant a coup was in the making. As a rule, political succession in Soviet politics was very mysterious and unpredictable.

Some citizens continued their everyday routine thinking this was just another purge. Some observed the arrests of party officials approaching their cars. It was difficult to determine where gunfire originated. Three men were shot and fell to the ground, followed by a volley of return fire that found its fatal mark on party officials and their bodyguards. Pedestrians scrambled for cover as three heavily armed vehicles and troop carriers roared by and surrounded a street intersection where most of the activity occurred. Party members held their hands up when ordered by army officers. They were searched while standing near their vehicles. Camera crews stood ready to film all of the activity. When car trunks were opened and searched, they revealed weapons and printed material hidden inside. Camera crews exposed gory details with close-up shots of killed KGB agents. Network snipers found their mark on all counts. They shot and killed several party members, their guards, and three KGB agents. High-powered pistols used in the murders were exchanged by forensic inspectors, then carefully planted in the hands of dead suspects. On cue, video crews filmed living and dead suspects, cleverly incriminated by treacherous evidence. The staging appeared seamless.

A quiet street near Gorky Park had its solitude destroyed moments later when military police and KGB officers raided homes of remaining suspects. Network agents shot and killed two more KGB agents and one party official. Bullets were riddled all over the area. Used weapons were once again planted on dead suspects as before. Video crews followed police as they entered apartments. They filmed large caches of weapons and confessions, brutally forced. Two party officials were beaten unconscious when they resisted arrest. One barely survived in critical condition. Kristoff appeared on the scene when his father radioed him after danger from crossfire ceased.. He now understood what his father described three days earlier. It bothered him to see corpses of KGB agents who were killed for enhancing the credibility of the operation. They were young men with families.

Kristoff began writing his report for public consumption. He was surprised that he still had control of his emotions. His story would appear in Pravda the next morning with several photos to enhance public interest. He truly understood there was no turning back. He wanted to be assured his column would satisfy his father the following morning. Written accounts of revolutionary events attract public support. Credible composition using persuasive commentary were skills Kristoff had perfected. He knew it was all lies and this bothered him, but he also understood propaganda wins revolutions.

The following morning, he would meet his mother at the airport, just prior to his flight to New York. He pleaded with her to leave with him. She understood his concern but would not leave her husband in Moscow. They had other plans. At 10:05am, Aeroflot Flight 307 was airborne. Kristoff was on his way.

That same morning, in his Kremlin office, Chekov was reading a report Orlov had written. He squinted, even with his glasses.

"Well done, Captain Orlov. It is very unfortunate that we lost five of our agents. Make certain their families receive full compensation." The KGB took care of its members better than any other government agency.

Orlov acknowledged Chekov's request.

"Yes sir. I have arranged for that. Will there be anything else, sir?"

Orlov did not expect the response he received.

"Yes. I want you to replace some of our old recording equipment. That tape you gave me was not the best quality. I have been informed by the morgue that Vlasov is still alive. He has a pulse and a severe concussion but is expected to survive. Please investigate." Orlov's heart pounded with fear, but he managed to respond with his steady demeanor.

"Yes sir. We will investigate."

When Vlasov was brought to the morgue, an examination revealed that his heart was still beating. Unknown to Orlov, Chekov was immediately informed by authorities.

Believing Vlasov was killed during the raid, Orlov reported his name to Chekov as being one involved in the assassination conspiracy. Vlasov's recovery presented major problems for the network. His survival was the operations's only flaw. Vlasov's reported death was premature. The assassination conspiracy was effective but now a surviving witness could contradict its veracity. Orlov's hoax was now a possible liability. This is an example of how intensive planning to confuse your enemy can be reversed by one unfortunate mistake. Orlov was devising plans to have Vlasov's medical recovery terminated as soon as an opportunity presented itself.

Meanwhile, Chekov had arranged to have Vlasov placed under heavy guard around the clock. Unknown to Orlov or anyone else at KGB headquarters, during early morning hours, Vlasov was moved to an undisclosed location at the personal direction of Chekov. He ordered another patient moved into Vlasov's room without informing the hospital staff or his agents of the switch. Orlov understood Chekov would interrogate the lone survivor when his condition improved. Of the twenty-five members targeted by the Network, Vlasov was the only one with close ties to Chekov. The remaining survivors were political opportunists who Vlasov frequently manipulated. Chekov had a taped voice, purportedly that of Vlasov. Better yet, he had Vlasov, still alive, although temporarily incapacitated. Chekov wanted his testimony in order to determine the motives behind this planned assassination. He knew Vlasov would cooperate.

Orlov left headquarters to meet his commander in a television studio. The video crew was editing film of political enemies, dramatizing their conspiracy and corruption. This was all intended for public consumption. Fomenting public outcry or uprising after the videos were broadcast was his intention. If military force was required to control demonstrations, he would order army personnel to support and sympathize with protesters. That would be an important signal. Military endorsement of public sentiment, especially in regard to charges of corruption, theft, tyranny, and now the assassination conspiracy, would favor the network cause. The Commander could have staged a protest using network sympathizers but he favored an organic movement, not one manipulated. He preferred listening to the pulse of public opinion, believing that at some point, massive demonstrations could be exploited.

The political ramifications of glasnost favored his network. Revolutions need public support for credibility. Unlike free and open societies, where demonstrations are common, in Russia they can be dangerous and deadly. Orlov understood the commander's strategy, but did not share his idealism or optimism concerning glasnost.

Orlov's thinking was inclined not to favor too much transparency. He believed openness was not something citizens understood. Historically, it was not part of their political culture. Transparency could backfire, especially if communist hardliners ordered agitators to stir public outcry on their behalf. Orlov believed it was a gamble to democratize citizens too soon. He preferred Network control should be firmly established before democracy is unleashed.

Orlov anxiously waited for video crews to complete their editing of daily events for evening broadcasts. He was anxious about one surviving witness and had the unfortunate task of informing his commander. Vlasov's survival was not foreseen. He was a close associate of Chekov, Orlov's superior and adversary. Fear of Vlasov's ability to contradict network actions now became a major problem. When they convened to discuss aftershocks, Orlov spoke with real concern about addressing their problem.

"Our operation's only flaw is the survival of a man by the name of Vlasov. His close relationship with Chekov makes him a dangerous witness. They are political allies. He must be targeted for termination. He is now in a coma but will survive."

The commander listened intently. Getting access to Vlasov would be very difficult. The commander thought of a woman who was head nurse at the military hospital. Her father was an army officer who served under Captain Rypchensky's command during World War II. A meeting with his former officer would be arranged. He believed his daughter could locate Vlasov and would cooperate with the network. Immediate attention and action was required before Vlasov gained consciousness. The commander was upset by the news. Finding Vlasov consumed him.

Activity levels during the last forty-eight hours were endless and very intense. Problems emerged faster than solutions could be found. Pressure was mounting.

Orlov maintained his composure.

"The hospital has informed me that he was on the fifth floor. The intensive care unit is monitoring his condition." The commander correctly assumed this information was inaccurate by now. Chekov certainly would have him moved two or three times for security reasons. He would have to contact the nurse and have her investigate his whereabouts.

Fortunately, Commander Rypchensky knew the KGB chairman from their military experience in World War II. Chekov was a man with few friends because he could not be trusted as a friend. He avoided personal relationships as much as possible because he believed they could compromise nationalistic security. His loyalty was to no one. His career was his only consideration taken seriously. Chekov's private feelings would rarely get in the way of good intelligence work. This was clearly an important reason why Communist Party members, familiar with his personality traits, promoted him to lead the KGB.

Commander Rypchensky decided to initiate a personal call with Chekov, his former subordinate. Having a sense of what chatter was in the pipeline was critical. After arrangements were made for their meeting, he ordered one of his aides to deliver a case of French cabernet from his extensive collection, knowing Chekov enjoyed his libations. He also understood Chekov's paranoia would be agitated by his former army superior requesting a meeting. He therefore clarified his intentions with a credible purpose. A solid reason was the plot to assassinate recently elected Party Chairman Mikoyanov. Knowing Chekov's thinking at this juncture was important. The Commander could compare his reading of Chekov with other KGB operatives, especially Orlov. Maybe undercurrents could be revealed.

The commander understood his nemesis was very capable of creating dire consequences. His immediate purpose was to determine if he could garner any information on Vlasov, whose whereabouts and life or death status was critical. If he failed, he knew he could depend upon the services of one woman he had known personally for many years. She was dependable, trustworthy, sexy, beautiful, and someone whose intimacy with Chekov was less intense than her feelings for the commander. She was a woman who could circumvent Chekov's personality disorder.

Chapter 18

The American Embassy in Moscow was an electronic nightmare leading to breaches in security and privacy. Americans knew very well that Soviet agents worked with construction crews and had wired the building for intelligence purposes. American electronic tracking devices could isolate equipment hidden in concrete walls. For this reason, embassy staff had to use special electronic codes that would block any recording of their messages. Under these conditions, intelligence became problematic. This particular day was more active because political turmoil had been rampant during the past twenty-four hours. The following conversation occurred between an embassy official and his assistant before addressing the entire intelligence staff:

"Make sure the jamming equipment is operating properly." The aide re-checked the devise used to prevent any monitoring. He signaled a thumbs up. Then the embassy official motioned for silence by waving his arms and gesturing with his hands. "OK, I want your undivided attention. Move closer so I don't have to speak loudly." He motioned with his arms for them to move closer. He paused and looked at his entire staff with a serious gaze. When their attention was focused on him, he commenced speaking.

"We have received orders to take as much liberty with our leisure time as legally permitted. This means you are to visit every museum, restaurant, park, statue, or any other establishment that is not off limits. Speak to citizens if you are so inclined. In other words, you are to hint, suggest, or imply suspicion in the minds of agents who will be following you, so expect it. You are not to discuss this order with anyone. Absolute silence! For sure, our diplomatic immunity will be tested. I will not entertain any questions. Remember, you are not to discuss this order with anyone. That is all."

The American personnel looked at one another and quietly left the room. The orders were clear to those with knowledge of the Soviet underground. Confuse the KGB. Create suspicion. Divert KGB operations so precious man hours would be used following Americans around the streets of Moscow. KGB manpower was currently stretched to its limits. Most agents were working around the clock, while Soviet network agents successfully avoided detection of their underground activities, with assistance from powerful Russian officials. The strategy was working; however, there were limits to this tactic. At some point, its effectiveness would cease to exist. For this reason, network KGB agents arrested American embassy employees for spying, believing this ruse would convince their enemies that Americans were indeed somehow involved. Distractions of this sort would cost the KGB valuable time. To add even more credibility, some of those arrested were deported as spies. Multiple diversions might consume valuable time that allows network conspirators to complete critical operations for a successful coup. As suspicion spreads, more paranoia is created. The unknown factor was, how long could this charade continue before the truth emerged, exposing network strategies? No one really knew the answer to that question. Revolutions are vulnerable to events whose impact is unpredictable.

Chekov followed his gut feelings. He had strong instincts. Activity levels were too high and he sensed something was wrong. His telephone was ringing more than usual. He almost refused to answer the last call when his secretary asked him if he wanted to speak to Sophia. There was no last name, only Sophia. Chekov motioned affirmatively as his secretary closed his office door. He picked up the receiver. "Hello, Chekov here." His voice was hospitable since Sophia was one of his former lovers. He seemed relaxed and flattered that she would call him. Their last rendezvous was about a year earlier. He had pleasant memories.

"Are you that busy that you refuse my phone calls?"

His response did not indicate any suspicion. "Sophia, how are you? It's been much too long."

Her experience with powerful men was extensive; she was beautiful, sexy, and very intelligent. "I am fine. Just returned from Canada. My sister lives there and we had a nice visit. I am well stocked with your favorite vice besides me." She laughed at her own humor.

Even Chekov managed to smile. Her voice was pleasant and made deeper from smoking. "How kind of you to keep me in your thoughts. I would enjoy seeing you again. When will that be?"

Sophia did not hesitate. "I am free tomorrow. Why don't we meet at our usual place, if that is all right with you?"

Chekov was rarely impulsive but this was pleasure not business. He welcomed her suggestion. "That would be a great way to end my week. It has been hectic around here. Seven o'clock work for you?"

Her sexy voice responded. "That would be perfect. See you then."

Chekov was rather pleased as he placed the telephone down. This woman was a wonderful diversion from his workload. He looked forward to their meeting. For several years, Commander Rypchensky had studied Chekov's personality. Everyone has their weak spot and for Chekov, it was beautiful women; he could not resist. Sophia's sexy charm would serve as a starting point for finding Vlasov before it was too late. Recent violence involving the death of KGB agents and the arrest of those charged with conspiracy, left Chekov drained of his usual energy. He believed time spent with Sophia would revitalize him. He left his office with a smile on his face.

Chapter 19

Russian bureaucrats were known to have a preference for sexy and glamorous escorts. It was common practice. Attractive woman cavorted with several highly regarded Soviet officials. Sophia was very selective with her men. She always had a special place in her heart for Commander Rypchensky, but their relationship never moved beyond that of friendship. His life was always expanding to higher levels of power and he had little time for extramarital affairs, even with a woman as attractive as Sophia. Besides, he loved his wife and had no reason for betraying her love. If he could not justify an action or behavior, he saw no reason to become sexually involved with another woman. Sophia seemed to understand and even admire his approach to life but always wished that just once he would cave in during a weak moment. For this reason, she would always acquiesce to his requests.

He planned to meet with her prior to her rendezvous with Chekov. The commander arranged to have Sophia driven to an isolated, private cottage that he used on occasion for meetings with agents or officers working on military intelligence. She was always impressed by the precautions that had to be taken whenever she hobnobbed with high officials. This meeting had special meaning because her love and admiration for the commander was always restrained but she knew that he was attracted to her. Women know that feeling. Sophia never doubted his feelings for her were genuine, however, he managed to restrain his masculine impulses. Would today be any different?

Her attire was elegant. A lavender lace dress, highlighted with snow white trim covered her shapely body. A multi colored scarf tied the colors together. Pearl white necklace with lavender ear rings finished the look. Sophia knew how to dress, especially after many years of modeling for high society fashion; for any occasion, she looked stunning. Her figure was full but firm and she maintained her shape and good looks over the years. When her driver approached the cottage, she felt a sudden urge that unnerved her. He was the one man who could melt her walls and inhibitions. She was very excited at the thought of embracing him. To her surprise, the commander was waiting as her car came to a stop. He was dressed in his uniform and looked as handsome as she remembered. He opened the car door and greeted Sophia very affectionately while escorting her inside. When he looked at her he imagined they were both contemplating similar thoughts. She approached him and placed her arms around him without hesitation, something she had never done before. His response was more than she expected when they kissed passionately. The stare exchanged with one another indicated they had crossed a line in their long relationship. Their bodies were charged with wonderful chemistry. There was little question as to the next move. He lifted her firm body to a bedroom where they consumed each other for the next hour. Their long-denied passion for each other had exploded into intense lovemaking that was long overdue. At last they were more than just friends.

The commander waited for their chemistry to cool before he commented on her meeting with Chekov. Sophia was waiting for the transition from intimacy to intelligence. She knew it was forthcoming and for the first time it bothered her because of the closeness she felt at that moment. He sensed her mood and as much as he tried to avoid sounding professional, he knew his effort was wasted. His preoccupation with critical network demands altered his mood. Intimacy was not an emotion he could always display with integrity. Sophia was momentarily confused. Her relationship with the commander had been overpowered by her personal feelings. She realized the man she truly loved was uncomfortable with their situation as well. They stared at each other and realized how their lives had been affected by their act of passion after many years of restrained friendship. They embraced and savored the closeness they now shared, however, both could sense their new relationship was just an interlude.

For Sophia, he was the love she never knew, but always wanted. Her life had been spent looking for a man with his character and quality. She also concluded at this point in time, she had best relish any intimate moments with him whenever possible. Their long friendship had allowed them the advantage of knowing each other's feelings, especially when their emotions peaked. Difficult as it was, they retreated, placing their passions and emotions aside. Explaining his feelings and obligations to a very special friend followed.

"Sophia, please forgive me for my misguided passion. You will always have a special place in my heart. You must know that. But our relationship must not go beyond false expectations. You must also know, I will always treasure our friendship."

Sophia sensed intrigue was imminent. "Tell me what's going on? Obviously you are asking me for assistance and you know my trustworthiness. But for what purpose?"

The commander did not hesitate. "You should know. You deserve to know because you want what I want, a free and open country. Would you agree?"

Sophia nodded. "Yes. Please continue."

He had to craft his words carefully. He held her close and said. "I am using our strong attraction to each other for a noble goal. Believe me Sophia, all those occasions we shared together, we shared as friends. And they were wonderful. I always chose to refrain from loving you because I love my wife and still do. Now I need a favor so I wanted to give you something in return, something you've always wanted but I would never offer. But today I surrendered because we both have something to gain, something you and I have always wanted, something more important than our feelings for one another. I need your assistance. It's critical that you know how important this is." She remained motionless and didn't know what she felt at that moment. In her mind, she played back his words and processed them carefully.

"What is your noble plan?" He placed both of his hands directly on her shoulders and looked straight into her eyes. "To bring freedom and reforms to our country. I know this is what you also want." He then pulled her close to him. "I would never place your life and safety in jeopardy without informing you of the dangers involved. You are a very special friend. A genuine friend."

Strangely, Sophia did not feel used. She realized he was clarifying his personal emotions. What feelings he did retain for her were genuine, of that she was confident. She believed his shared love for her was honest even though there was a caveat involved.

"Tell me what needs to be done. No more explanation is necessary." Both understood their life choices were limited. It was time to place their feelings aside and move to a practical and professional relationship.

He took the first step by smiling and recalling their last meeting in Kiev where they had dinner with friends. It was an interesting evening because the commander's uniform had been soiled by a clumsy waiter and they laughed recalling the episode. Sophia's recollection was that he removed his jacket and had his valet replace it with another uniform that was missing a button. Later that evening she sewed a button on and they laughed at the silliness and small talk shared with their friends. He gradually and patiently realized it was now time to transition to present reality and the important task at hand.

Her role was dangerous and critical. He nervously glanced at his watch, grasping for words. Sophia never looked so beautiful, gazing at him, patiently waiting for his request. He was confident of her ability for the task at hand. Vlasov had to be found. Sophia listened intently as he detailed the latest information on Vlasov's whereabouts. However, before he explained her mission, he believed it was necessary to explain what his overall mission was as well.

"I am leading an underground operation to overthrow our totalitarian oligarchy. Violence has begun and will get worse each day. During our latest operation, a man by the name of Vlasov was wounded in an exchange of gunfire and violence. He took a severe blow to the head. We thought he was dead, but he survived. He's in a coma but is expected to make a full recovery. Now we have to locate him and terminate him. He's a critical witness who can expose our underground strategies. Chekov is hiding him. Your task is to locate him before he talks to Chekov. The last we heard, he was transferred from the veterans hospital to another building. Before he comes around, we need to get to him with a disabling drug. He won't feel a thing."

Sophia did not flinch. Her role was made clear: Locate Vlasov. The method she used would have to be determined before her meeting with Chekov. She was a master at making situations unfold. Her questions followed.

"I am meeting him tomorrow evening at seven o'clock. Do you want me to use an electronic device for monitoring our conversation? My cigarette lighter is perfect. I could inform him of a few rumors I learned in Canada while visiting my sister, about growing political dissent to whet his appetite and build his trust."

The commander listened carefully. Sophia had good instincts, however, he was not sure if he agreed with her tactic and questioned her about it. "Is this wise? He is dangerous enough without making him more paranoid. You would place your life in danger."

Her response was direct and convincing. "Let me worry about that. I can handle Chekov." She winked, then continued. "Our conversation will revolve around rumors of discontent within party factions. Information already written in Pravda. Nothing he is not aware of, just conjecture, but for a paranoid, conjecture can be reality. It will get him talking, especially after a few drinks."

He looked at her, realizing how a clever woman's mind operates. This woman was smart. Her instincts were on target. Intimacy reservations set aside, he pulled her close to his chest, stared into her eyes and kissed her gently at first, but suddenly their passion returned. Their bodies charged once again. She whispered into his ear, "I love you."

Sophia began her career in ballet and transitioned into modeling when she met a wealthy New York advertising mogul in Manhattan. He was recently divorced and as many wealthy American men were discovering, Russia had an abundance of beautiful women, looking for their future elsewhere. Sophia was an educated women who knew what she wanted and this man could finance her dream of starting a modeling agency. There were hundreds of beautiful women Sophia knew from her extensive travel throughout Europe and the Americas who would model for her in the future. She shared her business plan with this man and he agreed to finance it with an understanding they split their profits equally. Sophia agreed, but there was a caveat to their contractual document that she would not accept. He wanted more than she was willing to give. She thought her refusal of his advances would destroy their business arrangement, but this man was also a smart businessman who believed Sophia's business model was a winner.. Their contract was signed and her agency began with a tremendous advantage. Her partner was an expert in advertising.

In their first year of business, profits exceeded expectations. In the next five years her modeling agency was considered one of the best worldwide, with accounts in all major cities known for fashion.

Sophia was smart enough to invest her profits in Manhattan real estate. This business expanded and she eventually acquired a residential and commercial real estate licence. Her good fortune continued in real estate as well. In two years she bought the remaining shares of her model agency from her partner. Her personal wealth was now in the billions of dollars.

Sophia's life never found time for establishing a personal relationship with any man. This was her only regret. When she met Commander Rypchensky in Paris, he was a young army officer. After meeting him, Sophia felt a strong connection and asked him if he could join her for dinner. When he told her that he was engaged to be married, she was silent then asked him. "How long have you been engaged?" His response shocked her. "Last evening. I am returning to Moscow late tonight." Her heart stopped for a moment. Then she said without hesitation. "Unfortunately I am one day too late. I would like to meet you again, maybe in Moscow. My card." She was surprised when he said.

My flight is four hours from now. Maybe we could have dinner together." She agreed. They found a cafe where conversation was encouraged. Hours flew by quickly. Their connection was obvious but so was their reality. Before he left for the airport, she said to him. "I wish we had met sooner. You have made me feel so comfortable. Your fiancé is a lucky woman." He thanked her and squeezed her hand. The one man she could have loved for a lifetime slowly disappeared into the night.

Chapter 20

Olga Kinski was a brute of a woman who dispensed orders in similar fashion as a drill sergeant. But behind those coarse manners and appearance was a very warm and caring individual. She had met Commander Rypchensky on several occasions during her father's military service and remembered how her father always praised him. So when she was approached by a military attache requesting her presence at his office, she was pleasantly surprised. When her hospital duties as head nurse ended for the day, she was driven to army headquarters where she was escorted to a beautiful lounge. When she entered, her father was seated, waiting for the commander. Before they could speak, the commander entered with a pleasant greeting. He then personally escorted them to a private dining room where they enjoyed being served an assortment of beverages and delicacies while commiserating, mostly about their Ukrainian roots. The commander was enjoying himself because he had fond memories of Sergeant Kinski and his comrades. Prior to his daughter's arrival and out of respect for Sergeant Kinski, the commander had explained his plan for finding Vlasov and how Olga could play an important role. Sergeant Kinski assured him there would be total cooperation. Olga was dependable. She thought their meeting was for the purpose of discussing recent political disturbances between Russian and Ukrainian nationals. Olga did not expect, nor was she prepared, for anything more dramatic.

"Olga, your father and I have shared an interesting history. I am sure you have heard many stories before."

Olga smiled. "Yes, Commander, many times."

He continued. "You must be wondering why I have invited you. Your father has told me how efficiently you direct operations at the army hospital. Well I have a special request for you regarding information which needs to be kept top secret." Olga had been informed of the network by her father but did not realize how she would be involved. She was aware of many Ukrainians who were devoted to the underground movement. She listened intently as the commander explained her assigned task. He spoke slowly and emphatically.

"An important member of the Politburo, with KGB connections, was critically wounded recently and hospitalized in your building. He was secretly moved to another location. His name is Vlasov. We must find him and terminate his ability to talk to authorities who are anxiously waiting for his recovery. Your task is to locate him for us. We will do the rest." Then, looking directly into her eyes, he asked, "How soon can you locate him?"

Olga was silent. She thought for a moment and then said without any sign of uncertainty: "Twenty-four hours, maybe less."

The commander looked at her, smiled as he held her hand and said, "Start immediately. Contact me at this number when you can confirm his location. Now you must both excuse me because circumstances at this very moment are critical and my services are needed elsewhere. Some day we will make time for a more relaxed and enjoyable gathering. Thank you for your loyalty."

The commander excused himself while Sergeant Kinski and his daughter sat in silence. Olga's fears were disguised behind her bulk. She did realize the importance of her role and was honored to be selected by the commander. She looked at her watch. It was 5:45 pm. She had twenty-four hours to locate Vlasov. Now the commander had two women working to locate a key witness who had to be terminated before Chekov could question him.

Before returning to her hospital duties, Olga called to arrange a night shift in the pharmacy department. When she arrived, she checked pharmacy prescriptions for outpatients and found one without a name or address. She ordered her subordinates to bring her ledgers listing recent admissions, without any mention of Vlasov. She browsed through the entry ledger to check all patients currently listed or recently admitted. Vlasov's name did not appear, but, she noticed, a patient was moved from an assigned room and released. No name was entered. Her subordinate on duty informed her that a man with a head injury was moved to another location, not disclosed. His name was deleted from a list of recent arrivals. She recalled a similar incident once before when KGB agents moved a dissident with a head injury to a mental hospital where he died days later. She understood Vlasov's head injury placed him in a coma. Quiet bed rest was required until his consciousness returned.

In the pharmacy ledger for outpatients, she located two prescriptions listed, one, a loop diuretic, to be administered to help reduce pressure inside the brain, the other, an anti-seizure drug, administered intravenously, to avoid any additional brain damage. The patient had to be Vlasov. Prescriptions were called in by doctors, to be administered in evening hours or early morning hours. These two prescriptions were stored in the pharmacy for pick up at some future time.

She relayed this information to Commander Rypchensky. He asked her to find a way to duplicate the prescription syringe containers and labels so he could substitute fatal drugs, one pentobarbital, used for euthanizing terminally ill patients or military personnel, suffering and dying from extreme wounds. Moments later, Olga walked to the emergency entrance. Hidden in her purse were two empty prescription syringes with official labels which she delivered to a waiting network agent.

At eight o'clock, the phone rang. It was the call she was waiting for. The doctor's prescription matched those listed in the ledger.

The prescribed drugs were refrigerated in a bag containing a printed address label. She immediately informed the commander who now had confirmation of Vlasov's location. The commander would do the rest. Within two hours the original prescriptions would be retrieved by KGB agents for delivery to Vlasov later that evening.

Olga completed a pile of paper work before leaving when her shift ended. She felt satisfied about her accomplishment. Before returning home, she stopped in a popular eatery and treated herself to her favorite meal, a Reuben sandwich. When she returned to her humble abode, she was very pleased with herself. The intrigue gave her a rush.

Chapter 21

Chekov had arranged to have Sophia driven to their rendezvous, a small café, Cafe Pushkin, located near the Kremlin. It was a Russian version of a disco, but served good food and drinks to a variety of patrons, mostly government bureaucrats who worked for the military or KGB. Chekov was seated at a table he reserved in a corner, hidden from crowds and clatter. Then as now, Russians love to drink and smoke. They were fond of American cigarettes. Chekov preferred Pall Mall and smoked at least two packs a day. He saw Sophia enter; her attire was a silver green dress that matched her eyes. She complimented her attire with an elegant scarf neatly tied around her neck and shoulders. Her stunning appearance attracted looks from several patrons whose heads turned as she approached Chekov's table. He stood and embraced her with affection. Chekov was also a very handsome man. Sophia's attraction to him was apparent although she knew her feelings were purely physical, not emotional as with the man she truly loved.

Chekov began by saying, "You are more beautiful than words can describe." Sophia was flattered; she enjoyed being the center of attention. Chekov ordered champagne and caviar for starters and they commenced what he thought would be a beautiful evening. Sophia was tempted to look at her watch but realized how Chekov was very keen on body language. She made herself aware of his every movement. Commander Rypchensky had coached her. Gestures that were dead giveaways had to be avoided. She felt pressured, knowing Vlasov had to be found. Was it possible that her meeting with Chekov would not produce desired results? Thinking about it made her anxious.

She planned in advance to use her recent visit with her sister in Canada as a starting point for their discussion. She then remembered her gift for Chekov, intentionally forgotten in the car. It was just at that moment when the chauffeur who had driven her approached their table with a colorful bag containing a large bottle of Seagram's Crown Royal. A perfect opportunity to present her gift to Chekov and relate news from Canada. She had pre-planned this gift gesture, including the chauffeur's delivery, as a seamless transition for their conversation. The spontaneity of the moment was flawless.

When they were comfortably settled, her comment followed.

"It is the largest bottle they market. Should keep you in stock for a while." Men standing and talking near their table could not take their eyes off her, which pleased Chekov. Sophia also noticed and smiled, looking at the very large bottle of Crown Royal whiskey. Chekov thanked her for the gift by raising then gently kissing her hand. He motioned for the waiter to pour champagne. He then proposed a toast.

"To our loving friendship." She sipped her champagne and maintained eye contact with a friendly smile before tasting the caviar.

"I love this caviar. So delicious! Where do they purchase it?" He smiled and touched her hand with affection'

"Nothing but the best for my good friend. Nestrovia!" He raised his glass.

They drained the first bottle and Chekov ordered the waiter to open another. At the other end of their conversation was Commander Rypchensky. Sophia's pearl-white, diamond-crested cigarette lighter was fitted with a built-in transmitter. Half way through the second bottle she noticed his giddy behavior emerging. Now was a good time to ask him a question.

"So what's going on? In Canada I was informed there is some discontent among Soviet personnel working in Toronto. I am not certain of details, but you must have read this as well. Is this a generational conflict, old versus young? It disturbs me hearing news like this but I have no way of knowing the truth." She maintained her composure as she lit a cigarette and patiently waited for his response. Chekov maintained his silence while pouring more champagne; he did not appear suspicious.

"We have everything under control. We've experienced events that are disturbing. Too much activity makes me nervous. But we will soon know who and what is behind this activity." He lit a cigarette while the waiter served more caviar. Sophia raised her glass and they clicked them together. He smiled and touched her hand with affection. Then he continued.

"One of our agents will soon reveal important information. When he talks, we can arrest conspirators. He remains unconscious but doctors have assured me he is making progress and believe he will make a full recovery within a day or two, maybe sooner. We have him under guard in a private residence. Under the circumstances, hospitals are too insecure."

Sophia could not believe what he had just revealed, without significant effort on her part. Ascertaining the location of this private residence now became urgent. But how? Maybe champagne and more champagne would have to be consumed for this purpose. She could drink champagne with little effect. She wasn't certain about Chekov, but noticed that he matched her sip after sip. How long would this take? She thought consuming caviar might mitigate the alcohol affect.

With the second bottle of champagne, Chekov became loquacious and giddy. Sophia knew he was on his way. She was enjoying herself and felt a wonderful high that also made her sexual juices flow. She smiled at Chekov and observed a man very relaxed when he asked, "Why don't we dance?" She used her sensual body contact to illicit information, hoping champagne would induce more verbosity. It was a slow foxtrot. A perfect opportunity for her to press her body close to him. Advantage Sophia. His sexual response was firm against her lower stomach. This man was primed. He kissed her lips. They were on their way.

She whispered, "Your body is talking to me." She looked into his blue eyes knowing that alcohol and lust were now controlling his behavior. She had similar feelings when she said, "I won't be able to make love to you if you are preoccupied. Forget about everything else. I want you all to myself for a few days. Is that possible?"

Chekov was amused and before he could respond, her sexual charms disarmed him. "What comes first, business or pleasure? My time is limited. I said, I want you all to myself. Have I made myself clear?"

Chekov was flattered.

"You will have my undivided attention. All of it, but first we will make a quick visit." He kissed her on the lips, while her mind recalled what he just said: "quick visit." He was feeling no pain.

"I have a hunch today is my lucky day, in more ways than one." Their dancing ended when he escorted her to their table. Sophia waited patiently and prudently. Ascertaining the location of this hideaway was critical.

She feigned her annoyance with him.

"I certainly hope our 'quick visit' is not going to take too much time." Chekov kissed her, looked at his watch, then sipped more champagne. She took advantage of his mood by placing one hand on his while the other reached under the table cloth, messaging his leg and thigh. She moved closer to him and whispered, "Let's get this business done and leave plenty of time for us. I have to be in Vienna Monday morning for a fashion show." Chekov motioned to the waiter and then signaled for his driver to prepare his car for departure.

As they walked out, Sophia asked.

"Where are you taking me?"

Without hesitation, Chekov responded, "To my summer chalet on the river. It is not far from here."

Sophia cleverly stalled and motioned toward the ladies room.

"You will have to excuse me. I cannot wait another minute."

Commander Rypchensky was now aware of Vlasov's location and ordered his men to Chekov's chalet. Fortunately, there were several women ahead of Sophia, waiting to use the facilities. More time consumed. When she returned to leave with Chekov, he did not appear suspicious. He was reminded of their last rendezvous when he smelled her perfume. Just then, Sophia remembered that her gift of Crown Royal had been left under their table.

"The Crown Royal. I didn't carry that bottle all the way from Canada for nothing." Chekov laughed and ordered one of the waiters to retrieve his gift. Meanwhile, more precious time was allowed for network agents to reach Vlasov. Chekov was still consumed with thoughts of making love to her, motivated more by the essence of perfume. For Sophia, it was mission accomplished.

While Olga Kinski sat at her desk, completing paperwork, she was informed the unnamed patient's prescription would be retrieved by KGB operatives momentarily. When they arrived, she signed the prescription order. When they left, she called Commander Rypchensky to warn him. The timing was perfect.

Network operatives arrived about one hour before Chekov's agents. They posed as medical providers who had prescriptions ordered by a medical team treating Vlasov. There was no suspicion when the delivery arrived since an order had been called in earlier by doctors, who unknowingly were caring for a key witness. When they were greeted at the door, network agents had substituted a fatal drug that instead of relaxing Vlasov, would deliver him to a hallucinogenic stupor that would eventually kill him.

Chekov arrived about thirty minutes later. He was excited to speak with Vlasov but was informed by those attending him that he had suffered a relapse, followed by a fatal heart attack. Chekov was stunned. He returned to his car where Sophia was waiting. He stared at her as she checked her appearance in a compact mirror. Even under stress and sensing dire circumstances, her objective had been successful; she teased Chekov: "That champagne has whetted my appetite. When can we . . ."

Chekov interrupted her without apologizing. He was disturbed when he said:

"I must leave. There are urgent matters to attend. I will have my driver take you back to your hotel. I will call you later this evening." Without another word, he directed the chauffeur to drive Sophia to her hotel, then rushed to his cottage. He felt something had gone wrong at the last minute, which always made him suspicious.

When Sophia arrived at her hotel room, there was a beautiful bouquet of flowers with a note: "Sophia, you are wonderful in so many ways. Love CR." Next to the bouquet was an envelope containing a ticket to Paris with another note: "Avoid Vienna. Not safe for you at this time. We will see you in Paris." Sophia burned both notes in an ashtray and flushed them down the toilet. She immediately proceeded to check out. Her flight was leaving Moscow in two hours.

KGB medical teams had performed an autopsy on Vlasov and discovered that potent drugs had been administered by attending doctors, just before his death. Chekov concluded, the prescriptions were altered, not by the pharmacy where they originated. Those who delivered the drugs were imposters who replaced the prescription with drugs that would cause death. He began to weave together a scenario that explained what happened. He was angry and determined to find those responsible. His failure to secure the operation also haunted him. He thought of Sophia. Was she involved? He ordered his agents to pay her a visit at Hotel Catherine and escort her to his cottage. Once again, his agents were too late. She left a note for Chekov at the front desk.

"My assignment to Vienna was cancelled. I have been reassigned to Paris and must leave to prepare for the show. I was fortunate to find a flight. Will contact you when I return to Moscow. Fondly, Sophia"

Her cancelled flight to Vienna had been rescheduled to Paris, one hour earlier. Now Chekov had every reason to believe she was part of a conspiracy. Was he duped? If so, she was the bait who fooled him. Very smoothly planned. But by whom? His conclusion was only one man could devise such a clever scheme. But he had to be certain, only because a mistake could result in bad blood between two very powerful men.

Discretion was difficult for Chekov, but he understood its importance at critical moments, especially when feeling anger. His composure was steady. One careless mistake must not be followed by another. In intelligence work, two negatives do not make a positive. Defeats and disappointments must be minimal and temporary. He had learned these realities early in his career as an intelligence officer. His one cardinal rule had been violated by allowing his personal feelings for an attractive woman to blindside him. He even smiled, thinking of Sophia and how she manipulated him with her charm. Her sexual prowess combined with too much champagne had disarmed his usual awareness. She was so close, yet so far. Her feminine charm was clever and effective. No woman he knew could be so persuasive and alluring. Now his desire for her was more intense. Next time their rendezvous would be on his terms. Sadistic behavior was not considered an aberration with Chekov. He felt confident in his temporary defeat.

Olga Kinski had returned a favor to her father's hero who had once saved his life. The commander was touched by her loyalty and relayed a message to her via her father that future opportunities to serve the network would be available. He assured her that her services would be utilized and even claimed an element of danger would be involved. Little did he realize that Olga was excited by the possibilities danger offered her uneventful life.

Chapter 22

At the Kremlin, meetings were scheduled among Communist Party leaders to discuss issues that had surfaced and could be major obstacles. The process for settling political controversy by hardline communist circles was drastic, if not deadly. Mob mentality ensued, practically routine for resolving fundamental political differences in the Kremlin. "Murder methodology" varied as well. The public did not have to be informed of deadly deeds perpetrated by authorities. People simply disappeared. Then, maybe weeks later, a sickness or accident was revealed that explained the demise of powerful men. It was an efficient system. Implementation was crucial, especially timing and location. Police state politics was dangerous business.

Network politics however, resorted to consensus and consultation. Ideas were constantly examined for feasibility including democratic exchanges with a Russian twist. Network leaders soon realized circumstances required drastic changes in their style of decision-making. Transition of power to Network legislators required autocratic leadership. Democratic principles could not be implemented at this time.

When Party Chairman Mikoyanov addressed his elite network colleagues, they listened with keen interest.

"Too many of our best citizens are defecting. We cannot afford to lose the cream of our nation." He was referring to writers and artists whose contributions were critical for maintaining a national dialogue. These intellectuals maintained and promoted social progress with their constant flow of unwavering dissidence. Without their analytical public dialogue, critical issues never surfaced. There was no cross-examination. Everything was secret, causing tension and suspicion. Transparency would be impossible.

In fact, those who dared to challenge conformity were regarded as disloyal. Intellectuals feared violence would escalate making their emigration from Russia more challenging. Therefore many escaped into Poland and Czechoslovakia during the commotion. Mikoyanov realized his democratic mindset would have to face reality. He referred to an outspoken dissident, Revchenko, a gadfly who asked many questions, constantly challenging conventional thinking. He stirred the pot. Party hardliners despised his contrary personality. Reluctantly, Mikoyanov realized he would have to appear more authoritarian. Resorting to autocratic leadership was not his preferred style. He had no choice and would declare martial law until tranquility returned.

When Commander Rypchensky finally spoke, he sounded an alarm. Methodology was about to change. He also concluded it was time to set aside consensus politics. Decision-making had to be swift and precise. Democratic deliberation under current perilous circumstances was dangerous and unproductive.

"We must acknowledge, the KGB is on our trail. Our network may be unraveling. Revchenko warned me this would happen. We must act with Machiavellian determination or we will be destroyed."

Mikoyanov then interrupted. He concurred with the commander.

"Half of the Central Committee is with us, at least philosophically. If we act soon, there is a good chance for success. Unfortunately, this means acts of violence against our enemies must be swift. If they are eliminated, we can control every move against us. This goes against my core beliefs, but if we do not act, our enemies will, and with vengeance."

Orlov then spoke.

"I totally agree. This is not an easy task but I see no other way. Kill or be killed. It's come down to these extremes. I have prepared a list of names for this very moment. If we hesitate, everything we have worked for will be lost."

The commander added his consent.

"You are both correct. We have no choice." Deep in the commander's mind he thought of his family. His wife, son, future daughter in law and even future grandchildren. He kept his thoughts to himself, realizing his network had also reached a point of no return. His comrades would be shocked if he revealed any contrary action or thoughts of defecting. Everything he worked for would be lost. Fear for his family was eating away at him, however, his military discipline managed to win over his internal emotions. He was confident that network operatives were experiencing similar feelings of skepticism. He reminded himself that honorable revolutionaries throughout history made sacrifices for future generations. Referencing American leaders who placed their sacred honor above personal safety of their families and property. This was not a time for second thoughts. Timidity was unacceptable. His determination and fear of failure motivated him to move forward. It was simply a matter of life and death. Knowing he would be a primary target, he ordered his most loyal subordinates to protect him and his family.

Orlov then informed Mikoyanov.

"In order to protect you, Mr. Chairman, we will have to 'kidnap' you and your family. Your association with our network cannot be known at this time." The strategy was to maintain his innocence and neutrality. He would then announce an agreement leading to a cease fire and creation of a new democratic constitution. Transition of power from the Communist Party to freely and democratically organized political parties would follow. Elections would then be announced.

The commander looked nervous when listening to Orlov's recommendation because he realized that during the interim period, his role as military leader would oversee hundreds if not thousands of citizens with divided loyalties. They would have to decide which party to follow, and the military would have to keep the peace. He displayed emotion, rarely observed by his staff.

"What we are about to undertake frightens and displeases me." He paused and looked directly at his officers. "Hopefully our acts of violence will eliminate the curse of totalitarianism. Turning our citizens against one another will bring suffering and death to many patriots. I don't see any other way to dislodge our entrenched enemy. If there is a God of mercy and forgiveness, I hope He is with us at this historical moment."

Mikoyanov listened carefully to his commander, walked to the window and stared outside at the Kremlin's Byzantine architecture. All eyes focused on him. After a prolonged moment of silence, he turned and faced his network leaders. Motioning with his arm for his network soldiers to get on with their tasks, he ordered them, "Go! You know what has to be done. Hesitation is our enemy." Then he turned and faced the window, adding, "I will pray for our success."

Orlov and the commander did not waste any time. Their plan was set months ago and finally the order was given to commence OPERATION NETWORK. Within hours, officers of the high command were assassinated by network agents using silencers on their Tokarev 7.6mm pistols. Officers of the KGB were poisoned by contaminated food in their dining hall. In the Kremlin, government officials and major power brokers, were arrested and imprisoned for treason. Some were shot during attempts to escape.

Chekov was informed by loyal KGB agents that Mikoyanov and his wife were detained after their arrest.

"Sir, Chairman Mikoyanov and his wife have been taken hostage, in handcuffs."

Chekov's office was buzzing with activity, but he remained unusually silent. He paused to think through the crisis. He then barked out an order to his aide.

"Find Orlov! I am having a staff luncheon tomorrow. Hand deliver him this invitation." His thoughts led him to believe he smelled a rat. He had questions only Orlov could answer. Then he called an emergency meeting of his staff to investigate latest developments. He wanted a comprehensive report of all international connections between known conspirators and western powers, especially American intelligence.

"The conspiracy attempting a coup must be identified."

He believed enemy forces would have to act rapidly before their momentum was lost. Chekov was not convinced that international forces were responsible for the multitudes of activity overwhelming KGB personnel. He suspected dissidents conspiring against powerful and privileged elites. He was part of that elite. He ordered his best investigators to prepare a report and to have it on his desk within twenty-four hours, after which he would discuss the details with Orlov. A fundamental question Chekov wanted answered was:

Were the increased activities in intelligence warranted or were they fabricated wild chases leading nowhere? His hunch lead him to believe these activities were contrived to create a smoke screen cover for conspirators.

Up to this point, Chekov had no reason to suspect his subordinate. Their working relationship had not revealed any misdeeds. That was due to Orlov's ability to cover his tracks one way or another. He understood how Chekov's mind processed information. Orlov's knowledge of his superior kept him one step ahead, at least up to this point. Orlov, however, realized he could no longer disguise or conceal his intentions. It was time to act with deliberate speed before opponents struck first.

Orlov concluded Chekov's gut instincts were approaching critical mass. He was correct. Chekov believed conspirators were operating within a brief time frame. Their success would depend upon all moving parts flowing with precision.

Fortunately, Orlov not only had prepared explanations for Chekov, but, more importantly, believed he still had Chekov's confidence. When the KGB Chief went out of his way to invite Orlov for lunch to discuss the entire matter, a warning flashed across Orlov's mind. The invitation was written on fancy stationery, hand delivered to Orlov. He was unnerved after reading its contents. Chekov's intentions were not miscalculated. In all his years serving Chekov, Orlov never had been formally invited to have lunch with his autocratic chief. Theatrics was a vehicle Chekov would employ for exposing hidden agendas. Orlov could not flinch. He expected the upcoming luncheon would be used for a grueling face-to-face questioning. Chekov was a very skillful inquisitor. Orlov knew very well he had to be alert.

Feeling threatened for his life, he decided to share his alarm with Commander Rypchensky in advance. They met later that afternoon in army headquarters. Fearing their offices were wired, they decided to converse while walking through army corridors. This was not a time for careless or unforced errors revealed by electronic recorders placed randomly throughout the building. The commander suggested, very seriously, that Orlov wear a recording device while dining with his boss. Orlov was reluctant due to fear of Chekov's suspicion. He preferred wearing a bullet proof vest.

When Orlov was informed of Sophia's part in finding Vlasov, his only comment was: "Chekov never enjoyed being duped, especially by a woman." Sophia's unannounced departure left Chekov in a sour mood. His frame of mind made him more daring and dangerous with his decision-making. Commander Rypchensky was also aware of Chekov's irritability. Sensing imminent danger, he was compelled to outmaneuver his powerful nemesis. His plan was to disrupt the luncheon Chekov planned by having his own "luncheon." He would invite military police, fully armed, to enjoy lunch in an adjoining room, within reach of Orlov, if the need arose. The idea was to deny Chekov any logistical advantage with his plans. Orlov was informed by the commander that having lunch with a man who was ready to kill at the slightest sign of betrayal was dangerous.

Orlov then asked the obvious: "Why not eliminate him?"

The commander hesitated before he responded.

"I also thought of this, but too many innocent people could be killed if we do not take control. Chekov's agents will also be there to protect him. He rarely makes himself an easy target. However, I will seriously consider your suggestion. Be prepared for the worst. I also believe Chekov would make a high profile prisoner for our cause. His reputation is filled with so many evil deeds. The publicity following his public trial would propel our coup in the direction we need for public approval."

Orlov understood the wisdom of his commander's thinking. Arresting Chekov and using his tyrannical reputation would work in their favor. The commander would make a final decision concerning Chekov's future status in less than twenty-four hours.

While being served in the dining room, they plotted the next day's event. Commander Rypchensky decided he would also entertain members of his loyal staff, mostly women, during an informal luncheon earlier the same day. The strategy was to occupy the dining room with employees who would maintain a noise level that would create a normal atmosphere. Nothing out of the ordinary.

During similar occasions, friction between army and KGB personnel stirred, usually caused by bruised egos involving protocol. During these rare moments, army officers never flinched. Their powerful status was feared by KGB agents who would not expose themselves to military retaliation.

As a precaution, network operations were suspended prior to the luncheon. All violent acts toward enemies of the network were placed on hold. Current reports indicated network leaders managed to control governmental operations. Atrocities previously committed by network agents were cleverly screened from public scrutiny. Tranquility, however, was temporary. One final piece to the puzzle was Chekov. He was a major player who had to be neutralized or eliminated.

On the following eventful day, the dining hall was filled with loud chatter. Commander Rypchensky thought it wise to intercept any possibility of violence directed at Orlov. He instructed four marksmen with concealed weapons and stationed them in strategic locations in the dining hall. He preferred a large crowd for what he had planned. Journalists would be present to write an account of events, while photographers and video crews prepared for unknown drama. The outcome was controlled but elements of uncertainty were also present. Not knowing what to expect created an intense atmosphere.

Chekov's suspicion of Orlov and Rypchensky was confirmed the previous day by an agent who followed them to a private dining hall. Adversaries on both sides had been identified. The element of surprise would be critical. Army officers and staff seated themselves at four tables situated around the dining hall, while other officers milled around a bar. Chekov was seated with his agents waiting for Orlov to appear. Chekov's plan was to arrest and handcuff his subordinate after he was seated. He relished the thought of humiliating his subordinate.

However, before Chekov's party of six had an opportunity to act as Orlov approached, army personnel, escorted by six military police, nonchalantly gathered in front of Chekov's table. The officer in charge announced the following statement directed at Chekov:

"Colonel Chekov, you are under arrest for conspiracy against the Soviet Communist Party and for conspiring to assassinate our elected president, Andrei Mikoyanov."

Absolute silence filled the dining hall. When military police attempted to place handcuffs on Chekov, he forcefully resisted, ordering his agents to assist him. When they moved to free him, military police moved in, pointing their weapons at KGB personnel. All were cuffed. Video crews lost no time recording the entire event. Kristoff, seated with his father, could not believe what he heard and observed. His written account of the drama unfolding before him would include the following comment from Orlov, directed at his superior.

"Your torture and murder of innocent victims is over. I hope you rot in jail." Journalists would highlight that comment on the front page of Pravda. Chekov cursed Orlov, spit in his face and was immediately restrained. Chekov and his agents, all handcuffed, were escorted out of the dining room, surrounded by Army officers and military police. No shots were fired. Chekov, despised by citizens familiar with his savagery, was referred to as, "public enemy number one." Kristoff would use that comment as a headline. He was thrilled this happened before his departure for New York. His father's timing was impressive. The arrest was filmed by media crews as it occurred, all for public consumption that evening. Chekov's disgraceful arrest was a major story highlighted by military police escorting him to prison in handcuffs. Kristoff could not be more pleased with his father's brilliant plan for disabling and arresting a corrupt public tyrant.

"Enemy number one" would be televised throughout the Soviet Union. With the arrest of Chekov, the coup was now in motion for the world to see.

Chekov's fatal mistake was he waited too long before acting. Orlov had cleverly camouflaged his underground movements, and in so doing, allowed the network time to neutralize the KGB's intelligence capabilities. Arresting Chekov could not be delayed any longer. He was too dangerous. Commander Rypchensky would not make that mistake. If Chekov was allowed one more opportunity to strike, he would, and with deadly force. The commander realized Chekov's luncheon was a ploy. He also surmised he and Orlov were being followed the day before by Chekov's agents. The commander was certain Orlov, his closest aide, would have been arrested or killed. Chekov had belatedly connected all the events of the past month. But the commander struck first, with media present, to enhance public awareness of their coup's intentions. However, there were still many factions of established power and entrenched party officials who would have to be uprooted.. The coup was still incomplete. The commander feared rogue military factions could form, organized by corrupt officers and hardline party officials. They could be very dangerous opponents and would not remain idle. Their elite life styles were made possible by control of profits received from vast national monopolies. They were the "robber barons" of the Soviet Union whose lavish life styles would be defended to the bitter end. Chekov's cadre stretched throughout the Soviet republics, hidden by corrupt officials who benefitted from their collusion. Acting as mobsters, they would react accordingly. The commander, wary of this reality, now had to prepare for the worst. Retaliation by hardline terrorists would be violent. They were not just corrupt politicians, they were criminal thugs.

Chekov's arrest incited counterrevolutionary violence that forced corrupt officials to stage riots throughout several republics. Organized criminals and party members would use their wealth and influence to bribe officials at all levels to protect their interests. Civil disturbances, especially in Ukraine, where anti-Russian sentiments increased, became another concern. Chekov's infamy throughout Soviet republics was well known. Even in prison, he could remain a threat. Ideologically, many followers of hardline communism were actually fascists if judged by their political behavior. There was little difference between their beliefs and fascist thugs in Nazi Germany.

Chekov's supporters fought back causing violence to spread. Network radio and television announcements were broadcast to expose their evil intentions. Chekov's name was publicized and made synonymous with the Cheka, who were notorious secret police during the communist revolution. Chekov and Cheka were made enemies of the state. Radio and television reports announced: "A powerful force of evil has been defeated with the arrest of Chekov."

Press releases informed the public of Chekov's violation of human rights throughout the republics. Public opinion was directed against forces of tyranny from all sectors of soviet bureaucracies. Would public support follow? That would depend. How much influence remained with corrupt officials throughout the spectrum of power?

Hardline communists quickly implemented ruthless counter measures. They had everything to lose and would fight with determination. Public safety became an issue as forces on both sides spread fear and directed acts of violence against one another. Spontaneous public marches displayed flags of all republics. Commander Rypchensky supervised martial law to protect demonstrators from random acts of violence.

The commander also focused on personal matters. His first thought was the safety of his family. As planned, his son was assigned a foreign post at the United Nations Soviet delegation in New York. Before his departure, Kristoff expressed his satisfaction at being an eyewitness of recent events, which he cleverly expressed in print media. He was, however, anticipating his surprise visit with Nadia, performing in New York.

The commander also arranged his wife's departure to Paris, where she would be safe with her family.

Next he would have Chekov securely transported to Kiev where Ukrainians would assure his isolation from his elitist Russian allies, who would not hesitate to use force in attempts to release him from prison. If that should materialize, Ukrainians were ordered to kill Chekov. The commander did not want him to see the light of day. His death would make him a martyr. He was more valuable alive.

Foreign journalists began to speculate when they observed military personnel filling Moscow's streets. A British journalist was frightened when speaking to his colleague.

"What the hell is going on here. This is unbelievable!"

Shots were heard and explosions caught pedestrians off guard. They fell to the ground. Another journalist commented:

"If this isn't a coup, then what the hell is it!"

Army officers remained loyal to their commander. They were immediately mobilized to code three, internal threats to national security. Swift decision-making was critical for containing opposition forces. Strategic military and commercial centers were occupied by network leaders. Military and commercial airports, rail stations, naval bases, and centers for television and radio communication and commercial centers for distribution were ostensibly under the control of network personnel. Within twenty-four hours, the entire nation could sway toward civil unrest, or even worse, civil war. Network agents had preplanned multi-media broadcasts that proclaimed peaceful transformation of power. The hope was that positive information would encourage pubic support throughout republics, where demands for autonomy and cultural heritage were expressed through demonstrations, all televised to garner public attention and support. To encourage even more support, each republic was encouraged to announce their independence. The belief was, once the Soviet Union was shattered, its mastery of control would be impossible to reconstruct. Republics would refuse any attempts to return to communist dictatorship.

Many KGB personnel and their cronies went underground. Bureaucrats who were trapped between two opposing factions, hastily decided their political fate. Those who hesitated with their realignment and failed to commit to new slogans of perestroika and glasnost were detained. Public announcements were made during raids against "communist terrorists" aka, enemies of freedom. Increasing public support was vital. Those who resisted could expect some form of unfavorable public response. Network operatives wanted to be perceived as protectors of civil liberties and social justice. Economic and political freedom were topics of editorials and other media outlets. Outspoken enemies were arrested. Coup leaders, anticipated favorable public sentiments. The army's role as peacemaker was critical. Military police assured law and order were maintained. The coup appeared to be under control.

The commander realized democratic traditions in the Soviet Union were practically nonexistent. Network government officials would struggle without institutions to guide them through this crisis. Leadership was crucial. Was Andrei Mikoyanov capable of the task before him? When Mikoyanov and his wife were released from their staged house arrest, television crews and reporters recorded the event for public consumption. He was championed as a national hero of a Free Russian Republic.

Political succession in Russia was often filled with uncertainties. New leaders, whether warranted or not, inherited sins of autocratic predecessors. Democratic institutions could not flourish with Tsars and communist dictators as role models. Transition to free press and free enterprise were also problematic. The commander was under no illusions of democratic harmony. As a student of Russian history, his limited expectations for success mitigated his optimism. He was frustrated when unexpected circumstances presented his people and nation with dangerous alternatives. Russian political history clearly demonstrated that without democratic traditions and culture, the possibilities for returning to autocratic leadership were very real. The commander was hopeful that Mikoyanov could be a transitional, benevolent autocrat, until democratic institutions could be nurtured by a new generation. His confidence diminished as events unfolded.

Network leaders proposed using the Chinese economic prototype as a realistic model for transition toward perestroika. The Chinese utilized principles of economic democracy, where market forces of supply and demand, would replace the command structure. This evolution would transform and transfer production to private sectors. Over time, Chinese entrepreneurs would become decision-makers, which was the first step toward economic democracy. The time frame had no limits. The gradual transition of wealth from the public sector to the private sector would unleash a spurt of economic expansion in China. The hope was that political democracy would follow years later.

Unfortunately, in the USSR, sinister, plutocratic elites absconded billions of rubles that Network leaders intended for employment of millions, working on infrastructure projects in every republic. That was the economic plan, post revolution. Use accumulated wealth to finance the transition away from communist economic principles. However, Russian kleptocrats had been laundering billions in foreign accounts. The commander realized vast sums of revenue were scammed. Getting access to those funds would not be an easy task. The commander assumed his role would be that of power broker, not CEO. He lacked confidence in network leader's ability to manage monumental fiscal and monetary issues. In retrospect, network leaders realized their economic deficiencies, especially, financial planning. The Commander was well aware of one 18th century American financial genius, Alexander Hamilton, whose services during America's critical period, could have been utilized for this occasion. What he needed was a financial officer who could reorganize their national debt.

Maintaining the appearance of economic justice and opportunity was critical. If the economy was stable, political reform would follow as basic needs were being addressed. In order for the revolution to move to the next stage, a massive infusion of cash was necessary. These funds would have employed millions in construction, energized a private banking system, and oversee sale of public assets to private ownership. This was the idea behind perestroika. It never happened as planned. The revolution stalled, caused by corrupt and ignorant communist officials.

The net worth of the Soviet Union, measured in natural assets, is trillions of dollars. That wealth was being squandered and mismanaged by men who did not implement financial principles practiced in capitalist economies. This blind spot by Network leaders was their "Achilles heal". Basically, communist ignorance of capitalist financial principles, mitigated their success. Successful revolutions must incorporate economic growth. Network leaders, for a variety of reasons, were unable to achieve this goal. Their revolution stalled, leaving their forward progress in jeopardy.

Chapter 23

Nadia was performing with the Bolshoi in Manhattan when Kristoff arrived. He was advised not to discuss details of his new assignment with anyone. To quell rumors, his father made certain his position as Soviet UN press officer was made public. The circumstances required discretion, not secrecy. Reprisals were feared if his departure was interpreted as defection. Media reports communicated by Pravda and other network publications, reported minor disturbances not political turmoil. Network media consultants chose to limit activity until stability and controls were in place. This also meant limited contacts with international media outlets. However, foreign correspondents in Moscow had reported incidents of violence. Official network releases were withheld until new leadership was in control. Under these tense and uncertain circumstances, Kristoff was made aware that Soviet UN employees were a mixture of friend and foe. He had to be cautious.

Since Nadia was not informed of his visit, he looked forward to surprising her. Even while turmoil in their native land continued, his joyful anticipation was not diminished. One powerful emotion motivated him more than anything else; his love for Nadia. Holding her in his arms would assure him their future had real possibilities. His control of their safety was limited. Who could he trust? Unknown dangers would have to be dealt with one day at a time.

Nadia's plan to defect and live in America now made more sense. Her vision and dream was now his as well. He arranged to have flowers sent to her at the Embassy Hotel with a note that read:

"Nadia, I love you and hope you are in good spirits. Love, Kristoff." His heart raced as he approached her residence. When he knocked at her door, she peered through the opening and saw

Kristoff standing outside smiling. How quickly the door opened with outreached arms that she flung around him. Tears of joy rolled down her cheeks as they embraced; both were at a loss for words. After holding each other with lots of kisses, he closed the door. His loving stare was not received as expected. He sensed something was bothering her so he asked without reservation, "Is something wrong?"

Nadia looked into his eyes, smiled and said, "I am pregnant with your child. We are going to have a baby."

Her smile pleased Kristoff. He always wanted children and this was wonderful news. "Then we must get married." He drew her close and looked into her blue eyes.

"Will you marry me, Nadia?"

Teasing him with a kiss, she responded, "I thought you would never ask." They embraced and settled themselves on a love seat. Her soft voice followed.

"I found a Russian Orthodox Church in Manhattan. We must have a church wedding. My father would have insisted. You know Kristoff, I wanted to call you but waited until I met with a doctor. I wanted to make sure everything is normal. I saw him two days ago."

Kristoff was overjoyed.

"That sounds wonderful. Let's go to the church and set a date."

Nadia settled back and placed her hands on her stomach.

"One morning I woke and knew there was something inside me. I have not danced for about a month. My role was changed to assisting our lead choreographer. He's been so kind and understanding. They will all want to come to our wedding celebration." Nadia told Kristoff she would return to Russia before the baby was born. Her mother was excited for her and Nadia wanted to be with her when the baby arrived. Kristoff was frightened by her plan to return. Political upheaval appeared imminent and could explode without warning. He tried to coax Nadia to stay in the States but realized she was determined. She rarely spent time with her aging mother and wanted her to experience her first born grandchild. Like Kristoff, Nadia was an only child, so he understood her reasons. The Soviet Union was filled with many one-child families, for a variety of reasons.

They were married three days later; her troupe attended. After the church ceremony, a celebration was arranged in the hotel lounge. She scheduled a flight to Moscow in three weeks. Kristoff would remain in Manhattan. He wired the following note to his father:

"To my loving parents. Nadia and I were married in New York, on October 1st. Expecting our child. Nadia is returning in three weeks. I will return before the baby arrives. Love, Kristoff." Two days later, after speaking with his father, an arrangement was made. Kristoff would remain in New York for two months before returning. His abbreviated mission would be explained in Pravda as follows.

"Kristoff Rypchensky officially reassigned as chief editor."

His parents disagreed with his decision to return, but understood his desire to be with Nadia, especially with a child on the way. The commander's wife tried to persuade her husband to cancel his flight. She even called her son and pleaded with him, but he told her, "I must be with Nadia." Circumstances in Moscow were unstable. Political violence escalated between network and communist factions. The commander had to plan several contingencies to protect his wife who delayed her plan to leave for France until Kristoff and Nadia were settled. She was nervous about domestic instability. The commander arranged 24 hour security for their residence. Factions resorted to violence. Targets became personal.

Within political circles, news of Chekov's arrest spread. His detention in Kiev isolated him from his former allies, who were scattered but still determined. Media exploitation was working in favor of network policies. Network radio and television broadcasts were constantly informing and educating , utilizing propaganda to persuade public opinion. Hardline opponents, however, were not retreating from their principles, flawed as they were. They countered with nationalistic responses.

"Preserve the Soviet Union." They called their opponents, unpatriotic, terrorist enemies of the state. Surprisingly, military protocol and discipline were maintained, mostly due to loyalty for Commander Rypchensky. The central government's newly elected leader, Mikoyanov, addressed the public with daily press conferences designed to appeal for calm. He was successful in portraying a neutral position until his network could secure government control and authority. One of the most clever strategies suggested by Orlov, and followed by network policy-makers, was to isolate Mikoyanov from aligning himself with any faction. He wisely remained a spokesman for unity and patriotism, leaving many citizens satisfied. However he had to be very discrete with his political power. Political winds were trending toward liberalization. When he announced two new policies of glasnost and perestroika, public response was favorable. Political speech and private ownership were legitimized throughout several republics. More openness would lead to press and broadcast freedom. However, rogue militias were organized by KGB agents and several high-ranking air force officers supported by special forces paratroopers, who allied themselves with hardline party leaders. Communists were fighting to protect their political status and privileged life styles. Defending their selfish interests motivated them into a formidable enemy. The Commander feared this reality. A civil war was imminent. Network opponents understood what was at stake. If their reforms appeared too radical, their momentum could be stalled. They would not gain ground by hastefully implementing reforms. A delicate balance was required.

When violence exploded in Moscow and other cities where opposing forces exchanged gunfire, the Commander had to call out more troops. In one incident, over forty were killed or injured in crossfire battles. Some included civilians. The line was drawn. Mikoyanov would have to step up and lead. He tried the role of peacemaker without much success. Neither side would make concessions. Military presence was everywhere.

There were interludes where no one really knew who was in charge. A political vacuum left powerful men on both sides of the political spectrum contemplating their next move. It could have been the best of times for all republics, but unfortunately, evil forces instigated acts of violence. Would Russia's future avoid a violent civil war? Would Russia forfeit an opportunity for political and economic change? The commander's authority over the military was critical for maintaining law and order. However his concern was now more focused on his wife and growing family.

Mikoyanov decided to announce a ceasefire where both sides could meet and attempt compromises, hardly a familiar concept within soviet political circles. Would the body-politic be open to making concessions that could possibly result in a coalition government? When a cease fire was accepted on both sides, the question that remained was, how long? One advantage for network leaders was the declaration of sovereignty announced by newly independent republics. This news was broadcast throughout all republics. The Union of Soviet Socialist Republics, aka USSR, was for all practical purposes, dissolved. This was a very critical step forward that would be difficult to reverse.

Events within the Soviet Union were in flux. Network leaders and organizers were working to control violence and cultivate public support. One problem was Communist party bureaucrats and the institutions they represented could not be easily dismantled.

Massive resistance from party loyalists continued. Many citizens were accustomed to and depended upon meek offerings from state-sponsored safety nets. Entitlements supported thousands of "foot soldiers" who were low level members of the Communist Party. Their basic needs and security were subsidized by state socialism. The revolutionary government would have to outmaneuver their communist counterparts with employment, income, and security. Mikoyanov announced a massive public works program directed at construction and repair of roads, bridges, tunnels, pipelines, air and sea ports, neglected for years. Millions of good-paying job opportunities were announced. To finance these expenditures, vast quantities of Russian natural gas and oil would be sold to European energy conglomerates. Large supplies of Russian gold would also be sold at market prices high enough to mitigate burgeoning deficits. It was a New Deal program, Russian style. These expenditures, combined with massive cuts in military spending, would help to move the economy forward. The only question now was, could network leaders move fast enough to fill the vast political and economic void caused by the implosion of a command economy now under the leadership of a quasi, authoritarian leadership. Revenue was scarce, caused by excessive fraud. European banks would not extend credit to a revolutionary government in flux and with no established credit. It appeared revolutionary goals were in doubt.

Chapter 24

Six weeks after Viktor and Yolanda enjoyed their love fest in a Manhattan hotel, Viktor established a routine of visiting her which caused suspicion among enemy agents. Their relationship crossed a threshold, even though both understood circumstances made a normal relationship impossible. New York City offered a variety of locations for them to meet and talk about future plans. The KGB observed them and predetermined their motives were underhanded. A handsome Russian KGB agent falling in love with a very attractive American CIA agent was off everyone's radar. Why was it something no one could imagine? Cold War hostilities were too severe to allow loving relationships between "enemies". Whatever the reason, Viktor's behavior raised a red flag. He should have known better. Personal needs and obsessions overpowered his discretion.

One rainy afternoon, Viktor planned to meet Zelensky and Yolanda at Jake's Pub in Lower Manhattan. As Viktor approached his car on the Lower East Side, he noticed what he believed were KGB agents following him. His instinct was to avoid them at all costs. When he looked back and noticed two men gaining ground, he turned and ran as fast as he could, knowing his car was at least four blocks away. Suddenly a car screeched its brakes. Two men jumped out. Viktor avoided one but ran directly into the other agent whose grip was strong enough to drag him into the back seat of their Mercedes where he was roughed up by another agent. They did their best to make him uncomfortable.

The agent in the front seat spoke first, in Russian. "You know, Viktor, we have been following you for the past six weeks. You are playing tricks on us. Why not tell us the whole story? Otherwise I have orders to eliminate you. Understood? You will never see your whore again. Tell us what you know and you will be released."

Viktor, out of breath, struggled but responded: "What have I done to make you suspicious? I am only doing my job. If you want the truth, I have fallen in love with this woman. Do you understand love? That is the truth. I want to be with her. She has given us computer secrets. I have done my job."

The agent holding Viktor screamed, "You are lying." They lost their patience and concluded he would not divulge any information without assistance. Suddenly, Viktor felt an injection in his arm. He was familiar with the drug because he recognized the smell. He wouldn't be able to control himself. He was drifting into a semiconscious state. His mind surrendered to the drug; his will to resist ceased. Helpless, he revealed everything when the agent repeated his question.

"Viktor, what have you been doing under cover? Tell us."

He began his response slowly. The powerful drug slowed his speech. Gradually, words followed. "KGB working for Soviet underground. Mission overthrow Soviet government. Control central committee, politburo. Spreading misinformation, keep enemies off balance."

The KGB agent made sure his recorder was working properly. "Who is in charge of this operation?"

Viktor was fading fast. "Ze . . . Ze . . . Zelen . . . Zelensky." Viktor finally passed out. The agent grabbed him and shook him vigorously. The other agent blurted out.

"How much was in that injection? You may have killed him. See what you can do to revive him."

By now Viktor was slumped into unconsciousness. The agent holding him said, "He looks dead. Can you feel a pulse?" There was no pulse. "No, he is gone. Poor fool. His heart stopped. What do we do with his body?"

The agent in charge responded with contempt: "Go uptown. Throw him in the Hudson River. Zelensky's next."

In lower Manhattan, Zelensky and Yolanda were seated in a pub sipping cold beer. Zelensky kept looking through a large window, hoping Viktor would appear from the subway exit. After repeated glances at his watch, he sensed something was wrong.

"It is over one hour; he is never this late. Something must have happened." He motioned to the waiter, whom he had befriended.

"If Viktor should arrive, please tell him to call us." He gave the waiter a large tip.

"Yes, for sure, thank you sir."

A quick subway to Penn Station, then LIRR to Huntington Station. Zelensky did not hesitate to move quickly. They returned to her home and waited for a telephone call. Yolanda's emotions were released. Zelensky tried comforting her even though he had a strong feeling Viktor was in serious trouble.

"Do not worry. He will show up." Then he thought, if not, this means I am next on their list. Zelensky, however, had planned for this possibility. He turned to Yolanda while grabbing his trench coat.

"You can reach me at this number. Call from a pay phone only. They are probably looking for me as I speak. I must leave now."

Zelensky realized his comrade was probably dead because he knew Viktor would not cooperate and that agents would heavily drug him. Yolanda sensed the worst as she watched Zelensky entering a taxi. What she feared most had become reality. Her emotions were numb. Her professional and romantic involvement were being monitored. She felt responsible for Viktor's disappearance. Guilt overpowered her.

Early the following morning, Zelensky heard a CBS radio report from a hotel room on the west side near the bus terminal. New York City police found a body floating in the Hudson River, just north of Battery Park. Police reports described the body as a white male, six feet, one hundred and seventy-five pounds, dark hair. No name was announced. That was his comrade. The description fit him perfectly.

Zelensky made contact weeks before with international agents working for the network throughout Europe and Canada. The Canadian government had arrangements for immigrants displaced by political turmoil. Lists of Russians and citizens from other republics could find asylum through arrangements made with immigration officials. Zelensky took advantage of this opportunity. He purchased a one-way ticket to Montreal from New York City. Before he boarded the Greyhound, he called Yolanda to inform her. When she answered the phone he told her he was at LaGuardia, in case her phone was being monitored. Then he paused. He was at a loss for words. She waited for him to say something but he remained silent. She called him out. "Zelensky! Please tell me if he's alive. I must know." There was no reply. Then she heard the receiver click his silent answer.

Chapter 25

It was late morning in Manhattan when Burkov heard official reports of Viktor's disappearance and death. Within an hour, a written report was delivered to him that described in detail what happened. Zelensky's name was mentioned as co-conspirator. When Burkov read the report, he felt his prejudice against Viktor was justified. Learning of Zelensky's escape made finding him a priority. Burkov's phone rang. UN headquarters informed him that a journalist for Pravda had recently arrived and would report to his office for his first assignment. Two hours later, Kristoff arrived in Burkov's office for his initial meeting.

Burkov's first impression was positive. He was aware that his father's status may have enhanced his credentials.

"So you are the writer I have been waiting for. Your first assignment is to report the death of Viktor Romanoff. It was suicide. Get that out as soon as you can. He was an alcoholic. His body reeked of alcohol. Here is a written report you can use for reference."

Kristoff was shocked by the abruptness of Burkov. There were no signs of sympathy. No formalities or small talk; this man was all business. Kristoff realized his written report would be scrutinized carefully. He responded to Burkov's order. "Right away." Then he asked. "Are there any details I should know that may not be in this report?"

Burkov was not prepared for that question. He surprised Kristoff with his direct response. "This man was a traitor. He was part of a network attempting to overthrow the Central Committee and Politburo."

Kristoff could not believe what he was hearing. He was filled with fear for his parents. Now he understood why his father had reservations about foreign assignments, including New York. He thought he was protecting his son from imminent danger. Hardly the case. Kristoff's mind raced but he managed to appear calm while pursuing his line of questioning with Burkov. "Any names revealed?"

Again to Kristoff's surprise, Burkov responded.

"Yes, only one, Zelensky. We are looking for him at this moment. He will be able to identify the nucleus of this insurrection." Burkov stood, paused, and stared into Kristoff's eyes before his stern warning:

"This information is not to be revealed to anyone. Understood?"

Kristoff responded immediately. "Yes sir! Absolutely!"

Burkov was abrupt. "Now I have important business to attend to. Move along." Kristoff was shocked by this news and expected UN communications would inform his father.

Kristoff excused himself. He realized his writing assignment had to project a message of loyalty to the party and government, and would be carefully reviewed by Burkov. A secretary directed him to a room equipped with new IBM word processors. She demonstrated how easy it was to use. Kristoff was impressed with the technology. In Russia he was using old typewriters that broke down quite often. He was able to complete the article in about an hour, making sure he projected an image of Viktor that conformed with Burkov's instructions. When he was about to leave, an aide entered and asked Kristoff if she could use his word processor because her work station had experienced a blackout. Kristoff was very cordial and introduced himself. She stared and he could tell she was flirting with him so he used this to his advantage.

"Of course. You can use this processor. I have just finished." Then he returned his stare to her and asked, "Did you know Viktor?"

He didn't expect much of a response but she offered some unexpected information. "The only thing I can tell you is Viktor was handsome and had a beautiful girlfriend. I met her at a cocktail party. How could I forget her! Yolanda Spieler. It's very sad. Rumors were that she is a CIA agent. They were close, very close. I hope she had nothing to do with Viktor's death. It's so sad."

Kristoff wisely decided not to discuss the matter. Instead he made a mental note of Yolanda Spieler's name. "Do you know where she lives?"

She responded: "On Long Island, that is all I know."

Kristoff motioned for her to sit at the computer as he offered her his chair. He thanked her again, and before leaving, quietly said:

"It might be prudent for all of us to keep this information to ourselves for security reasons; I'm sure you understand."

She smiled and responded, "Yes, of course."

He wished her a good day and proceeded to his office to edit his written account of Viktor's death, making certain the final copy would meet with Burkov's approval. When he left the UN, he walked uptown and found a quiet pub where he could have a beer and sandwich. Close to the bar there were several telephone directories, adjacent to phone booths. After several minutes of searching, he located Yolanda Spieler's telephone number and address. He wrote the information on a small slip of paper. She was listed in Dix Hills, Huntington, Suffolk County.

He dialed her number. After just two rings a woman answered. "Hello."

Kristoff was caught off guard by her voice. Although she spoke in English, her voice had a very familiar sound. He thought he was hearing Nadia's voice. He responded before she hung up the receiver.

"Is this Yolanda Spieler?"

Her response was instant, like a person waiting for a long lost friend.

"Yes! Who's calling?"

Kristoff sensed her nervous response.

"I am a friend of Viktor's. It's very important that I speak with you. I believe you know what is happening in Russia. I am willing to drive to Long Island and meet you at a location of your choice." Silence followed. He thought he lost contact but she suddenly responded.

"How do I know I can trust you? Look what they did to Viktor!"

Kristoff's response was instant. "That tragedy makes it even more important that we meet. You must trust me." He waited for her reply, knowing she had to believe and trust his response.

"Yes, I would like to talk to you also." She paused, then continued.

"You can meet me at the Milleridge Inn, located in Jericho. I don't have the exact address."

They arranged to meet at 7:00 pm that evening. She would be wearing a navy blue suit with a light pink silk blouse.

She advised him to ride the LIRR to Huntington Station, where he could rent a car. He left Manhattan early so he could have time to drive around Huntington and Sea Cliff where he was informed, a large Russian population resided. He wanted to see for himself and did find Long Island's north shore charm appealing. He was impressed with the area, and wished Nadia was with him, knowing she would love it as well. After two hours of sightseeing, he headed for 585 North Broadway in Jericho, location of Milleridge Inn. After several wrong turns he managed to find the restaurant and located a parking spot. From a table, adjacent to a large window, she observed him as he walked to the entrance. He was dressed in a sport jacket, collared shirt, no tie and looked handsome as he approached the main entrance, where upon entering, was warmly greeted by the hostess.

"Good evening sir. How may I help you?"

In his best English, he said, "I am having dinner with Ms. Yolanda Spieler. I'm a little late." She motioned for him to follow. He didn't know what to expect when he walked toward her table. Yolanda observed him approaching, holding a brown leather writing portfolio. As Kristoff walked closer to her table, he was stunned by her beauty. The CIA recruited her for a reason. He would soon conclude that her fluency in Russian and sharpness of mind were also factors.

"Are you Ms. Spieler?"

She nodded affirmatively, and in perfect Russian responded.

" Yes, very nice to meet you." He appeared comfortable with her voice. Her welcome was graceful and seemed genuine. Kristoff stood quietly until she motioned for him to be seated. He was uncomfortable when he sensed anguish in her abrupt question.

"Who are you? How do you know Viktor?" There was sadness in her voice.

His response was barely audible. He leaned close and spoke almost in a whisper, to protect their conversation.

"I did not reveal my name on the phone. You should understand why." He paused before continuing.

"My name is Kristoff Rypchensky. My father, Commander Rypchensky, is leader of an underground network in the Soviet Union. His life is in danger unless he is informed of recent breaches in their security. I met Viktor in Moscow just over a year ago, during a meeting with members of the press and KGB intelligence officers being stationed here in America. We had dinner together and enjoyed our meeting. Viktor was a remarkable man. I am saddened by his death."

She responded with:

"You know he was killed by KGB. They are looking for his coworker, Zelensky. If they find him they will torture and kill him, just like Viktor." Her eyes began to tear and Kristoff tried his best to comfort her. She continued.

"I knew Viktor was in trouble. It is partly my fault. I may have exposed him to more danger." Then, unable to control her composure she said.

"We were in love. I told him his status in the KGB would not make it easy for us."

Kristoff understood her emotions but he felt compelled to pursue his line of questioning.

"I am very sorry for your loss, but you must understand that Viktor would want our network to succeed. I need your help. Please Yolanda. You must help me. It is possible for me to help Zelensky qualify for asylum."

Suddenly she appeared suspicious and realized her emotions may have revealed too much information.

"Can I trust you? Maybe you're KGB. Look what happened to Viktor. I am concerned and frightened for my safety."

Kristoff understood her fear. "Trust me. I am part of the network. To verify, check with the CIA. They will confirm my story. Please call to verify. Give them this code word and number. They will respond with N13. That is my code number."

She wanted to believe him but decided to call.

"If you will excuse me, I will do just that. I must be certain." It didn't take too long. When she returned to the table, he noticed many heads turning to observe her beauty. Her tension began to subside. She then reached for something in her purse.

"I have a telephone number. Please be careful. If they find him they will kill him." Kristoff thanked her and she responded:

"I hope you weren't followed." Their eyes met and momentarily locked together.

Staring into her eyes, he responded:

"I was careful. If there is anything I can do, please call. Here is a number. Ask for John. I will get the message. Call just before 8:00 am or immediately after 11:00 pm. It's a diner I frequent. We should both use public phones." He paused and stared.

"Yolanda, I am very sorry about Viktor. He was a good man who wanted what I want. To be happy and free." Then he shared his personal information.

"My wife is expecting our first child. I am very concerned for her safety. A year ago she was dancing in the Bolshoi. Today she is happy expecting our first child. She will return to Russia to be with her mother for the birth, but we expect to live here in the States. It's not easy living in a police state. Nadia loves America. I will join her next month. Our child is due in about seven weeks. I surprised her with my visit. We were married here in New York, shortly after I arrived. We are enjoying our honeymoon in New York City."

Yolanda's eyes teared. She felt joy and sadness as she reached out for his hand and squeezed it gently.

"That is wonderful news. That's what Viktor wanted. We discussed it." When their eyes met again they both felt something connect that was powerfully mysterious. The remainder of the evening was filled with good conversation and a delicious meal. Kristoff had managed to secure information, critical for his father's mission. He had to assure Zelensky's security.

When he returned to Manhattan, Nadia was sleeping. His love and bond with her was made stronger after meeting Yolanda Spieler, whose tragic loss magnified Kristoff's love for his wife and child. Yolanda Spieler's anguish altered his outlook. Tragic events had taken a toll on her emotions. Kristoff's empathy for her was sincere. She lost a man she loved. He felt restless as he quietly entered the bed where his wife was sound asleep. Her warm body calmed his mood. He gently kissed and embraced her. After the day's events, his love for her had appreciated immensely, never to be taken for granted. However, his emotions and love for his wife with child, were somewhat distracted by uncertainty and apprehension he could not comprehend.

Chapter 26

Kristoff and Nadia had been married for just over two weeks. He wanted to spend as many daytime hours with her as possible. They enjoyed Broadway shows and several other cultural experiences New York has to offer. However, work obligations were pressing. Nadia was almost seven months pregnant. She wanted to work with her replacement in the Bolshoi before returning to Russia. She also assisted her choreographer who was a close friend. He requested her transition be as seamless as possible. Kristoff insisted Nadia would not partake in activity that could affect her pregnancy. He was looking forward to being a father.

There was another important matter that had to be dealt with before she returned. Kristoff believed Nadia should be informed of circumstances behind Viktor's murder. This information might encourage her to remain in New York. That was his preference even though he knew she would refuse his request. She believed her mother's involvement was important, but he wanted to press his point one more time. While she was packing for her flight, he decided to share his concerns with her.

"Nadia, I must inform my father of recent developments here in New York."

She heard about Viktor's death from Bolshoi performers but did not understand his connection to the network. "Why, what is wrong?" Nadia sensed trouble and uncertainty in his voice.

Kristoff was angry with himself for getting her upset. However, she had to be informed for her own security. He moved toward her and held her close.

"Our Network has been exposed. It is just a matter of time before...." Nadia placed her index finger on his lips. She passed her warm hand through his hair and kissed his forehead.

"When I return to Russia, I will relay your message. We must focus on our new baby. Not to worry." She sat on the edge on the bed holding her stomach.

"I have not been feeling well lately. Maybe I should have left the ballet sooner."

Kristoff held her close. "You look tired."

Nadia reclined on the bed and pulled Kristoff down with her.

"You are going to be a papa in a few months.

Kristoff rubbed her stomach.

"Our child should be born in America. It is too dangerous for you to return."

Her response was immediate.

"No, Kristoff. I must see my mother one more time. I may never see her again." It was a difficult moment for both of them.

Kristoff tried one more time.

"With my father's life in danger, it is best for you to remain here."

Her response was firm.

"No Kristoff. I must see my mother. I am her only child. I want her with me. We need time together." She kissed Kristoff and held him close to her enlarged stomach.

He whispered. "I will miss being with you." Then he paused and said:

"My mother has arranged their apartment for your comfort. She found a highly recommended doctor. Promise me you will take good care of yourself."

Nadia kissed him tenderly and said, "As long as we are together when the baby comes." Kristoff held her close.

"I will return home as soon as my work is complete." They embraced and fell asleep in each other's arms. Two days later, Nadia would arrive in Moscow.

Her arrival in Moscow was made pleasant by the warm greeting she received from Kristoff's' parents, now her in-laws. The commander and his wife, Monique, were overjoyed when Nadia deplaned. She was the daughter they never had. Greeting her with words of love made Monique's eyes tear. When they arrived at their apartment on the outskirts of Moscow, Nadia asked: "Is it safe for me to talk?"

The commander responded. "Only, if it is good news."

Nadia smiled and said: "You already know the good news. But there is also news that is not so good. Your security may have been breached. Viktor was killed. Under sedation he may have revealed network operations and objectives. The KGB are now looking for his partner, Zelensky."

The commander was very concerned but tried his best not to show it.

"As long as he can remain isolated, we still have time. If I know Zelensky, the KGB will never find him."

After a brief stay in his apartment, the commander left Nadia and his wife. Monique wanted to get reacquainted with her daughter-in-law, and now with a new grandchild only weeks away, they had much to discuss and plan. Monique also arranged transportation for Nadia to visit her mother. She also thought her mother could stay with her in their apartment so they could spend some quality time together.

"I would really like to visit with my mother. I haven't been with her for almost a year. Would you mind?"

Monique's warm smile responded.

"Whenever you are ready. I can take you now if you like." Nadia was so thankful. She missed her mother and knew she would be thrilled to be a grandmother. Nadia telephoned her mother to make sure the time was convenient for her. She was surprised that her mother answered so soon. Apparently she was anxiously waiting for her daughter to call. Nadia was pleased to hear her mother say:

"Now is a good time." The drive would take about twenty minutes.

When Monique and Nadia arrived at her mother's apartment, tears of joy flowed down their faces. They both cried and held each other. Monique could not hold back her tears. "My darling daughter. How I have prayed for you to come home to me. God heard my prayers." When they released themselves from each other's grasp, Nadia introduced her mother-in-law.

Monique smiled and offered a comment.

"I know how it feels to have only one child. My son adores Nadia. As you can see, their first born is on the way."

Nadia's mother Valeri smiled and nodded affirmatively.

"You must have tea. I made Kyiv cake for you." It was Nadia's favorite. A recipe from her Ukrainian ancestors, created by the Karl Marx Confectionary factory in Kiev. They sat and discussed family moments. Nadia's father died a year earlier in a construction accident Her mother cleaned offices in the Kremlin during evening hours and would be unable to visit except for Saturday afternoons and Sunday. Her meek salary barely covered her expenses.

Valeri was direct with Nadia. "You should stay in America where you can be free. The life you seek is not here." Monique took notice. She had similar sentiments. Her choice was of course France. Monique then offered to drive Valeri every weekend to her apartment so she could be with Nadia. She graciously accepted.

Then, as only her mother would notice, Valeri stared into Nadia's eyes and said:

"My darling, you look tired. Are you feeling OK?" Nadia did have a difficult pregnancy at moments. She believed she may have injured her groin during her last ballet performance, just before she learned of her pregnancy. Her mother insisted she rest. Monique agreed and decided to leave so Nadia and her mother could be together. They would have about three hours before Valeri had to leave for work. Nadia preferred staying with her mother but would return to Monique's apartment on the weekend. Monique understood and quietly left. Mothers understand these moments.

Nadia sat with her mother who had photo albums of their family. She viewed photos of her parents when they were just married and realized her good looks were a gift from a very attractive couple. Her mother placed her hand on Nadia's stomach. "Do you have any pain in the lower region? I see you wince every now and then. Is everything all right down there?"

Nadia did not want to upset her mother, but she responded with the truth. "Before I realized I was pregnant, I had just performed. I think I strained a muscle in my groin. Periodically it hurts."

Her mother held her close. "When I am at work, I want you to rest in my bed. I have a heating pad. Low heat only, if you feel any pain. Then her mother looked at her and inquired with a very serious voice.

"Why did you ever decide to return? I would have found a way to come to America to be with you. You should not have traveled so far under your condition." She gently hugged her daughter. "Tell me about your husband. Is he a good fellow?"

Nadia smiled. "Yes, momma. He's wonderful. You will love him. He is so good to me." Then without thinking she said.

"He also wanted me to stay in New York. Bad things are happening. You must not say a word or we could be arrested." Nadia felt obligated to inform her mother of impending danger.

Now her mother was upset.

"So why did you return? If you knew this, why did you return."

There was no sure answer, but Nadia said, "Yes, you are correct. I never thought of asking Kristoff's father to help you get special visa to visit America. Family emergency. I should have thought of that." Her mother escorted Nadia to her bed and they both rested and talked about names for the new baby. Her mother was not an alarmist. She realized and accepted many obstacles of life in a police state. No need to make her daughter feel concerned about future unknowns. Nadia felt so safe cuddled close to her. Before she dozed off into a deep sleep, she heard her mother's favorite remark: "What will be will be."

Chapter 27

The manhunt for Zelensky was intensified. Fortunately, his anticipation of being uncovered forced him to preplan his escape. Through CIA contacts with Canadian intelligence, Zelensky's political asylum was arranged in Montreal. For the time being he was safe; however, KGB agents had contacts in Canada. Russian hockey players were defecting to Canada where lucrative contracts were offered for their professional skills. Zelensky had to be careful. Russians would allow defections but could also demand Zelensky's repatriation. French Canadians love their professional hockey team. Choosing between super star hockey players and a Russian spy could be problematic for Zelensky. His only option would be to inform Canadians of the coup in process.

When Commander Rypchensky had been informed by Nadia, that Zelensky's security was endangered by Viktor's capture, Kristoff became involved via communication with his father. Kristoff was ordered to compose a letter for the purpose of securing Zelensky's political asylum in Canada. He could not wire the letter to his father for security reasons. His father trusted his writing skills. They discussed pertinent information during a telephone exchange. Kristoff would sign his father's signature and mail it to Canadian authorities for immediate resolution.

Network leaders limited release of news that could be intercepted, until they were confident their opponents were incapable of retaliation. The opposition's power remained a threat. If Zelensky was exposed and interrogated by authorities, revolutionary leaders would be identified. Their success would be in jeopardy. Certain acts of violence and revenge, from both sides, would immediately follow if leaders of the coup were exposed. Kristoff had to write the letter using an old typewriter he purchased. Using equipment from UN headquarters involved too much risk. He immediately began his composition, using his father's identity and addressed to:

Office of Canadian Prime Minister.

VERY URGENT: IMMEDIATE ATTENTION REQUESTED

October 18, 1988

Dear Sir,

As Commander of Military Operations in the Soviet Union, I request your immediate attention concerning a political crisis of monumental proportion. Currently, I am leading an underground movement whose goal is to replace our current totalitarian regime with a freely elected democratic parliament and prime minister. I can assure you, officers under my command are prepared to follow my lead. However, we must act immediately, with precision and protect our secrecy. As of this moment our intentions are considered to be conjecture. Our opponents have thus far been contained. However, we are now facing a situation that is very problematic. A certain agent of ours, Nicolas Zelensky, has defected to Canada with complete knowledge of our political intentions. His current status qualifies him for political asylum. However, our opponents have demanded his repatriation for reasons that are not justified, nor in accordance with Canada's long tradition of honoring amnesty for those who would be persecuted for their belief in political democracy. If Mr. Zelensky is repatriated, he will be drugged and tortured until he reveals our underground. This will place thousands of our citizens at risk, since our political opponents will react with ruthless brutality and contempt. Our country could be torn apart by a violent and dangerous civil war.

Please contact your American allies to confirm my request. They have worked with us to achieve what all freedom-loving citizens of our fifteen republics demand. Freedom from persecution and national sovereignty for republics whose cultural heritage has been destroyed. These values are fundamental to our cause.

The Soviet Union is a most imperfect union, incapable of providing natural rights ordained by a loving God of mercy. We have suffered for centuries under absolute monarchs and twentieth century totalitarian dictators. Our political, social, and economic freedoms must be fulfilled for our citizens who have suffered for generations. Together we can make our world a better place.

Please join us by expediting our request.

Respectfully yours,

Commander Alexander Rypchensky

Soviet Military High Command

Kristoff reread his letter. He was direct and concise. He did not burden Canadian authorities with uncertain words or requests. Their response would have to be swift under these urgent conditions. His father was pleased with his written precision and clarity. Kristoff turned his attention to another important task. Arranging his return to Russia to be with Nadia. He regretted leaving New York. The city was saturated with energy he never experienced before. However, returning to his loving Nadia, with child, trumped all other thoughts.

Chapter 28

United Nations Soviet headquarters was buzzing with activity. Most of the staff had met Nadia and knew she was expecting. Even so, Kristoff did not think his request for returning to Moscow would be granted under any circumstances. He was pleasantly surprised when his office secretary informed him.

"Good morning Mr. Rypchensky. I have good news for you. Your request to be with your wife was approved by Secretary Burkov. I have made arrangements for your flight. It departs at 6:30 pm on Saturday. If that is not convenient, please let me know." Stella was an efficient secretary who was fond of Nadia and was also fond of children. She told Kristoff she looked forward to being a grandmother someday. Apparently, Nadia's training and recommendation of Stella's daughter for an opening was well received by the Bolshoi staff. Her daughter's acceptance was quite an honor. Stella's gratitude was displayed when she said:

"Kristoff, we are so thankful to Nadia and you as well for assisting my daughter. Without Nadia's training and encouragement, this would never have happened. I feel I owe you a big favor. Thank you so much."

For whatever reason, Kristoff thought he might need a favor sometime in the future so he asked Stella for her private telephone number, which she readily provided. He also wondered whether she had anything to do with his request being approved. Stella's affinity was obviously genuine. She motioned to Kristoff to come closer. Stella had suspicions after overhearing a discussion between Burkov and KGB officials. She revealed her concern when she handed him a card along with a baby shower gift for Nadia.

"Please read the card before you leave. It's from all of us."
Then while shuffling papers, she whispered, "Kristoff, be careful.
Your request was initially rejected by Burkov, but KGB specifically
requested that your return be approved. Something seems wrong."
Kristoff surmised that Stella was one of many network employees
his father had spoken about. He thanked her and understood the
importance of her warning. His guess was that KGB operatives in
Moscow were planning to use him as bait to get to his father. He
would arrange alternate plans for his return.

He glanced at Stella with a warm smile and thanked her for the
gift and card. She quietly advised him to be vigilante. She knew
from her vast experience as a clerical worker how the system worked,
and encouraged Kristoff not to sacrifice his safety when it could be
averted. Then she stood to say good bye and embraced him while she
whispered, "Contact your father. He will advise you." He listened to
her advice and made plans to contact his father using CIA network
communications.

It was 3:00 am Moscow time when Kristoff finally spoke with his
father. Hearing his voice made him want to be with his parents. Now
he understood Nadia's reason for wanting to return home to see her
mother, maybe for the last time.

Unfortunately, elements of danger were now threatening
Kristoff, his new wife and parents. His father made it clear that he
did not want Kristoff to be trapped by his enemies. "Kristoff! Good
to hear your voice. This is not a time for you to return. Much too
dangerous."

Kristoff disagreed. "You know it is just as dangerous for me here;
if they can kill Viktor, they can kill me too." His father realized
Kristoff made a strong point so he made the following offer.

"I will arrange a different flight for you into Helsinki where a
personal jet will fly you to Moscow. Do not board your existing

flight. Understood?" Before Kristoff could respond, his father's concern could be heard in another question.

"When is your flight scheduled to depart?"

When Kristoff answered, "Tomorrow at 6:30 pm, " he sensed fear in his father's voice. His father ordered him to another flight.

"Go to Finnair at the same time and I will have your flight arranged. You will land in Helsinki where you will be met by a pilot who will fly you to Moscow. Understood?" His father was pleading with him.

"Yes I understand. See you in Moscow. Give mom and Nadia my love."

The commander signed off, saying

"You can never be too vigilant under current circumstances. Be safe."

When the phone clicked, Kristoff felt a fear that had escaped him until now. He realized how little control one has over circumstances constantly in flux. Up to this point, the Network seemed to be on schedule. Now the future was dependent upon a combination of factors that could implode. There was cause for feeling uncertainty and fear. Revolutions create unpredictable twists that are almost impossible to forecast.

Before Kristoff returned to his apartment, he used a public telephone to contact Yolanda. If Zelensky was captured, his plans might have to be changed. Yolanda answered the phone after switching on a machine that would garble tracking devices. He asked about Zelensky and learned there was no contact made with him. He continued with:

"I am returning to Moscow tomorrow to be with Nadia. Our child will be born soon."

There was a deafening silence. Had he said something wrong? Then Yolanda responded hesitantly.

"How wonderful! You must be thrilled. Maybe we all can celebrate when you return."

Kristoff sensed her muted response was conflicted. Something was not right. He noticed a preoccupation in her voice. She had expressed Viktor's desire for having children. Was she feeling a motherly instinct? Kristoff recalled their last meeting while having dinner on Long Island, where she revealed her loving relationship with Viktor and how they were making plans for a future together, including children.

Kristoff understood Yolanda's sadness about Viktor's tragic murder. Rather than probe her emotional pain, he chose to remain silent. His thoughts focused on Nadia. He did however sense Yolanda was withholding information about her relationship with Viktor. When their telephone conversation ended, he could not comprehend why his feelings of intrigue remained. At that instant, he was reminded of childhood moments, when his father's stories left him with mysterious sentiments that were eventually revealed. Something was missing.

Kristoff decided to call Stella and probe her knowledge of Viktor and Yolanda. She was aware of information that might be useful at some point. Her work at UN headquarters provided her with inside information. He was pleased when she answered his call. They decided to meet for a drink at a pub uptown near her apartment. She was seated at a table drinking a vodka when he entered the pub.

"Good evening Stella. I hope I'm not too late. I am still learning the bus schedule."

She smiled. "No problem. I'm enjoying my vodka. How is Nadia feeling?"

He called Nadia almost every chance he had. "She's doing well. The time difference between New York and Moscow makes calling her inconvenient. I want her to get her sleep."

Stella claimed experiencing similar issues communicating with her daughter. The waitress brought Kristoff a vodka. He looked at his watch and realized he could relax and maybe discover some interesting information.

"Over a year ago, I met Viktor in Moscow. Had you ever met him?"

She responded. "Yes, I met Viktor shortly after he arrived here in New York. He was likable, friendly and very handsome man. We often had coffee together. He told me he met a lovely woman while working on an assignment. I heard she was CIA. They were seen several times at cocktail parties. A very attractive woman. They were a beautiful couple. He told me he was in love with her. He also shared some private feelings about his family history back in Russia. Quite tragic how circumstances ended for him. All he wanted was to live free, find the right woman, and raise a family." Kristoff responded.

"When I met him over a year ago in Moscow, he also shared with me his tragic family history. Then he came to America and is murdered. Why was he killed? What happened?"

Stella looked around before speaking, almost in a whisper.

"It was Burkov. He hated Kristoff. He was jealous, plain and simple. Kristoff had class. He was sophisticated. Burkov was a bully and was not refined. He felt Kristoff would one day replace him at the UN. That was the last job Kristoff wanted. What he really wanted was to defect and become an American citizen. Burkov had him killed. I'm sure of that." Stella then looked at Kristoff and quietly said: "There's one more thing. Viktor and Yolanda were secretly married. It doesn't matter now, but I'm sure they were truly in love. I could tell. So sad."

Kristoff responded with silence. Here in New York, thousands of miles from his native land, where revolution stirred, tragic consequences of Network intrigue continued. It made Kristoff imagine how the destiny of Viktor and his family was cut short by evil forces. A good man wanted a loving wife and family to live peacefully in America. Something so simple and ordinary was denied by a twist of fate. He wondered whether Viktor's widow could fathom the possibilities their futures could have produced. Kristoff also thought of his family and how their destiny would unfold. After finishing his vodka, he ordered another for Stella, thanked her and left the pub. It was a long walk to his UN office but he filled every moment with constant loving thoughts of Nadia.

Chapter 29

Flight 365 left as scheduled and Kristoff felt relaxed enough to sleep practically the entire time. He was well rested when Finnair landed in Helsinki. A pilot wearing a Soviet air force uniform approached him.

"Mr. Rypchensky, I am ordered by your father to fly you to Moscow."

Without any delay he led Kristoff to a taxi after his bags were retrieved. Military aircraft were located several miles from commercial traffic. It was not a pleasant day for flying and Kristoff did not look forward to a military flight after flying a comfortable commercial airline. There was no alternative. He climbed aboard, hesitating every step of the way. The military transport was gutted and fitted with luxury accommodations. There was little comfort flying a plane that appeared luxurious but rattled like an old worn-out truck. Kristoff was not impressed with Soviet aircraft after flying American 747s. When he arrived in Moscow two hours later, his father met him as he stepped out of the aircraft. They warmly embraced. The commander spoke first.

"I have mixed feelings about your decision to return, but I understand your reasons. Our situation is unclear. I believe we are targets of the KGB."

This information startled Kristoff.

"What are you saying? Should I get Nadia out?" His stressful voice was apparent.

His father could sense the strain. He responded authoritatively.

"You let me worry about us. Your wife is expecting any time now. You must be with her. I plan on living to see my grandchild."

Kristoff then asked, "Where is Nadia? I must be with her."

The commander did not hesitate.

"She is waiting for you at our apartment. Go quickly. The driver will take you now." Kristoff sensed urgency in his father's voice.

The apartment was located near Sokolniki Park, where Tsar Alexei Mikhailovich flew falcons who would hunt hares and other small mammals. He had fond childhood memories when he passed time in the park with his father, tossing a frisbee or kicking a soccer ball. Now he noticed adjacent streets were empty and appeared gray and somber, similar to scenes from black and white films. There was sparse activity in comparison to Manhattan, filled with life and energy. He finally confirmed Nadia's reasons for leaving her native land. It all made sense, especially for an artist, performer or intellectual who craves individual freedom of thought and expression. Russia was a world apart from democratic cultures; it was a lifeless city. Nadia knew better than anyone. Her world travel while in the Bolshoi changed her life. Now Kristoff shared her outlook as well.

When Kristoff arrived at the apartment, he noticed Nadia peeking out the door. She gingerly walked to him with her extended stomach and threw her arms around him. "Kristoff, how I have missed you. We are having a boy. Isn't that wonderful!"

Kristoff was still kissing her all over. He placed his hand on her stomach and smiled at their accomplishment.

"How do you know it's a boy?" Now he placed his ear on her stomach as though he would hear his son speak.

"The doctor told me." What she didn't tell Kristoff was the doctor's concerns over complications that would accelerate Nadia's delivery schedule. There was no time for discussion or explanation as

Kristoff would soon realize. Fortunately her nurse had requested an ambulance be on standby.

Within less than an hour, Nadia suddenly felt a surge of pain. Her attending nurse examined her, then calmly approached Kristoff.

"Your son is about to be born. You and your wife must leave for the hospital immediately. We have made arrangements." The nurse had Nadia placed on a stretcher and wheeled to a waiting ambulance. The hospital was only twenty minutes away. Nadia released a mild scream in the ambulance. She stared at Kristoff and he immediately felt something was seriously wrong. The turn of events, left him bewildered. He held her hand and looked into her glassy blue eyes as the ambulance rushed to the hospital. He noticed Nadia's painful grimace and called to the nurse.

"My wife needs your attention now. Please help her."

Nadia blurted out, "I can't make it. I feel tremendous pain." When they arrived at the hospital she was semiconscious and hemorrhaging. Attendants rushed her to a room on the third floor. Doctors were waiting and prepared for delivery. Nadia had lost a lot of blood; her semiconscious condition made her breathing very uneven. Doctors worked frantically to save her baby. Within an hour their son was born. Nadia was wheeled to a recovery room. Kristoff followed with his son wrapped in a blanket. He placed their son in her waiting arms. She wanted to bond with him as she held him close to her breast. Her body became listless from losing blood. A transfusion did not seem to change her condition.

Suddenly, a network agent raced frantically into their room. Kristoff sensed his urgency and inquired, "Yes. What is it?"

The agent was out of breath.

"You and your wife must leave immediately. We have made arrangements. You must leave at once. We have a nurse who will travel with you."

Kristoff could not believe what he was hearing.

"My wife cannot be moved. She's in critical condition. Are you crazy?"

The agent pleaded with Kristoff.

"Sir, as I speak, KGB agents are looking for you with orders to arrest you. Your father wants you both to be moved immediately." Nadia was still listless and hemorrhaging and her strength was fading. The monitor indicated her heart was very weak. The nurse was concerned but tried not to show any emotion when she commented, "Sir, we must not leave the hospital. Your wife is bleeding. She must not be moved."

The network agent vehemently disagreed.

"We have no choice. You will never make it unless you leave now. There is no alternative. KGB agents are searching for you. Your chances are best if you move your wife."

Kristoff followed the agent while wheeling Nadia's bed toward the rear exit elevator with all the tubes and medications still attached. The nurse followed with their newborn son. Meanwhile, KGB agents were methodically searching all rooms. Finally, they were directed to Nadia's vacant room. They missed her escape by a few minutes. One agent asked a nurse, "Where are they?"

One nurse responded, "Who are you looking for?"

And agent grabbed the attending nurse and pushed her against a bed.

"Who do you think? Rypchensky! Where is he?"

The nurse responded with fear: "They left moments ago."

Kristoff wheeled Nadia to a waiting ambulance. She was unconscious. He was trying to comfort her. The driver headed for the airport while the nurse pleaded with Kristoff. "Sir, you must take your wife back. She is bleeding. Please, sir. Hurry!"

Kristoff panicked. He yelled to the ambulance driver:

"Turn back! Please! My wife needs a doctor!"

Kristoff was informed by the agent who was driving that it would be best to have Nadia treated by a doctor who would meet them at the airport.

"We also have security there to intercept the KGB agents following us."

They did not turn back.

Nadia was motionless. The nurse handed Kristoff his son while she tried to revive Nadia without any success. Now the nurse began to cry when she realized Nadia could not be saved. She lost too much blood. Kristoff looked on in disbelief. His eyes welled up. The ambulance arrived minutes later at the airfield. Kristoff was in shock. Doctors were waiting and tried to revive her with a transfusion. Kristoff spoke to her while doctors continued their efforts.

"Nadia, Nadia, it's me, Kristoff." Blood covered his clothing. The nurse held his tightly wrapped son.

When Commander Rypchensky opened the ambulance door, his emotions crashed when seeing Kristoff crying, while holding his beloved Nadia. She expired in his arms. His father placed his arm around his son, while an agent looked on, then reminded them. "Quickly. You must hurry."

Kristoff would not budge. "No, you do not understand. My Nadia is . . . I must stay with her."

The commander then responded gently but firmly.

"Nadia would want you and your son to be free men. She would want you to take what is left of her, her son. You must protect him now. He is what is left of Nadia. Protect him and you are saving the most precious gift Nadia could give you." Kristoff was sobbing. Then with his arm around his son, he escorted him to a plane filled with network members and their families. An assigned nurse, Olga Smanski, recognized Kristoff's serious condition and injected him with a sedative. Kristoff's newborn son was now being cradled by the commander, who watched as his son collapsed in a seat. The plane taxied to a location adjacent to the airport where it remained until a few agents completed an important assignment before final takeoff.

Orlov greeted the commander as he deplaned. Security was everywhere. Network agents and military personnel had the airport completely encircled. Orlov was speaking to a former agent whose role became critical at this very moment. He was confident that agent Bostia would cooperate because of his personal needs.

"If you want to be with your family in Britain, here is your chance."

Bostia's attention was focused on Orlov like never before. Now, it was his time to return a favor. "What must I do?"

Orlov did not waste any time. "Listen carefully. We have little time." The roar of jet engines was everywhere. It was impossible to talk without shouting. Orlov was annoyed by the noise; he had to shout to be heard.

"Commander Rypchensky has four military transport planes ready to take off. Two of them will be empty. The other two are filled with over four hundred network members and their families. There is one seat for you."

Through the noise of jet engines, Bostia could barely hear, but acknowledged to Orlov that he understood. However, he was uncertain of his role. He shouted.

"What do you want me to do?"

Orlov cupped his hands over his mouth and responded.

"Contact the KGB. Tell them the flight numbers and destinations of the two empty planes." He then handed Bostia a piece of paper with all the information.

"They must be led to believe that we are on those planes. Understand?" Bostia acknowledged. "Now hurry. I will be listening in, so be convincing."

A black Mercedes pulled up with several agents. Bostia entered the car with Orlov. They each had a telephone to their ear. When Bostia delivered the assigned message to Orlov's satisfaction, he was driven to a waiting aircraft. The commander watched the planes take off and when his son's plane was airborne, he broke down and cried.

Two planes were scheduled to land in Kiev, empty of network members and their families. Instead they were carrying supplies for military operations with Warsaw Pact allies. The other planes, officially posted for Berlin, would be redirected to Stockholm, a safe haven for network families. From there, flights to London and New York had been pre-arranged. The revolution's success was still to be determined. Military support would decide the outcome.

When Commander Rypchensky coordinated flights of four Russian military planes, two were scheduled for transporting military hardware to Kiev for use by Warsaw Pact allies. The other two planes were for transporting troops. These two planes however, were filled with Network members and their families. Originally they were scheduled earlier in the week but Orlov recommended cancelling these earlier flights in order to synchronize their departure on the same day military hardware was transported to Kiev. The idea was to misinform airport authorities. The Commander was also aware of questionable loyalties within air force circles. He didn't trust them. He was confident with Orlov's designed plan to confuse specific flight schedules monitored by the air force. On the day of departure, network agent Bostia misinformed KGB authorities that two planes departing for Kiev were filled with Network members. Air force high command was immediately informed. Before officers of the air force ordered two planes destined for Kiev shot down, they ordered air traffic control to dispatch flight information that would cause a mid air collision. Miraculously, this did not happen because both pilots managed to avoid crashing seconds before impact. However, their miracle was short lived. Moments later another Air Force command was given to shoot them down. When the news was reported, air force officers tried to cover up their malicious deeds but recordings revealed their criminal behavior. Air Force officers in command were arrested and charged with war crimes. Media outlets made sure the public was informed. Several air force bases were occupied by army commandos. All flights were grounded. The public was made well aware that it was the army that represented the will of the people and would continue to protect their human rights. Propaganda was effectively used to improve public perception and more importantly, network families arrived safely in Stockholm. More flights were arranged to protect network agents and their families.

Network organizers exploited foreign capitals for publicizing their intentions to destroy communism. By taking advantage of free and open media, they were able to expose institutional and personal reasons for leaving the Soviet Union. Network demonstrations involving nationals from several republics were organized in European capitals. Many local supporters, especially college students, joined their call for freedom and justice. Berlin, Paris, Madrid, Prague, Budapest and London all joined a coordinated campaign to attack communist tyranny. Flags and colors of many nations participated.

Chapter 30

When Commander Rypchensky and Orlov returned to their offices in the Kremlin, Moscow's streets were filled with tanks, military personnel, and thousands of Russians waving flags. They were not hammer and sickle emblems of the Soviet Union. They were waving the tricolors of Russia, white, blue, and red. Throughout the Soviet Union, patriotic displays demonstrated similar loyalties to their republics, not the Soviet Union. It was the army's loyalty to their commander that protected the revolution up to this point. The duration of this revolutionary moment was yet to be determined. If the reaction of republics was any indication, the implosion of the Soviet Union was imminent. This outcome had been predicted by pundits for a variety of reasons. When the economy collapsed under the weight of bureaucratic incompetence and excessive military expenditures, leading to bankruptcy, the Soviet Union's era ceased to exist.

Network leaders throughout republics were feeling more confident by their display of local sentiments, opposing Soviet hegemony. A breaking point, motivated by frustration and anger, encouraged thousands of citizens to protest openly. Their experiences with totalitarian rule could no longer be tolerated. Many segments of the Soviet Union were bankrupt. Its command economy failed to produce goods and services demanded and expected by millions. Political freedom was also absent. If the streets of Moscow were any indication of what to expect, Russia would follow a different path. The commander anticipated Russia's future would be unstable. There were few democratic traditions guiding them. Centuries of Czars and seventy years of totalitarian communism had crushed opposition politics. Autocracy and authoritarian culture had smothered freedom of expression. Freedom's internal dynamic, powered by dissent, majority rule, and compromise, was missing. Soviet republics were suffering from the sins of ancestors, whose political intolerance and incompetence were impediments, making transition to democratic rule difficult.

Mysteriously, entrenched KGB personnel withdrew into underground political enclaves, where authoritarian culture and behavior was maintained. Revisions that would threaten their beliefs, comforts, and status were successfully resisted. Their loyalty to USSR had not been snuffed out. For generations, communist party membership preserved their status, life style, and national honor. Cunning political instincts, cultivated under one-party rule, emboldened them to protect their privilege and power. Concealing themselves in the darkest corners of Russian society, they conspired with like minds.

The commander understood this problem. He chose not to provoke KGB personnel, preferring to possibly utilize their skills and win them over. An assessment of their political ambitions was required. Whether they were willing to participate within a new political framework had to be determined. It was a gamble and he knew it. The unwilling would be replaced with his loyal followers. Loyal officials would assess whether old regime personnel would cooperate with revolutionary leaders led by Mikoyanov. Meanwhile, revolutionary constituents and their families had to be protected. Their security was a priority. Network leaders understood how reactionary forces could destroy their movement, resulting in the arrest and murder of thousands of their supporters.

There was one serious uncertainty that, if not addressed, would create problems for the commander: his nemesis, Chekov, locked up in a Ukrainian prison. Chekov had a strong cadre of loyal officers, whose rogue tendencies were very dangerous. Like an imprisoned mobster, Chekov's power could extend beyond prison. Tracing the movements of callous and notorious bureaucrats was a top priority. Their combined, hidden wealth, stolen over years of corruption, was capable of buying influence in key sectors of several republics, where poverty-induced desperation forced citizens to cooperate with communist reactionaries. Bribes for loyalty were common on both sides. Cynicism ruled political behavior. Idealism was largely absent. Pragmatic behavior was devoid of ethical considerations.

Flushing evil autocrats into the open was a top priority. Failure to eliminate their political influence would impede any chances for meaningful change. The commander realized he could have taken the low road and had all of them executed. This would have been much more efficient, similar to a reign of terror. However, he preferred exposing their criminal behavior to a free and open media, allowing public opinion to condemn them.

Orlov disagreed with his commander. His experience taught him KGB culture was both indelible and incorrigible, making it dangerous to delay their elimination. Why allow ruthless enemies time to organize their resistance? Massive arrests should be swift before it was too late. Disagreement between the two network leaders was eventually resolved. The commander conceded. His order now directed massive arrests of hundreds of apparatchiks who anticipated violent reprisals and took preemptive action, escaping arrests to live another day. Machiavellian tactics were utilized by all involved. Hesitation now became everyone's enemy. Kill or be killed. Violence was excessive. No one knew for sure who had the upper hand. For two weeks, urban warfare consumed cities with hundreds killed. Army loyalty was a pivotal factor in the end result. Public information on radio, television, print media, as well as loud announcements made on roving trucks weaving streets throughout urban settings expanded network propaganda. Photos with descriptions of enemies were provided for public consumption. Network planning had accomplished an important benchmark in winning public favor. However, Mikoyanov knew there had to be more than propaganda. Meaningful policy changes involving private ownership, profit-driven entrepreneurship, foreign assistance, and getting a handle on corruption were goals impossible to achieve without public support. The network's window of opportunity was closing. Without effective mass communication, control of public opinion would be lost. Propaganda, something their opponents understood and mastered, was used effectively to stall reforms. Revolutions are won and lost during these critical moments when unknown factors generate unforeseen results.

The most important strategy was to communicate with Russian citizens. The commander announced free elections would be held in six months for a new Duma that would represent all constituents and parties. Individual parties were encouraged to have their candidates listed within sixty days. He also announced a new constitution would be crafted by a blend of political leaders to clearly enumerate true democratic principles. These initiatives however could not be achieved within their preferred time frame. A tranquil environment was difficult to achieve due to political instability. Conducting free elections under these conditions was problematic. A basic component, law and order, was absent. Delays in democratic initiatives favored reactionary forces.

The media were celebrating and welcoming new freedoms for the first time. There were signs of optimism interwoven with skepticism. Opposition parties emerged from their underground secrecy. A feeling of liberation, never experienced in twentieth-century Russia, was moving more citizens into the streets. Party Chairman Mikoyanov received a gracious call from the president of the United States, who offered assistance during their critical transition to power. It appeared events were moving in a positive direction but Mikoyanov understood deep sentiments within totalitarian culture would not disappear easily. He organized special committees to encourage factions to offer their priorities for public deliberation.

Following the election of a national legislature, debate would begin and majority rule would determine public and government policies. This was a paradigm shift for Russia. The commander understood many uncertainties and obstacles. There were no models or precedents to emulate. Actions, not talking points, were necessary. The revolution's focus was blurred by uncertainty.

The commander's skepticism led him to protect his family from retribution. During the unstable transition, Kristoff was forced to emigrate with his son. The commander was deeply saddened by the death of his daughter-in-law. He felt guilty for what happened and wondered how Kristoff was coping with his tragic loss. He buried himself in work, striving to maintain his equilibrium. Meanwhile, his wife Monique was heartbroken and wanted to be with her son. She was filled with grief, especially when she was obligated to inform Nadia's mother.

Another critical task was introducing Russia's command economy to market forces. Russia's lack of experience in this area required assistance from Europeans and Americans. Arrangements were made to facilitate transitions in many economic sectors toward private ownership, while still maintaining government responsibility for infrastructure. Russian plutocrats emerged from underground economies. Their dominance would gradually monopolize industrial production and distribution. Russia's economy duplicated the American era of "robber barons" during the latter half of the nineteenth century. Opportunities for extreme wealth attracted former KGB bureaucrats who utilized their underhanded political skills. "Robber barons" employed them to manipulate opponents. Collusion between plutocrats and former intelligence officers would prove to be a major miscalculation of the network planners.

An unfortunate oversight. KGB officers could now gain access to vast opportunities for wealth, power, and privilege. The door to autocratic rule could gradually be reopened. KGB culture and experience with criminal minds was not wasted. Now it was used to usurp power from newly elected officials. The integrity of democratic government behavior was being undermined. The revolution was failing to achieve its stated goals.

Unlike the American Revolution, where men of merit assumed power, in Russia, duplicity and Machiavellian schemes replaced ethical conduct. Many participants were not men of honor. Tactics used by former European dictators were partially duplicated. As this insidious activity unfolded, Commander Rypchensky, and especially his wife Monique, made plans to leave for Paris on a moments' notice. His fighting spirit was strong, but could it overcome, an implacable force motivated by greed and power? He fought the good fight but was uncertain of the outcome. Ultimately, all might be lost to endemic forces beyond his reach.

There were, however, many good reasons to celebrate what appeared to be the Soviet Union's postmortem. Eastern Europe had dismantled the "iron curtain." The Berlin Wall was shattered and it appeared Germany would ultimately be united. Soviet republics began to celebrate their sovereignty, premature as it may have been. Their long-sought-after liberation from Russia's hegemony would allow for their future autonomy. They persevered for over three generations under control of Russian bureaucrats.

Tensions between Russia and the west would persist, but the revolution at face value had diminished the Soviet Union's super power status. Analysts could not at this time assess the final outcome. Would the Soviet Union survive or would the impact of dedicated underground networks dissolve the once powerful oligarchy and relegate it to history's ash heap? We know from decades of historical evidence, millions suffered and died under different brands of totalitarianism. The Russian experience is one example where centuries of concentrated power cannot be easily reconfigured. Throughout this political drama, private lives and loves of many citizens were exposed to suffering, persecution, misery, and death. Was it worth the cost? Historians will have to judge.

Chapter 31

The plane carrying Kristoff, his son, nurse, and network families landed in Stockholm. Many passengers applauded upon landing. Passengers prepared to exit. They were tired but filled with excitement. Kristoff noticed a woman who looked like his mother. He rushed to her only to find that she was someone else. He then felt a tap on his shoulder. It was Trushin. He had an envelope in his hand.

"We meet again. Always under strange circumstances." It was obvious that Kristoff was upset. News of Nadia's death had not been divulged to anyone but a few agents.

"Where are my parents? Are they alive?"

Trushin responded with confidence.

"They are safe and will remain unless they determine the revolution cannot move forward. You should know their decision within a year's time, maybe less."

Kristoff's response was angry and swift.

"Why didn't they escape? Why?"

Trushin could now see tears in Kristoff's eyes. He expressed sympathy for his tragic loss and tried to be reassuring with his response.

"If necessary, your father will leave. He wanted to secure the safety of his comrades first. That is typical of your father." He paused then continued.

"The revolution needs his presence and leadership. This has been his life's mission. He has planned for another faction to take over in his absence. Good men who will succeed." Trushin then placed his arm around Kristoff.

"You are my Godchild. I will always be available if you need me. My heart grieves for you." He handed Kristoff an envelope.

"There are visas, passports and tickets for you, your son and Olga to New York. There is also several thousand dollars in cash. Your flight departs from Stockholm late this evening. Your father is very concerned about you and your son. Maybe his letter will explain. May God be with you." He then embraced Kristoff affectionately and disappeared into the crowd.

Kristoff opened the envelope containing three visas, passports, tickets, hotel reservation, an envelope stuffed with cash, and a letter also sealed in an envelope. He began reading:

Dear Kristoff,

Your mother and I grieve the tragic loss of your beautiful Nadia. We will forever suffer the pain you feel. May your life find a new beginning in America. Someday we will be together again. I promise you. In the meantime, you must move forward. Nadia would want you to be happy. Your son is her parting gift to you. We will contact you soon. Take good care of our grandson.

Your loving father.

Kristoff and Olga boarded Scandinavian Air flight 311, bound for JFK. Olga had been cradling and bottle feeding his son for hours.

"Would you like to hold him?" She gently moved infant Nicolas into his waiting arms and placed the bottle in his hand.

"Here, you should experience feeding your son. He's a beautiful boy."

She then excused herself and walked to the rest area toward the rear of the plane. Kristoff would learn to relish private moments like this with his newborn son. When he looked at him he envisioned Nadia. Tears filled his eyes.

At Kennedy airport, Kristoff walked through the terminal. His infant son was sleeping. The bottled milk apparently was very satisfying. They retrieved their minimal luggage. A cab was hired to drive them to the Union Hotel in Garden City where his father had booked and paid for rooms. They settled in and he slept with the help of sleeping pills.

The next morning, there was only one person he could think of calling: Yolanda Spieler. It was 9:00 am when her phone rang.

"Hello." Kristoff could not respond. "Hello. Is anybody there?"

Kristoff's voice was barely audible. "Yolanda. This is Kristoff."

She recognized his voice. "Yes. Where are you?"

Her voice was clear and friendly. His emotions were uncertain.

"I returned from Russia earlier today. I need to talk to someone."

She sensed his urgency.

"Of course, but where are you?"

Kristoff felt very awkward.

"My son, his nanny, and I are at the Union Hotel in Garden City."

She did not think to ask any questions.

"I will be there in one hour."

When the call ended, Yolanda realized what Kristoff had said and, combined with the urgency in his voice, she realized something was wrong.

When she arrived, in just over an hour, Kristoff answered the door and immediately had flashes of Nadia. Apparently, he had taken too many sleeping pills. He hesitated and did not respond to her. She reached out and held his arm.

"Kristoff. Are you OK?"

He was feeling very lightheaded.

"Yes, I think so. My thoughts are elsewhere . . ."

He began to fade when Olga helped him onto a sofa. Gradually he regained his composure but suddenly began to cry, lowering his head into his hands. Yolanda held and comforted him.

"Please, Kristoff. Tell me what is wrong."

He sobbed uncontrollably.

"My Nadia is gone. My beautiful Nadia."

Olga could not escape the moment and also was filled with tears as she walked into the bedroom holding his infant son.

One week later, Kristoff planned to move out of the hotel. He, his son Nicolas, and Olga would temporarily move into Yolanda's home.

His son was awake and filled with life as he lay in a baby carriage. Olga lifted him and placed him into his father's waiting arms. Nicolas stared at Kristoff as he nursed a fresh bottle of milk. His father lamented.

"My son. Your mother was a beautiful woman but she is gone. Thank God I have what remains of her."

Just then the telephone rang twice. When he answered, Yolanda responded.

"Good morning. When will you arrive with Nicolas?"

Kristoff looked into his son's eyes.

"I have him in my arms now. He is all I have."

She understood his pain.

"We will work this out. You're not alone."

Kristoff knew his loss would take time to heal but appreciated her compassion.

"Thank you. We will be there soon."

Kristoff's parents called a week earlier and recommended he see a therapist as soon as possible. It was good advice and he immediately called and made an appointment with a psychiatrist in Garden City. All kinds of thoughts raced through his head. Grieving his loss of Nadia could now be shared with someone. He wondered if Yolanda would also seek therapy to cope with her grief. Their mutual tragedies were directly related to circumstances connecting them to network activities. They were young professional adults who at some point would seek out new relationships, of this he was confident. For all these reasons, they shared much in common. He just felt awkward and believed she would have similar feelings when they met the following morning. Interacting with her would have to be based on mutual respect and admiration. He asked himself how many men and woman could ever imagine being in similar situations. He never thought of therapy before but decided his parents were correct with their recommendation. Fortunately he immediately called a psychiatrist and due to a cancellation, was given an appointment the day before being invited to Yolanda's.

When the taxi drove him to the doctor's office his nerves were fragile. The doctor was in his forties and had a pleasant demeanor. Kristoff filled out forms and wrote an explanation for his visit as required. He included everything about his relationship with Nadia, their new son born in Moscow, her tragic death and his escape from Russia during an explosive and unpredictable period. But then he stopped writing. His mind froze. The doctor would have to pry it out of him. He hesitated to include personal information about

Yolanda. Was he violating her right to privacy? His brain stopped working for the moment.

The doctor welcomed Kristoff into his office where he was offered a comfortable chair. Dr. Molloy was reading his chart and written account filled out earlier.

"Kristoff, I see that you recently arrived from Russia under very difficult circumstances. My sincere sympathies. Your loss and the grief that follows will stay with you for a while. Try to share your grief with others. I always found that to be most effective. Is there someone you can confide in, someone who may have experienced a similar loss?" Kristoff could not believe the incredible questions asked by Dr. Molloy. It was as if he knew everything that happened; information Kristoff did not reveal. He responded to the doctor's comment.

"Well doctor, you have touched upon an incredible point of information that I must share. An American woman I met, about my age lost her husband as a result of circumstances related to what is going on in Russia. I cannot discuss particulars except to say that she was married less than a year. She is grieving his loss." The doctor's comment followed.

"Well this is interesting. You have someone to share your grief with. Do you have a problem with that?"

"Not exactly doctor. It's just that…" Kristoff did not know what to say next. The doctor responded.

"You stopped for a reason. Would you like to share your reason with me so I can assist you?" Kristoff relented to the doctor's observation. He must have "read" his body language.

"Yes doctor you're correct. You see I think there might be an attraction between us. I must feel guilty for having these feelings.

It's much too soon. Is this normal? How should I feel now that my beautiful wife is gone?" The doctor then asked.

"Is this woman also beautiful in your eyes?" Kristoff hesitated before responding.

"Yes she is attractive. I remember when I first met her that we had a connection. Our eyes locked. It was a strange feeling." Then the doctor added an interesting comment.

"If your wondering what's normal, there is no normal for every human interaction. Your emotions are very subjective and unique to your situation. Would you agree?"

Kristoff responded. "Yes I agree. Then my feelings of guilt are normal?" The doctor responded.

"Why are you feeling guilt? Can you explain your reasons?" Kristoff thought about it.

"It's just that Nadia did not get a chance to live and enjoy our marriage and new son. She was robbed of her life by an event that we could not control. I feel partly responsible." The doctor understood.

"There are many parts of our lives where our control is very limited. You escaped from a country experiencing revolution. Controlling your particular situation was made more challenging. Your acquaintance with this woman who is grieving the loss of her husband was not conducted for selfish motivations on your part. Am I correct in that assessment?" Kristoff immediately responded.

"Absolutely! I needed information to protect my family in Moscow. I cannot go into all the details." The doctor understood.

"So your feelings of guilt are not caused by selfish or sinister reasons. They are caused by your feelings of loss. Under the circumstances I am certain many husbands would experience similar emotions." Then the doctor offered another observation.

"There are many reasons why men are attracted to women. Maybe your attraction to her stems from her qualities, maybe you see similarities that remind you of Nadia. In other words, her attraction could be more than physical. Could that be a possibility?"

Kristoff was amazed at how this doctor's mind analyzed so instantly and correctly. He was incredulous.

'Yes, you make a good point. So my feelings should not be interpreted negatively?"

"That is correct. In fact, maybe she will feel similar emotions. You have both experienced tragic losses. Both of you are fortunate to have one another, whether that means you end up just friends or something more. Share your grief and remember your humanity. Take one day at a time. Don't rush anything. I wouldn't recommend living together. Allow yourself some space. I am sure she will agree. Time will heal both of you. Get on with your life. Nadia would want that."

"Doctor, this woman has invited us to her home to live until I can find a job and a new home for my family. I have accepted her offer. Should I reconsider?" The doctor did not hesitate.

"Under the circumstances, accept her offer but explain it's only temporary and that as soon as possible, you plan to find your own place. I am sure she will understand. Now is a time to think about your future. I am sure your wife would want you to find a new life. She would want you to be a good father to your son. Your contentment and fulfillment with your life is really up to you. Be patient. Be in the moment. Take one day at a time. Things will work out."

Kristoff felt so much better. He thanked the doctor and arranged for another appointment in two weeks. His mind was clear and his spirits improved. The doctor was right. Nadia would want him to move on.

Yolanda's decision to marry Viktor was sincere. Free of pretense. She concluded their commitment to each other should not be postponed. Being married to a man she truly loved overpowered her. Rather than attempt to control her destiny, she surrendered to her emotional love. When Viktor asked her to marry him, she did not hesitate. She believed they were destined to be husband and wife. When she learned that Viktor's child was inside her womb, she understood that his family's legacy would endure. Their child would be a confirmation of his life. She was joyful in her anticipation of being the mother of his child. Their rendezvous with destiny was now complete.

Yolanda did not disclose that she was pregnant with Viktor's child. Her conditions would eventually be obvious. There was no need for any announcement at this time. When the taxi arrived in her driveway, with Kristoff, Olga, and Nicolas, Yolanda approached with a genuine welcome. Kristoff envisioned Nadia with him and Nicolas. His watery eyes glanced down at Nicolas cradled in his arms. He gradually redirected his look, studying Yolanda's eyes, then her entire face. Extending her arms, she embraced them all. Kristoff gently placed his son in her arms. Olga smiled, but could not hold back tears. More assured, Kristoff forced a smile as he looked into Yolanda's beautiful eyes.

"Will you have us for a while?"

— The End —